First published 2013
by Starting Gun Books,
Auckland, New Zealand.

National Library of New Zealand Cataloguing-in-Publication Data

Price, Tony, 1965-
No Way Back / Tony Price
ISBN 978-0-473-26407-9
I.Title.
NZ823.3—dc 22

Cover design by Mary-Ann Attree
Cover image: Tony Price
Printed by Lightning Source

NO WAY BACK

TONY PRICE

ONE

He kept his head down and pushed deeper into the shadows. The situation had changed so rapidly, so dramatically that he was still unable to think straight. And being more than half cut wasn't helping. They'd all had far too much to drink.

It had happened so quickly, with no time to consider right or wrong. To work out a better way. To think it through. He'd been forced to act and he already regretted his actions. Deeply.

Kieran was dead, of that there was no doubt.

His temple throbbed and his heart literally hammered in his chest as he risked a quick peek out of the darkened hiding place. He saw no one and pushed himself back into the shadowed nook of the ferries lower deck.

The *Kestrel* was a double-ended wooden vessel with two levels, about forty metres long and almost a hundred years old. And he had to get off it somehow – quickly and unseen.

He risked another look. The throbbing in his temple intensified and he shook his head to try and clear it away. From his hiding place he could only see a short way around the lower deck in either direction. The lighting was dull with patches of deep shadow. There were good places to hide, for both himself and anyone who may be seeking him.

Again he saw no one.

The *Kestrel* was still and quiet, bobbing only gently. It had been tied up alongside the wharf at downtown Auckland now for less than a minute. He didn't know if it had finished

1

working for the night or not. But a fresh boarding of passengers would be a disaster. He couldn't be found here.

With trembling legs he stepped out of his hiding place again. The gangway off, to leave the ferry in the normal way, was on the upper level. But he couldn't risk using it without being seen by the crew. So he crept towards the harbour end of the vessel with no real purpose.

A creak from the upper deck made him duck into a shadow and freeze. He waited breathlessly. Muffled noises above filtered through from the Auckland end of the ferry. People were coming. Panicking, he darted away from the sounds and found himself almost at the bow of the, currently, seaward end of the boat. But he couldn't go any further. That was where it happened. Kieran's blood was still on the deck around there. He stopped, looking around desperately for a way out. For some way off the bloody boat.

Then he saw something. A ladder ran down the side of the wharf into the water. If he could get over to it somehow he could climb up and reach the wharf. He moved forward, gauging the distance. It was a good two metres from the side of the ferry to the ladder. Not a long way but he would have to jump. He lean out over the railing, looking first around the curving deck of the ferry for signs of life. No one emerged from the gloom, but he could clearly hear voices now. More drunken revelers were boarding to catch the ferry back to Devonport.

He needed to move quickly.

Staring over the side he found the water dark and murky, sucking endlessly at the massive pylons that held the wharf up. But the tide was out so the lower level of the *Kestrel* sat well below the wharf's surface, offering him a terrifying opportunity. If he could reach the ladder he could escape. But if he missed the jump he would fall into the water and be sucked between the ferry and the wharf. He wasn't a strong swimmer and he was still quite drunk. He would probably drown. Even in his current state he knew jumping was a bad idea, but he could think of no other way out.

With a final glance down the ferries deck he carefully climbed the rail and positioned himself. There was a ledge on the outside of the ferry that afforded him a tenuous foothold, only half the width of his boot. Stepping down he initially slipped and had to scrabble back over the railing before finally managing to wedge his boot roughly into place. He wished he was wearing sneakers, but he would never have been allowed into any of the pubs or clubs wearing them.

He tried to steady the butterflies in his stomach but fear gripped him tightly. Balancing on the ledge wasn't ideal but it did bring him significantly closer to the ladder. He took a deep breath, gripped the *Kestrel*'s rail as firmly as he could with one hand, and stretched out towards the ladder. It was still too far. Only about half a metre separated him from freedom. His temple continued to throb wildly. When his hand on the rail slipped slightly he drew himself nervously back to the ferry.

More noises above. The new passengers were moving around the upper level without a care in the world. He could hear them laughing and joking, just as he and his friends had been doing earlier. He tried to block out the sounds – and his memory of the terrible event that had so unexpectedly unfolded.

It was now or never. He needed to get off the ferry before anyone came down to the lower deck and saw him. He had no choice, time was against him. The ferry would depart soon. He released one hand again and stretched it out. He bent his leg, ready to thrust off the railing – and he jumped.

Time seemed to stop. He tumbled through the air gracelessly as the outstretched hand reached the ladder and he grabbed at it for all he was worth. His left boot hit a lower rung and slipped off the barnacle encrusted steel. Twisting in the air he wrapped one arm around the side of the ladder and forced his other hand through the space to lock onto a rung. His body smacked into the ladder and both feet flailed momentarily in the air.

But he held on, dangling precariously in space, cursing softly to himself.

Clinging desperately to the cold and slippery ladder he gingerly raised a leg, his pants scraping along the sharp barnacles of the lower rungs until his foot finally found purchase. He almost cried aloud in relief. Awkwardly he set himself on the ladder and then climbed around to the other side, beneath the wharf and into the shadows. Almost immediately a whistle sounded and he felt the ladder shudder as the *Kestrel* came to life and began to move away.

He scrambled higher up the ladder, pulling himself into deeper darkness beneath the wharf and waited for the lumbering old ferry to begin another repetition of its endless cycle. It would sail again to Devonport before returning to downtown Auckland, relentlessly plying this same course as it had –dozens of times a day, every day– for the last three-quarters of a century. The water beneath him churned and sucked and eventually the *Kestrel* was gone.

It became quiet again.

His nerves were almost completely shot and his head was about ready to explode, the pain at this temple reverberating like a cannon. Yet still he waited.

After nearly ten excruciatingly long minutes he rounded the ladder and cautiously ascended. The wharf above him was an open area, covered by a corrugated tin roof and barely lit. But the darkness would continue to be his friend as he slipped quietly between the wooden benches and made his way to the gates. The ferry terminal was quiet once again and only one man was seated in the little office beside the only entrance and exit. He was reading, it was late, and he was expecting only a few more customers. And they would all be coming from Quay Street, not from the wharf.

Moving silently away from the main entrance he would climb the big iron fence and cut across Queen's Wharf behind the main entrance – reversing the route that he and his friends had used to get in there earlier.

He felt slightly more confident now, away from the ferry. But he still had no idea where he would go once he got clear of the area. His heart continued to race in panic as he desperately tried to understand just how his entire world had so quickly become so incredibly messed up.

He knew that he had to get out of Auckland. That was the only thing he could think of with any clarity. Disappear. Escape. Get as far away as he could, as quickly as possible. He had to put distance between himself and that damned ferry.

He wasn't going to go to jail. Not again. He'd had a small taste of it once before and was terrified that it would destroy him. He couldn't live like that. No way, no how. He would have to run. And hide.

Perhaps forever.

TWO

"I have never met such a self-serving bunch of wankers in my life. Why the hell do we keep coming to these goddamn stupid dinners?"

I just stared at him, more than a little bleary eyed. It was late in the evening and Brent was winding up into yet another of his meandering, bigoted rants. Usually I would disagree with him, just for the sake of taking an opposing view, but I was tired and kept my mouth shut.

"These pricks don't know shit, and yet here they all are, slapping themselves on the backs, kissing up and stroking each other's egos like their lives depend on it." He pointed across the room openly at a short, chubby man with a pixie haircut in a brightly coloured shirt. "I mean, take that little prick. That bloody ass-bandit, Armitage. He should never have won the fucking Qantas trans-Tasman sales award. He couldn't bloody find Australia if it bit him on the ass."

"He's got a good Aussie team," I said.

Brent glared at me. Most mere mortals' would quiver when Brent Barclay glared at them like that, but I just rolled my eyes. He ignored me.

"He's a prick, and a fucking pillow-biter. There's far too bloody many of them in this industry. And that bitch . . ." He pointed again. This time at a buxom woman wearing oversized rectangular 'I-think-these-make-me-look-intelligent' glasses sitting only two tables away. "That bitch couldn't find her way to Auckland airport with a GPS up her twat . . . and yet, somehow, she manages to win a pair of Global Explorer round-the-world airfares. I mean, for fucks sake, how is that possible?"

I couldn't answer him. Frankly, I was just as surprised.

"And yet here I am, with the best performing corporate agency in the country –that's right– in the whole fucking country, and all I get is a lousy block of plastic from Air New Zealand for selling a shit-load of bloody premium space."

He pointed at the offending award on the table beside us. Presented for Top Sales of Premium Class seating it was, in fact, exactly that – an engraved block of plastic. Not even smoked glass, as they had been in previous years, but obviously plastic. It looked cheap and probably was. "Life's a bitch, big fella," I said. "These award ceremonies sure aren't what they used to be."

He looked at me again and morosely shook his head. We've both been to well over a dozen of these annual gala Travel Industry award dinners and the prizes were definitely getting worse every year. Back in the day, when we both first became travel agents, almost everyone in attendance, regardless of how well they operated their business, would walk away with a couple of free domestic airfares – or at least a few nights in a flash hotel somewhere. But these days, with airlines and operators all struggling to make a buck, and the intrusion of the bloody internet, you couldn't even lay your hands on one of those little plastic model airplanes. And the endless free drinks stopped quite a few years ago.

"You want another beer?" he asked.

I'd already had a couple more than I should and shook my head. It was going to be hard enough dragging myself up and into the office in the morning as it was. "No. Thanks anyway. I should be going."

"Come on, don't be a girl. I've got a night off. You're not gonna piss off and leave me with all these pansies?"

I smiled. Brent and I have been friends forever, which is probably why I so easily ignore his perpetually homophobic and expletive-laden rants. You just get used to it. But we haven't been out all that much since he got married last year.

It's odd really. I never thought any woman would tame him. I checked my watch. It was late, but not that late. "Go on then. But it's the last," I said.

"You're a soft-cock. Harden up," he called back over his shoulder as he snaked his way between the tables. People moved aside as they always did when Brent ploughed through a room. He was a big guy and carried a real aura of superiority around with him. It's one of the things that's helped to make him a very successful businessman – in addition to his obviously charming personality.

The hotel ballroom was vast, with over a hundred tables beautifully set out across it. But the evening was drawing to an end and only about half the attendee's remained scattered about the place. As I gazed about the room, Linda, the new Picarso Rent-a-car sales rep glanced my way and then started moving in my direction. I looked away quickly tried to decide what to do. But I didn't move fast enough and only got a couple of steps towards the open doorway out onto the hotel's balcony when she called my name.

"Adam. Hey, Adam. How's your night going?"

I turned and smiled. "Linda, hey. Didn't see you there."

"It's been a good evening, hasn't it?"

"It has, yes. This is your first gala, right?"

"Yeah, very glam. It's nice to dress up a bit."

I looked at her. She was very pretty and, feeling the knot of guilt in my stomach tighten, the form-fitting red evening gown she wore showed off some spectacular curves. But I couldn't think of anything else to say and just nodded meekly. Her dark hair was down, flowing over bare shoulders, yet I found the heaviness of her make-up distracting. Usually she wore very little. She didn't need much. There was an awkward silence before we both spoke in unison.

"So, are you–"

"Look, I've been–"

I looked away, unable to meet her eyes. Standing near the doorway I gazed briefly across the balcony to the lights of Devonport glittering onto the Waitemata harbour. The awards dinner was being held at the Hilton Hotel in downtown Auckland and we had a spectacular view over to the North Shore.

I turned back to Linda and bit the bullet. "I'm sorry I haven't called you."

Her response was surprisingly warm. "That's okay. I know how busy you are."

But that's just the thing. I haven't been busy. Again I didn't know what to say. We had a couple of dates and they actually went pretty well. It's just . . . how do I put this. Linda's really nice, but she isn't . . . well, she isn't the one.

"I had a good time," she said. "You're easy to talk to, and fun. So . . . you know. If you want to . . ."

"Yeah," I said, hating myself as I spoke. "We should . . ."

And then Brent returned, brashly interrupting and saving me from myself. He thrust two fresh bottles of Heineken into my hands and turned quickly to Linda.

I cringed as he reached out to take her hand in his massive paws.

"Well, Hello young lady, I don't believe we've met. I'm Brent Barclay of Barclay and Dodd. You must be new to the industry."

She blanched in surprise. Brent does this thing when he first meets attractive women where he takes one of their hands in both his own, draws them in close and stares intently into their eye's. It's a test. Depending on how they react he knows immediately whether he has a chance with them or not. I've seen him do it hundreds of times over the years and he swears it always works. He was doing it to Linda now. She recovered her poise quickly and didn't pull away.

"Brent, hello. I'm Linda DeWalt, I recently started with–"

"Wait," he interrupted. "Don't tell me. You're not an agent are you? You're with one of the suppliers."

"Yes, but–"

"Don't tell me, let me guess?"

He still had her hand tightly clasped within his own and drew it towards him, almost to his chest. He leaned forward slightly, towering over her, appraising her brazenly. I smiled apologetically as she glanced briefly my way.

"You work for one of the coach operators," Brent said, "Trafalgar, or possibly Insight?"

She held his gaze. "Close, but we're more self-drive."

"Ah-ha. Rental cars, then. Hmm . . . Not Avis or I'd have met you by now. Not Budget, you're too classy for them. So it has to be Hertz. Am I right?"

She gave the appearance of seeming suitably impressed, but shook her head. Smart girl. The Barclay and Dodd account would be worth a lot of money to any rental car outfit. But Brent wasn't finished.

"No, really? Hmm . . ." He glanced over at me. "And yet you seem to have already met this lowly reprobate."

She smiled and offered a vague shrug.

"Wait, wait, wait," he said. "You're working the leisure agencies. Low-end stuff, chasing the retail holiday sector."

She nodded, broadening the smile. "I'm with Picarso."

Brent's effort to not make a face was poor. Picarso Rent-a-car was relatively new in New Zealand, focused mainly on inbound holiday-makers. The name was a simply dreadful word-play on 'Picasso' –the contemporary Spanish artist– and 'car'. Yes, really. Their cars and vans were all brightly coloured with supposedly contemporary art-like over-the-top decals. It would be fair to call them garish, but the cars were all well maintained and well-priced. Great for the leisure market.

"And you actually went and called on this guy? I'll bet you haven't got a single booking from him yet."

Had anyone else bad-mouthed my business like that I like to think I would have asked them to step outside. But Brent is my friend, has been since we first met at primary school –far too many years ago– and, well, I was used to it. I knew he was only prodding me playfully. And besides . . . he was right.

"It's still early days . . ." she said.

Brent threw his head back and laughed. His raucous bellow filled the cavernous room. Half of the remaining dinner guests turned to stare like frightened sheep. "So, my lovely Linda, can I get you a drink?"

"Actually I have one somewhere, I must have left it behind. Perhaps I could . . ." she tailed off as she gently tried to withdraw her hand from his grasp. He released her and with a playful smile she turned and left us to find her drink.

Brent's head tilted to one side as he watched her move away in the form-hugging dress. "Nice ass," he said without turning.

"She's half your age."

He reached out and relieved me of one of the beers. "Bull-shit. She's easily north of thirty. But damn well preserved."

"You're a married man."

"What are you, my mother?"

"I'm done," I sighed. "I'm going home."

"No you're not. I just bought you a beer."

He leaned over and clipped my bottle with his. The ping was more a dull clunk with both bottles still full. He tipped his head in salute and chugged down almost half the bottle. I took a pretty long sip myself.

"So," he said. "You've met that one before tonight?"

"I have, yes."

He fixed me with his intense gaze. "You took her out, didn't you?"

I sighed. I'm so transparent. "A couple of times."

"You nail her yet?"

"No."

"Goddamn, you're so slow. Maybe I should have a crack."

I said nothing. He looked over at Linda again, across the room, appraising her openly. Then he grinned at me.

"You are such a sap, Adam Holt. What was wrong with her? Too chatty? Too needy? Too intelligent? Too easy?" I just frowned at him, but he wasn't done. "She seemed damn nice, but there's always something with you. It's either true love or nothing. I will never understand that. Why can't you just fuck 'em and enjoy yourself. You're such a blouse."

I didn't want to go there. Not again. Debating my love life with Brent was always a no-win discussion. "So how's your new Oz team working out?" I said.

"Don't try and change the subject, you putz. Answer the question. What was wrong with her?"

I took another long sip of my Heineken and shrugged. To be honest I really didn't know myself. I definitely liked her. She was easy to talk to; we had quite a bit in common, but, well, I don't know. As I said before, she's not the one.

Fortunately I never had to answer the question though.

"Oh, fuck-no. Hold me back, will you," Brent said.

I immediately saw the problem. Harold Armitage was mincing his way towards us. Brent had pointed him out only minutes before. The short, chubby guy who won the trans-Tasman award. Openly gay and annoying as all hell. Especially when he'd been drinking. He called out from metres away.

"Barclay, you big brute. Nice block of plastic you picked up there. It should look super in your cabinet."

"Fuck off, Armitage," Brent replied.

"Charming. You are always such a good sport. And Mr Holt, so lovely to catch up with you again."

"Likewise, Harry," I said, making him frown. Everyone knew he hated being called Harry but I'm not much of a fan myself.

"And did Milford Trips and Travel pick anything up this evening? I don't recall seeing you on the stage."

He was needling me. He knew perfectly well that my agency had no chance of taking home any awards. I said nothing and just shook my head.

"Oh, that's a shame. Maybe next year?"

"Fuck off, Armitage," Brent said again. They eyeballed each other for a minute, then Armitage shrugged.

"So . . ." he said. "Have you replaced the Commonwealth Bank account yet, Brutus? That must've really taken the steam out of your trans-Tasman volumes."

I cringed. Armitage had recently taken the CB account off Brent's agency – along with two of his best staff. It was a huge account, worth hundreds of thousands of dollars. Brent had been apoplectic. It was still a very open wound.

Brent stepped forward, picking up the Air New Zealand award from the table and leaning over the smaller man. He pushed the block of plastic up under Armitage's chin. "Fuck off, Armitage," he repeated yet again. "Or I will ram this fucking piece of plastic so far up you your spotty little Asian boy-toy will never find it."

Armitage went white. He hadn't anticipated the sheer venom of this response. A quick glance at me received no more than a raised eyebrow. I wasn't going to defend him. He backed up half a step and nearly tripped over an Asian man who had suddenly appeared behind him. Brent curled his lip and let out a muted snarl. Armitage's boy-toy boyfriend snarled back. There was no love lost there either.

We called him Cato. I think his name is actually Jerry or Jarrod or something equally European and bland but there is an industry wide joke that he's actually Armitage's man-servant and bodyguard – much like the 'Cato' character from the Pink Panther movies. He certainly acts the part.

"He's not worth it," Armitage said, gently placing his hand over the much younger man's arm. The glaring match went on for a few moments more and then Armitage shook his head, sniffed in disgust and turned to walk away. Cato stayed for another few seconds, locked in a staring death-match with Brent. Then he raised his right hand to his forehead and made the 'L' shape. Loser. Brent snarled again and stepped forward. Cato bristled and gave a small 'come on' wave. I let out a deep sigh and stepped between them.

"Let it go, you two," I said tiredly.

No one spoke or moved. The tension grew and I suddenly wondered if stepping in was such a smart move. Just as I thought it was about to explode Cato abruptly blew an air-kiss at Brent and spun away from us with the grace of a dancer. Brent started to go after him, shaking with anger, but I blocked his way. He stopped and expelled a snort.

"That went well," I said.

Brent grunted and took a long pull on his beer. "That little piece of shit. What was he thinking?" I just shrugged as he stared angrily past me, silently plotting a dastardly revenge.

I drank some of my beer, thankful that nothing more had come of the unfortunate meeting. Brent had already had a bit of a row with his business partner, Marguerite Dodd, earlier in the evening –I have no idea what about– and the thought of seeing him lose his rag again tonight made me feel drained.

Over his shoulder I spotted Linda, a glass of wine now in hand, starting to weave her way back through the tables in our direction. I slugged back most of the rest of the beer and popped it down on the nearest table.

"I have to go," I said.

He saw where I was looking and glanced over his shoulder. He shook his head. "You've got to be kidding? She's gorgeous. How could you not want to hit that?"

"I'll catch you later. You'll be at footy on Sunday?"

"If you're not gonna take a shot, then I will . . ."

"Knock yourself out."

He just shrugged. Linda was halfway to us.

"Behave yourself, Big Guy," I said and started to turn.

"Adam, hey . . ." I stopped. "You're not driving, are you?"

"Nope, I'll grab a taxi."

He looked beyond me, through the balcony doorway towards the harbour and gestured with his head. "You could always take the ferry."

I just stared at him. His expression was unreadable. I couldn't believe he would say something like that. Not after all this time. Frowning, I shook my head, but said nothing. Linda was only three tables away now. I let the bizarre comment go and turned away, slipping out to make my escape.

That was the last time I saw Brent Barclay alive.

THREE

"Yes, Mrs Coddington. I do understand." The voice on the other end of the line was insistent and I ran my fingers through what was left of my thinning hair. "I'm so very sorry but, rest assured, we'll get this sorted out just as soon as we can."

I looked over at Julie and feigned strangling myself with my free hand. Julie is my Office Manager at Milford Trips & Travel and entirely irreplaceable. Although very plain to look at, with bushy ginger hair and very pale skin, she has a wonderfully warm smile and is simply brilliant with people. All our customers love her. She offered me a fake smile of sympathy and turned away. I shifted in my seat and resumed placating the annoying woman. "Yes, Mrs Coddington. I fully appreciate that a harbour-view room should actually have a view of the harbour. There must have been some kind of mistake. I will sort this out for you."

It only took another three minutes to get her off the phone, which is actually a pretty good result. Usually I end up trapped for hours. As I put the phone down I groaned loudly – fortunately we didn't have any customers in the shop– and then dug around in my outbox pile of folders. I found the Coddington's booking file about half way down and turned quickly to the accommodation reservation. Oh, thank God. The invoice clearly detailed a booking in a harbour-view room at the Sydney Marriott. It wasn't my fault . . . this time. I dropped the file on Julie's desk.

"Would you mind –please, please, please– calling the wholesaler and sorting this out? Apparently there is not even the smallest sliver of water from the Sydney harbour visible from the Coddington's room at the Marriott and she is feeling just a tiny bit perturbed," I said.

"Goodness me, the poor women," Julie said. "Don't worry, Adam, I'll move heaven and earth to rectify this insufferable tragedy."

My agency simply wouldn't run without Julie. She knows everything and everyone and never, ever makes mistakes. Why she is still with me after all these years I don't know. It's definitely not the money. I haven't been able to give her a raise in the last four years. "That would be perfect, Jules. Thank you . . ."

I returned to my desk, sat down and rubbed my temples. The hangover from last night's gala evening had severely drained my normally joyful effervescence.

"Would you like another coffee, Mr Holt?"

Kylie has a surprisingly maternal instinct for one so young. She's a lovely girl and, at only eighteen, is my agencies Junior Consultant. She won't last long though. They never do if they're any good. I am resigned to the fact that a bigger agency will poach her within a year. It won't be the first time, or the last. That's just how it goes. "Actually, Kylie, that too would be perfect, thanks."

I've always thought that Kylie, as a name, was an odd choice for a child with Polynesian heritage. You hear the name and immediately picture a tiny, blonde, Australian singer. Yet our Kylie was tall, dark and athletic –she's part Samoan– and carried herself like a model, upright and proud. She smiled as she slipped past my desk, out the back to put on the jug, probably thankful to have something to do. The phones have been very quiet of late and walk-in inquiries are starting to become rare. Business isn't good. I'm going to have to do something about it, but marketing isn't one of my strengths. Neither is business in general, really.

"Remind me again why we do this, will you, Jules?"

She was on hold to the wholesaler, the phone snugly held between her shoulder and ear. She didn't turn. "Because, Adam, we care about nothing more than making our customers dream holidays come true. Our work here is not just a job, but a true vocation. You and I, we are architects of blissful escape!"

Julie has been with me through thick and thin, ever since I first bought (thanks to a substantial –and yet to be fully repaid– loan from my parents) this damn travel agency. We've been in the same little square box –with its goldfish-bowl front window– in the tiny suburb of Milford on Auckland's North Shore for well over fifteen years. That's a long time in anyone's book and almost half my life. When I was a teenager the thought of becoming a travel agent never crossed my mind, but fateful events transpired, as they do, and things changed. I left the country instead of going to university and did the big O.E. (overseas excursion) around Europe and Asia. When I finally came home no one would hire me, until the old couple that used to own this agency saved my bacon and gave me a chance – but only because they were good family friends. They were wonderful people, very supportive. Yet I worked with them for only two years before they retired and sold me the business. Julie signed on as an office junior a week after I took over. She was a smart girl and has been pretty much running the show for me from the beginning. I have come to truly appreciate her relentless positivity along with her often amusing turns of phrase.

"Oh, yes. Now I remember," I said, playing along. "We are a special breed. Only few are chosen, or something like that . . ."

Kylie returned with my coffee just as my son drifted in through the front door. My sons name is Donald, would you believe. Like the Duck. Seriously. I had no say in the matter as, at the time, I had no idea he even existed. His mother christened him and good luck to you in getting her to explain why she chose such a lame name. But, fortunately, he's okay with it although he generally only answers to Don or Donny.

As he entered Kylie immediately perked up, straightening her skirt and pushing her long dark hair off her face. Julie and I laugh about this obvious crush, but Donny –as yet– hasn't seemed to notice.

"Hey, Big D," I said, trying to sound hip, and failing.

He frowned at me and didn't return the greeting. He flicked a casual nod of acknowledgement to Kylie and then shot Julie a

'Hey Jules' like he always does before slumping into one of the customers chairs in front of my desk.

"You look rough," he said. "Big night, huh?"

"Rough? Don't do that. This is me looking my best."

"I'm sorry to hear that."

Kids today. No respect. Donny is nearly twenty and presently studying engineering at Massey University up in Albany. He looks almost exactly like I did at that age, just a bit taller, and –if it's really possible, as I was his age in the 80's– hairier. His long, dirty blonde hair was scruffy, hanging well over his collar. Damn, I miss having hair.

"So what's up?" I asked.

"Nothing much, just drifting."

"Shouldn't you be at Uni?"

"Nothing on this morning."

"So maybe you should be studying?"

"Nah, I got it all." He tapped the side of his head, indicating that everything he possibly needed to know was happily stored away in the memory banks. To my great annoyance he was probably right. The kid always brought home near perfect grades and never seemed to be trying.

"So you must need something then?"

"Ohh, harsh. How could you think that?"

"What do you want?"

He hesitated, clearly considering the best approach. He had only moved in with me about three months ago after growing up with his mother and her various boyfriends. We were still getting used to each other as housemates rather than as estranged father and son. But it was coming together.

"We're a bit low on milk . . ."

I raised an eyebrow and just stared at him.

". . . and bread . . ."

Still I said nothing.

". . . and I could use a new car."

I smiled despite myself. Donny is a good boy. I love him, without question. He works part-time at KFC to bring in some getting-about cash, but is otherwise dependent on hand-outs from either me or his mother. I have been expecting this conversation for some time. I don't know how he's managed to keep the 70's vintage, boxy-shaped, old Mitsubishi Mirage that his mother's-previous-boyfriend gave him running even though it's obviously well past its prime.

"Did *Milly* fail her Warrant of Fitness?" I asked.

"Big time."

"How badly, big time?"

"Two tires are bald; there are holes in her exhaust; she needs new brake pads and rocker joints; and she failed on, umm . . . rust structure."

I nodded knowingly. In reality I understand very little about the mechanical workings of cars but I do know that being failed on a WoF for rust structure is pretty much the death knell for most cars. And the old Mirage had plenty of rust. One of the rear panels was held on with little more than duct tape. I wasn't surprised at all. Trouble was I'm a bit tight for spare cash at the moment and I really didn't want to have to discuss my financial woes in front of my staff. The shop was a simple open space. Everyone can hear everything that anyone else says here.

I frowned at him to bide time.

The phone rang. Kylie picked it up; Julie was still on the other line sorting out Mrs Coddington's grave issues. But that didn't mean they couldn't hear our conversation, so Donny and I just stared at each other like cowboys at high noon. Someone had to blink first. I couldn't afford to buy him a car and he knew it. I was still trying to decide how to frame my response when Kylie saved me.

"Bella on line two for you," she called out.

Bella is Donny's mother. We both rolled our eyes. "Thank you, Kylie," I said as I picked up the phone. "Do you have a GPS tracking system on him now, do you?"

"What?" Bella's voice snapped down the line.

"I have the prodigal son right here before me. Are you tracking him somehow?"

"You have Donny there, with you?"

"I have."

"Tell him I want my DVD player back. Today. Now."

"Hold the line please, caller."

I held the phone out towards Donny. I didn't have to say anything. He groaned and took it from me. "What?" he said quietly into it. He looked pained, closed his eyes and nodded his head. "Yes . . . Uh-huh . . . right."

Julie finished her call and glanced over, bemused. I shook my head at her and made a face. I was glad it wasn't me listening to Bella on the phone.

Donny slumped. "Yes, Mum. All right. I'll drop it over soon, this weekend," he said and then looked up at me. "Did you want to talk to Adam?" I formed a cross with my index fingers to ward off the possibility of having to take the phone back. "Okay, whatever," Donny said and hung up. We resumed our staring match as if we'd never been interrupted. "So . . ." he said finally, ". . . the car?"

The phone rang again. I wasn't quick enough. This time Julie picked up. I really didn't want to have this conversation with my son. Not here. Not now.

"Adam, I'm sorry but this call's for you." Julie said, saving me again. I told you she was indispensable. I shrugged at Donny and raised a finger to indicate that I'd be just a minute. I picked up the phone.

"Adam Holt."

"Adam, it's Gemma Vickers."

Gemma is a friend of Brent Barclay's wife, Sharon. They had tried to set us up over dinner once. Gemma lives out west. Titirangi or Green Bay, somewhere leafy with nice views. We got on okay. She was nice, albeit in a snobby country-club type of way. We had a nice meal, pleasant conversation, but she was definitely not the one either. Too high-maintenance.

I gritted my teeth. "Hey, Gemma. Nice to hear from you."

There was silence for a moment and I wondered what I'd said wrong already. When she finally spoke her voice was shaky. "Adam, I . . . umm . . . there's been a . . . a thing. It's about Sharon . . . and Brent."

"What sort of thing?"

"There's been a . . . umm . . . oh, God. This is so wrong. Brent's been . . . and Sharon, she's been . . ."

My heart froze in my chest. It's been a long, long time since I've heard anyone sound so shaken. "Gemma, calm down. What's going on?"

"It's already on the news, it's so awful. Brent . . . he's . . . they've . . . Oh, God. I can't say it."

"Say what, Gemma? What's happened?"

There was a pause, a moments deafening silence. "Brent's dead, Adam . . . I'm at the hospital with Sharon. It's just so awful, it just so . . ."

FOUR

"You can't park there, lad. This is for drop-offs and pick-ups only. What if there's an emergency?"

The old man berating me must have been at least a hundred years old, but he wasn't going to step aside. I briefly considered arguing the point with him, but decided against it. I went back to my car and moved it from outside the North Shore hospitals main entrance and found a space in the parking lot. Five minutes later, as I returned to the entrance, I steadfastly ignored whatever the old guy was muttering as I finally brushed past him.

"I'm looking for Sharon Barclay," I told the smiling women at the reception desk. "She came in late last night, I understand . . ." Her irrepressible smile remained firmly in place as she tapped away on a keyboard. ". . . in an ambulance," I added mindlessly. I was having trouble thinking straight. Gemma had told me where they were and I promised to come immediately, and I had. I could barely speak as I left the shop, only just able to express that Brent Barclay was dead and that I had to go. No one said anything as I walked out.

In no time at all the receptionist directed me to a ward on the third floor and gestured to my right, towards the lifts. I thanked her and ambled off on legs that felt like I was walking through quicksand. The full reality of the situation was starting to hit me. I was numb, wrought with disbelief. Brent couldn't be dead. That simply wasn't possible. This had to be a bad joke.

When I reached Sharon's room I hesitated in the doorway and drew in a shaky breath as I saw her there, sitting in the bed, side on to the entrance.

Sharon Barclay is a beautiful woman. There is no two ways about it. She carries, with apparent ease, the sort of beauty that literally makes men breathless. I still remember the first time Brent introduced us about a year ago. I was so bedazzled that I actually stuttered as she took my hand. She spoke with a faint Australian accent and carried herself like a model. Tall, self-assured and poised. But today it was not her beauty that shook me; it was her forlorn and vacant stare. Her face was bruised and lip cut. She sat upright, but hunched like an old woman with her arms wrapped defensively around her knees.

She looked broken.

"Sharon," I spoke softly.

Her head turned to me ever so gradually, as if in slow-motion. Her eyes were red-tinged and dull and the spark that had been so electrifying was missing. She didn't speak. I suddenly found that I couldn't move. The vision before me was so foreign, so unnatural, that I froze, hopelessly unable to comprehend it. Then the tragic certainty hit me like a brick. Brent was dead. His wife's joyless eye's told me everything. My best friend was dead and I'd never see him again.

As I stood there, staring helplessly at Sharon Barclay, I found myself vividly recalling a conversation I had with Brent during our last boys-only getaway. It would have been about a couple of months before Brent would meet his future wife. We were lolling lazily on deckchairs at the Sheraton Hotel on Denarau Island, Fiji. We'd flown up on agents discounted airfares and Brent, being a big supporter of the Sheraton group, got us a few complimentary nights. We lay there beneath the blazing sun drinking cold beer.

"I don't know how you drink that shit," Brent said, referring to my Fiji Bitter.

"One should always partake of the local brews," I replied.

"It's piss-water," he opined brutally, swigging his Heineken.

"So how's your love life, Big Guy?" I said to deliberately change the subject.

He grunted and said, "Better than yours."

I laughed. He was probably right. I waved my beer towards two very attractive women wearing tiny bikini's across the pool from us. "Maybe, but I plan on rectifying the situation with one of those lovely ladies before the day is over."

He snorted. "Won't you have to fall in love with her first?"

I smiled. "I already have."

"Which one?"

"I don't mind."

"Yes, you do. You're the fussiest bastard I know."

"Come on. Have you looked in a mirror lately? There's no ring on your finger."

"That's different, I know what I want. And I'm looking forwards, not back."

"What's that supposed to mean?"

He waved his own beer towards the beautiful bikini babes. "Neither on those two are sporty blondes, with green eyes, who read Stephen King and like to sing loudly and out-of-tune. They've got no chance with you."

I felt myself frown. "I'm not hung up on her anymore."

"Yeah, right. And my back isn't hairy."

I took another swig of my beer to let the comment pass. "So why aren't you married yet then?"

He paused, drank some more beer and actually seemed to reflect on the question. "Because I haven't found the perfect woman yet," he eventually offered.

I looked over at him. It surprised me that he appeared to be serious. "Go on then, enlighten me. What's your definition of the perfect woman?"

He glanced at me, an odd smirk on his face, then turned away and slugged back a little more beer before he answered. "Perfect is perfect. Just that. Nothing more and nothing less."

"That's not a definition."

He snorted and rolled his eyes. I waited silently, forcing him to respond. After another minutes contemplation he did.

"All right then, how's this? She would have to be supernaturally beautiful, tall and willowy, with skin softer than silk. A woman who turns heads without even trying. Preferably brunette. She would have to be my intellectual equal and she'd definitely have to be more than a little bit sexually deviant. Oh, and an exceptional cook too."

I had to take a minute to process all that. "Wow. Some list."

"A man's gotta have standards."

"So you're actually looking then? I mean, if you found this willowy, deviant, brunette chef you'd get down on one knee?"

This time he surprised me again by answering without hesitation. "Like a shot, Holt. When I find her I'll know it and when that happens I'll close that deal faster than a rat up a drainpipe."

At the time I wasn't sure he was being serious but now I know better. Only a few months later he found Sharon and, I have been led to believe, she fit his detailed requirements like a glove. Brent's perfect woman.

I stood and stared at her, there in the hospital bed, looking so lost and alone, and was unable to imagine her ever being that perfect woman again. My heart sank with pity.

Gemma suddenly materialized from a seat near the end of the bed. I moved into the room and saw a depth of horror in her eyes that actually frightened me. She shook her head silently and looked away, forlornly unable to hold my gaze.

I sidled up beside the bed, lost, totally bereft of what I should say to Sharon. I suppose I had come to try and comfort her but my mind was blank. I started to sit down on the bed, near her feet, but stopped, feeling uncomfortable. I moved forward. I wanted to reach out to her but then drew back. Touching her seemed wrong somehow. The realisation that we hardly knew each other hit me like a hammer blow.

It was less than a year ago when Brent had seemingly conjured her out of thin air one day and, true to his word, he closed the deal without hesitation. They had married quickly, supposedly on a whim, while holidaying in Fiji, back at the Sheraton Denarau, of course. I probably would have been Brent's best man, but he didn't have one. It was just the two of them.

Since then we'd both made every effort to get to know each other over dinners and social get-togethers. But Sharon –besides being impossibly beautiful, which I honestly still found a little intimidating– was also a very private person. And I am not an expressive type myself. I don't open up to strangers or bare my sole to just anyone. We were starting to get to know each other, and I liked Sharon, don't get me wrong. But, for now, we were really little more than acquaintances with only one common interest – Brent.

And now that common interest was apparently gone.

I finally pulled up a chair and sat down about mid-way down the bed. Close enough to hold her hand if she reached out, but not as close as I possibly should have been. My mind was still numb.

"Are you okay?" I asked.

She was staring blankly at the bump that her feet made in the blankets that covered her. She didn't reply, but just moved a little. It was sort-of a shrug, sort-of a nod.

"What happened, Sharon? Can you tell me?"

She shivered, closing her eyes. I waited. After about a minute she half-turned to face me, eyes still shut. "We were robbed . . . the police are calling it a home invasion, I think . . ."

Talking was obviously a struggle as her words faded away. Something terrible had happened and I didn't want to push her. But I needed to know. Brent, my best friend, was dead. I needed to know how . . . and why?

"Last night?" I prompted gently.

She stirred, her eyes opened. "Yes, around 1.00 am." I waited for her to continue. I didn't want to push her. Eventually she did, gazing vacantly over my shoulder. "He had just arrived home . . . from that thing at the Hilton. You were there too, weren't you?"

I nodded. I left the Awards dinner at about 11.30 pm. It would only have taken Brent around thirty minutes to get home so he must have stayed at the dinner for about an hour after I had gone.

Sharon continued hesitantly. "I was in bed, asleep. I woke up to shouting and noises from downstairs. I got up and rushed down, it had gone quiet, and there he was . . ."

I waited. She seemed to have become lost in the memory. I shuffled in my seat to remind her I was there. She started talking again.

"He was just lying there, on the carpet, just inside the front door . . . completely still. But he's never completely still like that. Never. He's always moving, even when he's sitting. Even when he's sleeping he's restless. Something's either tapping or jiggling. You know what I mean."

And I did. Brent had a certain energy about him. He was always in motion. I nodded again without speaking.

"I didn't see the blood, not straight away. He was lying in it. You know, face down, on top of the blood. But he was so still, I just knew, immediately . . ."

A nauseous sensation began to creep up inside me. I couldn't imagine Brent bleeding. He was indestructible.

"They'd stabbed him. More than once. The police told me they stabbed him eight times – all in his chest and stomach. Why would they do that, Adam?"

I couldn't answer her, I was too horrified. It seemed excessive to me. Surely one stab would be enough to ensure they could get away with whatever they wanted to steal. Gemma made a soft sobbing sound behind me and moved back to her chair. Sharon drew another deep breath and continued.

"And the police . . . they told me . . . Oh, God . . . that they used one of our own kitchen knives. Eight times, Adam. With one of our own knives . . ."

Our eyes met briefly. This time I looked away. A giant hand grabbed at my stomach and squeezed. I tried not to throw up.

For an eternity I couldn't meet Sharon's eyes. I couldn't bear to see the anguish in her. And I couldn't bear the thought of letting her see the anguish in me.

Finally I found my voice. "How many of them?"

She hesitated. "I don't know. I only saw one, but it felt like there were another two, at least . . . there were other noises, voices."

"You saw one of them?"

She turned her face away. "Yes . . ."

Horror tore through me. She was bruised, cut. The way she seemed so lost. This was more than just the trauma of finding her husband murdered.

"Oh, my God, Sharon. Did they . . . did they hurt you?"

Tears began to immediately bubble from her and she visibly crumpled, clutching herself tighter. She mumbled. "I don't want to talk about that . . ."

I finally reached out to her, offering my hand. Wanting to offer some small amount of comfort. But she pulled away, not wanting to be touched. The realisation of what she must have been through overwhelmed me.

"I'm so sorry, Sharon. If there's anything I can do . . ."

She began to sob. Desperate, wrenching sobs that made me feel desperately inadequate. I put my head in my hands and tried to wish it all away. Gemma rose and came to sit beside Sharon on the bed. Our eyes met again for a moment and I finally understood. Sharon must have been assaulted, or probably worse, by the burglar or, I shuddered, burglars. Gemma put her arms around her and hugged tight without speaking. The sobbing continued unabated.

I felt useless. I could find no words.

A million years later the sobbing eased. Gemma was still holding Sharon's hands and dabbing at her tears with a tissue. I tried to focus, but I was numb. Brent was gone. Murdered. I still couldn't really believe it. Unable to think of anything else to say I just offered my help again.

"Is there anything I can do for you, Sharon. I need to do something, anything?"

She drew a deep breath and exhaled slowly. "There really isn't anything. Gemma is here . . ."

"That's good," I said, for lack of anything else. We sat for another minute or so in silence. Finally she spoke again.

"The police said that they wouldn't release his name . . . to the media . . . until all of his next-of-kin are advised. But there isn't anyone else to tell . . . is there?"

I didn't have to think about it. "No, there isn't. You know his parents are both gone and that he's an only child. There's really just me . . . and you."

"What about his business partner?"

I leapt at the opportunity to feel useful. "Yes, of course. Someone needs to tell Marguerite Dodd. Would you like me to do that? I could do that for you."

"Would you? Please. I don't think I can."

"Brent has, uh . . . had, a lot of friends in the travel industry. I'd be happy to contact all of them for you too."

We lapsed into silence. There was so much else I wanted to ask her about what happened, but it just didn't feel right. Now was not the time. Her wounds were still far too fresh.

After sitting for another few minutes in silence I excused myself and slipped away as quickly as I could.

FIVE

"Look Adam, It's great to see you and all, but I'm swamped here. And Brent hasn't even turned up yet this morning."

Marguerite Dodd looked extraordinarily stressed for a woman that I'd always thought did next-to-nothing in running the business that bears her name. I shook her hand and gestured past her. "That's what I need to talk to you about, Marguerite. Can we step into your office for a minute?"

She looked puzzled. I very rarely came into the palatial Takapuna offices of Barclay and Dodd and usually Marguerite and I would exchange nothing more than the required pleasantries. I felt awkward, standing in the offices beautifully appointed reception area, under the gaze of the far-too-coiffured receptionist, while soft muzak gently butchered something –it may once have been a Fleetwood Mac song– in the background.

"Don't tell me. You two got good and hammered at the Awards dinner last night and you need me to be part of your cover story for whatever Brent's told his wife. Yes?"

"No, Marguerite. Nothing like that." I gestured again and she reluctantly started moving.

"So what is this? What's he done now?"

I didn't reply as we passed through the expansive offices. Barclay and Dodd is a corporate travel agency and couldn't have been more different from my basic three-person shop. The open-plan design revealed almost fifty consultants spread through a maze of inter-connected desks with low partitions separating them into little groups. The carpet was deep and plush, mood lighting on the walls highlighted various industry awards and certifications while potted plants were dotted around to lend a bit of greenery. It was a hive of quiet and purposeful activity as we padded across the carpet in silence.

Marguerite led me into her office, frowning, and moved around behind the desk to sit down. She waved towards a chair for me as I entered, closing the door behind me. Her office was chic and disheveled with files scattered in small piles around the room and flight booking printouts littering her desktop, although it somehow felt like it was set up this way just to make her look busy.

She was an attractive, sociable and likeable lady, in her early thirties, and her core role for Barclay and Dodd mainly involved serious customer schmoozing. An enviable lifestyle, I guess. If I believed everything that Brent had told me about Marguerite it was her parent's money that bought her this position of prestige in the travel industry. The Dodd's were old money. North Shore royalty. Marguerite was a dedicated socialite, with her image appearing in any and every public-ation and gossip blog that she could possibly manage. Although she had a state-of-the-art laptop on her desk-top I was led to believe that she used it mainly for googling her own name to keep track of her public profile.

I sat down and tried to figure out what to say. I had been trying not to think about it because the raw emotions within me were startling. Denial was currently the strongest of them. I just couldn't accept that Brent was dead. It did not compute. Brent was unbreakable, all-powerful. I simply could not conceive of how my life would be without him.

But Marguerite was impatient. "If Brent's got himself into something, uh . . . controversial, well, just spit it out. How bad can it be?"

I looked at her, she had one eyebrow raised and her arms were folded across her chest, clearly irritated. I had to stifle a smile as a memory hit me of how Brent often referred to her as 'Mistress Maggie' behind her back. She usually wore buttoned-up suits and her bottle-blonde hair pulled back in a severe, authoritative style of knot when she was in the office –as she did today– while she would literally let her hair down and unleash her cleavage when out on the town. With some effort I managed to shake away an image of her in suspenders with a whip.

"It's nothing like that, Marguerite." I said and then paused, trying to focus while still struggling to come to grips with how I could say this. "Look, it's bad news I'm afraid. Very bad news."

She went quiet. Something in my face must have finally registered. "Something's happened to Brent, hasn't it?"

I nodded.

"Jesus Christ, is he in hospital? Did you guys get drunk? That stupid, arrogant bastard. I knew he'd . . ." She stopped ranting as I shook my head. "Then what is it? What's happened?"

I took a deep breath. "Brent's dead, Marguerite. He was killed last night in a home invasion. After the dinner. Someone killed him. At his house. They murdered him . . ."

Marguerite just stared at me. "This isn't funny, Adam."

"No. No, it isn't."

"You're being serious . . ."

"I'm afraid I am."

"Jesus." She looked away, staring blankly around the office as if suddenly seeing all her own crap for the very first time. "Jesus Christ, this better not be a wind-up."

"It's not. I'm sorry."

"A home invasion? Seriously, that really happens?"

"It's hard to believe, I know."

"And they killed him . . ."

I didn't respond and left the news to sink in. While I could barely believe it myself, I could tell she was struggling to comprehend that her business partner would never walk in through the door again. She asked me to repeat myself: Where? When? How? I complied as best I could, outlining for her what little I really knew. Eventually Marguerite stopped asking questions and fell silent. I don't think they were ever really great friends, but you could see her usual self-assurance draining away.

When she turned to her lap-top and started tapping away I was surprised. After a minute she spoke flatly. "Home invasion leaves businessman dead."

I stared at her blankly.

"On the NZ Herald website . . . that's the headline." She was checking the news, possibly to be absolutely certain that this wasn't some kind of very bad joke. She read for a bit and spoke again without looking up. "There are no names yet. It just says a businessman and his wife, victims of a home invasion in Takapuna. How long do you think it will be before they release his name?"

"Probably not that long. He has no other family to inform. Just Sharon . . . and she, well . . . she knows."

"Is she okay? This isn't very clear."

"I guess she's as well as can be expected."

"What do you mean? She wasn't hurt, was she?"

I hesitated. Her situation seemed to me to be a very personal and private thing. Would I be betraying a confidence by telling Marguerite? Did she even need to know? She stared at me.

"Did they stab her too? Is she okay?" she asked.

"She was . . . uhh, assaulted. But not stabbed."

"Assaulted? You mean they beat her . . . or . . ."

I couldn't say it or meet her eyes.

"Jesus."

I nodded slowly, pretty sure she understood.

"God, that's awful."

"I know."

She was slowly becoming pale, staring at the computer screen and shaking her head. "This is terrible," she said. "We're not ready for this . . ." she trailed off.

I didn't understand, but chose not to respond or query her words. I felt that she must have been referring to the business, the agency.

Marguerite continued to stare fixedly at the computer screen and started to mumble softly, more to herself than to me. "This can't be happening. We've got big accounts coming up. Brent was all over them. Shit. And that bastard Armitage is . . . Jesus . . ." She trailed off, her words losing form.

Brent would never say it directly but in discussion his inference was always clear that, at Barclay and Dodd, he was the brains behind everything and Marguerite was only there because her family had money. I'd always considered his snide comments to be self-serving bluster, but maybe there was more to it. The look on Marguerite's face was eye-opening. She was really freaking out.

"I'm sorry, Marguerite," I said, more to remind her that I was still in the room than anything else. She lifted her eyes and gazed at me. A deep frown was firmly fixed on her face while her eyes danced with bewilderment.

Suddenly her demeanour changed. Drawing herself up rigidly she raised one eyebrow. "You knew him for a long time, didn't you?"

"Yes," I said, surprised by the question.

"Since you were kids, am I right?"

I nodded slowly.

"You two probably shared a lot of secrets over the years." She paused meaningfully and I suddenly went very cold. But she then abruptly slumped and shook her head softly, turning away. She looked back at her computer screen for a moment and then began to stare over my shoulder at the busy workplace beyond the office window. "It's all going to come out now," she said. "Everything . . ."

I didn't know how to respond.

"You think you know someone, Adam. But you never really do."

Her face went dark before she finally closed her eyes and took a deep breath, composing herself. Getting to her feet she stared at me grimly and stretched out her hand. When she spoke again her voice was careful. "Thanks for coming in. I guess there's not a lot more to talk about here, is there?"

I stood up and took her hand but the grip I offered was not returned. Her hand in mine was limp and cold, her thoughts already a million miles away.

"I'm sorry, Marguerite," I repeated simply and left her office.

I didn't go back to work, I couldn't face it. I was onto my third beer at home when the police dropped by to question me about last night. Two guys in suits with ID badges in little leather wallets knocked on my door. I spent thirty minutes with them but even now I couldn't describe them or tell you their names.

Their assignment was obviously to piece together Brent's last movements, but their efforts seemed perfunctory. I got the feeling they were pretty certain that his death had been a burglary-gone-bad and they just needed to get this extra info for the record. It was a depressing discussion.

I told them what time I had left the gala dinner and that I'd last seen Brent with Linda DeWalt. They took her contact details. I asked if they were going to catch the guys that did this and they respectfully assured me they were pouring significant resources into the investigation. But they wouldn't tell me anything about that.

They asked me, quite specifically, about any disagreements Brent may have had recently. I was only able to tell them about the argument with Harold Armitage and Cato last night since I hadn't caught up with Brent for a couple of weeks before that. But that squabble was nothing abnormal. Brent was always rattling cages. It was how he did business. He bullied people. He wound them up to expose their weakness and then he would find some way to exploit that weakness. He'd boast to me about his techniques all the time, and then call me a soft-cock because I wasn't ruthless enough. But even as I told the police about the argument I could see in their faces that they didn't consider it relevant. I had to agree. Surely it didn't matter who Brent had been arguing with previously. Sharon said it was a home invasion, a robbery gone wrong, a pretty random sort-of thing. Brent's petty quarrels beforehand meant nothing.

I asked if much had been taken but they wouldn't say. My question led to a brief discussion about what valuables Brent and Sharon were known to have in the house. Did they have a reputation for hoarding cash, or gold, or other valuables? No more so than any other affluent, egotistical, and vain businesspeople, I said. I would expect there are plenty of soft targets living around Auckland's North Shore. My openness on the subject drew frowns, which I immediately regretted. But it's one of my foibles. Rich, flashy people generally annoy me . . . and Brent, despite being my best friend, was one of the worst. He was one of those guys that had to be seen to be successful. He had the latest model SUV; only wore branded clothing and footwear; was a member at the trendiest gym; always had a tan and was forever showing off his newest model iPhone. His need to demonstrate his success was like a sickness that I simply have never understood.

Then they asked me if anyone could confirm my movements after the dinner. That annoyed me, but I had to accept that they were just doing their job. I told them that my son was here when I got home, he could vouch for my arrival time and that I went straight to bed. They took his contact details too.

I half expected one of them to mention Brent and my shared past, but they didn't. It was ancient history and they can't have made the connection yet. But I felt sure they would eventually.

After they left I returned to my fridge for another beer. It was Friday afternoon. A long, depressing weekend of anger, denial and self-pity awaited me.

SIX

Donny repeated the greeting into his headset's microphone for the millionth time. Sunday evening had been busy earlier but it was much quieter now it was late. "Welcome to KFC, please place your order when you're ready."

"D, my man," the voice crackled back into his ear. "What time are you finished tonight?"

Donny immediately recognised the lazy drawl. "Hey, Slouch. Now, man. Now. You're my last order."

"Awesome . . . so, what 'choo recommend tonight?"

"Just read the menu, Loser. It's all good shit."

The headset went silent and Donny checked the video feed. He could see Slouch staring at the menu board from the drivers' seat of his ancient Mini. It was a 70's model and had so many dents it looked like it had been used as an extra on Goodbye Pork Pie. Slouch's Mini was almost as crappy as *Milly* but at least it had a current WoF.

Donny sighed. It was right on 11.00 pm. He was tired; it had been a long day, a long weekend. His Dad had been really bummed out all weekend because his mate –a man that Donny had only met a couple of times– had died. Adam had been moping around the house looking lost. Donny didn't know what to do or what to say. He'd had a lot of practice consoling his mother over the years, whenever she broke up with her latest boyfriend, but this was different. Donny didn't think that his Dad would snap out of his funk anytime soon. He was hopeful that Adam would already be in bed when he got home and they wouldn't have to talk.

His headset crackled again. "You got anything ready to toss? I'm good for any kind of freebie," said Slouch.

"We're not closing yet, you cheapskate. You want food, you gotta order from the menu. You know that."

"Come on, D. I'm starving out here."

Donny waited a few seconds and then said, "Welcome to KFC, please place your order when you're ready."

The headset crackled back a mild obscenity.

Donny looked around himself. There were no customers other than Slouch currently blocking the drive-through. His only co-worker was slopping out the toilets and the manager was hiding away in what passed for an office out back of the fast-food restaurant.

"I guess I'll have the popcorn chicken then," Slouch's voice suddenly crackled in his ear.

Donny sighed again. Slouch was so predictable. He always asked for freebies and when he was denied he always ordered the popcorn chicken snack pack.

"Drive through to the window please," Donny said.

Slouch did so, as Donny bagged up the order.

"So, did you sort it with your mum?" Slouch asked as he handed over payment at the window, all in coins as usual.

"Didn't see her, man. I just dropped off the DVD player and had yet another freaky moment with the Grunter."

"Dude, that guy is one weird prick. Boy, but your mum can pick 'em. What'd he do this time?"

"Not much really. Just the dead-eyes glare. You know, where he locks eyes with you and doesn't say anything."

"Ahh, yeah. The mute zombie thing?"

"Almost. I walked in, and he was on the phone, and he just turns and shoots this glare at me. For no reason. Just really hostile. You know, like I just spat on him or something. And then he says, 'How long have you been there?' and gives me the evil eye. He's a real fun guy, that Grunter, you know."

"Yeah, a regular comedian."

"So I just put down the DVD player and legged it. You know, beat the hasty retreat."

"Smart move."

"Yeah, so what you doing now?"

"No plans, just gonna hang for a bit."

"Cool, I'll catch you in five."

Donny checked there were no other cars waiting and then slipped quickly out the back. His manager was a young Indian guy, only a couple of years older than Donny himself, whose nametag carried the moniker 'Johnno'. Donny was pretty sure that wasn't his real given name. Johnno's uncle was the owner. Nepotism at this KFC was alive and kicking. "Hey, Johnno. It's 11.00 man, I'm outta here."

Johnno didn't even look up from the game he was playing on his portable playstation. "Customers?"

"Nil," Donny said.

"Who else is on?"

"Estelle."

"Okay, give her the headset will you."

"Right, will do. Catch you later."

"Whatever."

He grabbed his jacket and found Estelle just stepping into the serving court. Handing her the headset he saluted in farewell. "You're in charge now, Captain. Be strong."

Estelle was the same age as Donny, and also studying at Massey University, but majoring in media studies. She sighed and nodded. "When are you next on?"

"Tuesday, day-shift, and you?"

"I got a week off. Back next Sunday."

"Ahh, lovely. Enjoy."

Donny stepped outside and took in a deep breath of relatively fresh air. Another shift done. He did a quick mental calculation. Minimum wage, six hours, hmm. Should have earned just about enough to pay for a two-litre bottle of milk. God, there just had to be a better way to make a living. He stretched and started to walk towards his car. He could see that Slouch had parked beside it, on the far side. He had his head down, greedily tucking into his chicken and chips.

Suddenly a voice cut through the night air. "Hey, you. Are you Donny?"

He turned, surprised. He didn't recognise the voice. A woman was standing next to a near-new, bright and shiny, Ford Falcon. An XR6, Turbo, with stunning alloys and sleek golden bodywork that shimmered in the restaurant's glow.

But then his gaze drifted to the woman herself. Donny's eyes widened. She was probably mid-twenties and wearing leather pants and jacket. His breath caught in his throat. This woman was mind-numbingly, smokingly hot. She had a sexy exotic look that made him imagine her as Jessica Alba's naughty sister. Dark-skinned, sultry, unobtainable. And he'd never seen her before in his life.

"You are Donny, aren't you?" she said in a seductive tone and walked up to him. He was momentarily lost for words. She smiled disarmingly and arched one perfectly sculpted eyebrow before dropping her gaze to his chest. "Ah-ha, just the man," she said as she read his KFC name-tag. Pirouetting on her toe she glided back to the Falcon. "Get in. I have something you really need to see."

Donny actually hesitated for a split-second. But he was a nineteen year old red-blooded male and this woman was spectacular. Easily the hottest lady he had ever seen – in real life, that is. How could he not follow? He glanced over at Slouch who was now looking up, craning his neck to get a better look at the gorgeous woman. Donny grinned at him, flashed his eyebrows and went to the car.

She fired it up the moment he slid into the passenger seat and was gunning it out of the parking area before his door closed properly. He clung to the seat and tried to act cool as the XR6 powered away up the road.

"Put your seatbelt on, Big Fella . . ." she purred while maneuvering the low-flying vehicle between two slower moving cars and accelerating heavily. He grabbed at it and clicked it firmly in place. ". . . and hold on." She had a slightly rural accent, like she had grown up on a farm or a small kiwi hick town, which Donny found a little incongruous. It wasn't the foreign-accented voice you would expect having laid eyes on her exotic and near-perfect exterior.

Less than a minute later they were turning, almost sliding in fact, onto the motorway. Punching her foot to the floor the car growled menacingly as she made it roar down the ramp and onto the wider, black tarmac. Only once they were cruising in the outside lane did she speak again. "Having fun yet?"

"Yeah, sure . . ." he said. Donny was shocked, but also very excited. It's not every day a beautiful woman picks you up in her awesome car and whisks you away. This was almost a fantasy come true. "Who are you?" he asked.

She smiled easily. "Who would you like me to be?"

Wow, what a great question. Donny's heart was already racing. He wasn't sure how to answer. The Falcon was literally flying north on State Highway One and at the speed they were going they'd be at Orewa in minutes. Donny didn't really care. He couldn't believe his luck. "I don't know. Do you have a name?"

She laughed. "Let's say I'd rather remain anonymous. So what would you like my name to be?" She angled her face, teasing him, one eye on him and one eye casually on the road. Donny took a deep breath. He couldn't take his eyes off her. "Anonymous is okay with me," he said.

"But you can't call me that."

"I don't mind, really."

She laughed again. "Go on, pick a name. Any name."

He couldn't think straight. Nothing sprang to mind. "Ahh," he mumbled.

"We could be Donny and Marie?" she suggested. "Like the Osmond's."

Donny cringed. He couldn't bear to think how many people, mainly those around his parent's age, had started singing *"Puppy Love"* when they met him. He hated the song and had never watched The Osmond Show in his life.

She laughed easily. "Perhaps not . . . So I guess Donald and Daisy is also going to be a non-starter?" He grimaced, nodding. He'd heard the Disney reference far too many times before as well. She laughed again. "Okay," she said. "How about . . . Susan, or Sue? Or better yet, I could be Suzy."

"Is that your real name?"

"Perhaps . . . or something like that . . ."

"Suzy works for me."

Her face lit up with a massive grin. "Then Suzy it is."

He nodded, unsure what to say next. "Great. So. Where are we going, Suzy?"

"Away," she said.

"Anywhere nice?"

"Nice enough."

They zoomed along the motorway. Albany village was well behind them now and the Orewa turn-off was only moments away. They were leaving Auckland, and rapidly. "Okay, umm . . . can I ask where?"

"All will become clear soon."

He thought about that for a moment. There were so many possibilities. Maybe she was a high-class hooker and his mates had chipped in to hire her. Or perhaps Adam was setting up some kind of surprise for his birthday, which was only next week. Or maybe, just maybe, she'd seen him somewhere before –he didn't really believe this, but was prepared to dream– and she just wanted him. You know, for a bit of wild, abandoned, sexual gratification. He suddenly thought of that old song by Heart, the one where the singer says that *'all I wanna do is make love to you'* so that she can get pregnant, because her hubby didn't have the juice. That would be just fine with Donny. And what a story it would make. He didn't even care that no one would believe him. "So, how do you know my name?" he said.

"That's not important."

"I'm just curious . . ."

But she didn't reply. They were coming up to the Orewa / Dairy Flat turn-off and she was checking her mirrors. She pulled off at the last minute. There was a roundabout at the top of the off-ramp that allowed drivers to either cross over the road-bridge or return to the motorway. Suzy pulled on the hand-brake and the car skidded to a stop just through the roundabout. The engine idled with a throaty purr as she turned to face him. "You got a cell-phone?" she said.

He nodded. Doesn't everyone?

"Show me."

He pulled his battered old Nokia from his jacket pocket and held it up. She stretched out a hand, silently asking for it. He wanted to please her so just shrugged and handed it over. She slipped it into a zip pocket on her jacket.

"Just the one?" she said.

He nodded again. It was a fair question. Quite a few of his mates had two or even three. Some just to reduce costs with cross-network calling. Some to keep track of multiple girl-friends. Some for other reasons.

"Okay then. So, here's the thing, and you're just gonna love this." Her smile returned, but this time Donny noticed that it didn't really touch her eyes. He said nothing. "You see, Sweet Cheeks, I'm kidnapping you."

"You're what?"

"Well, maybe I need to rephrase that. I mean, you're not really a kid, are you? You're what . . . eighteen?"

"Nineteen. Nearly twenty."

"Well, there you go. So kidnapping, you know, it just doesn't sound right. Does it?" Donny was confused, so he again said nothing. "I guess this is more of an . . . abduction, although you aren't exactly being held against your will, are you?"

He remained silent. Suzy smiled oddly and carried on.

"I'm pretty sure that you would have had to have been forced to get into the car for this to actually be an abduction. But you were more, sort-of, coerced. Not even that, really. I mean, I just asked and you came willingly. So . . . from here on I think it best that we simply consider this to be a holiday. Okay?"

"A holiday?"

"Very good. You're getting with the program."

Donny started to get a bad feeling. "And what if I don't want to take this holiday?" he said.

She smiled again, but something strange crossed her face. Like a dark cloud briefly whispering past on a sunny day. She leaned across towards him. He caught a hint of sweet perfume and more than a glimpse of her ample cleavage. He sat still, unsure of what was happening. Was this it? Was she going to kiss him? His breathing became ragged. She tilted her head again and leaned in a little closer, then placed one hand gently on his thigh. "Trust me, Donny," she said. "You want to get onboard with our little holiday."

He could barely whisper. "I do?"

"Oh, yes-siree you do." She squeezed his thigh.

Once again there was something slightly off in her gaze that, this time, suddenly scared him. Everything in her body language was as sexy as all hell, yet her eyes were dead pools of blackness. He drew back a little and flinched. "And, ahh . . . what if I don't?"

Her fist moved so quickly he could do nothing to block it. She struck him with a sharp, incisive jab low to his side, near his kidneys, so fast and so hard that white light flashed across his vision before the pain erupted inside him. He cried out and crumpled, doubling over, clutching his side. Then he was thrown back in his seat as the car abruptly leapt forward. When he was once again able to focus and look out the front windscreen they were almost at the Johnstone's Hill Tunnels, well past the old North Shore city limits. The pain was incredible. He'd been in fights before, but never had he felt something as intense as this. He returned his attention to the woman who had so recently dubbed herself '*Suzy*'. The radio was off, but she was singing softly to herself as if she didn't have a care in the world. The tune sound vaguely familiar to Donny.

It sounded like that retro song '*Holiday*' by Madonna.

SEVEN

"I hope I'm not disturbing you Mr Holt, I appreciate that you must be very busy."

I didn't recognise the voice. Julie had simply advised that I had a Lance Hopkins on line one. I struggled to recall if I'd ever made a booking for anyone named Hopkins. Possibly. But when? Where to? I couldn't remember. "No trouble at all, Mr Hopkins. How can I help you?"

"Please, call me Lance and, as much as I would love to book a holiday I'm not calling for that. I actually need to ask if you would drop by and pay me a visit."

"Ahh, okay. And that would be in regards to . . ."

There was a brief pause. "Mr Holt, do you mind if I call you Adam?"

Even though it was still early on Monday morning, not yet 10.00 am and I wasn't fully awake, I was at work where my default setting is automatically tuned to ready-to-please. "Of course not, please do," I said.

"Great. Thank you, Adam. I'm a solicitor. A junior partner in Greenwood and Associates of Parnell."

"Okay."

"Your name is mentioned within the last will and testament of our late client, Mr Brent Barclay, and I was hoping we could meet and discuss a few things."

"Brent's will. Discuss things?" I paraphrased mindlessly. I am nothing if not lightening quick on the uptake.

"Yes, that's right. Now, and I apologise for the lack of notice, is there any chance you could drop by and meet with me later this morning? Say at 11.00 am?"

"Ah, just a minute . . ." I pretended to consult my diary. I knew there was nothing in it for today, or tomorrow, or the next day but I wanted a minute to think. Brent must have mentioned me in his will. A feeling of unease swept over me. "Umm, Mr Hopkins, Lance. Brent's funeral isn't until tomorrow. Isn't it usual for a will to be read after that? What is this about?"

"I understand the timing may seem a little odd, Adam, but there is a small issue that I feel should be addressed as early as possible. And I do think it would be best discussed face-to-face if that's okay. I have just been able to confirm, as an interested party, that Mrs Sharon Barclay is able to drop by this morning. If you were able to join us I think there would be real benefit in a round-table environment."

My feeling of unease increased, but he obviously wasn't going to tell me anything over the phone. "Okay, then . . . yes, sure. I can make 11.00."

He gave me the address and bid me a fairly cheery good day. I hung up the phone slowly and sat there in stunned silence. What sort of provision would Brent have left for me? Money, shares, his old collection of girly magazines? I spent the next hour contemplating dozens of obscure possibilities.

Later that morning, when I walked into Hopkins's office, the first thing I noticed was the transformation in Sharon. I hadn't seen her since Friday morning at the hospital and the change was, quite frankly, mind-blowing.

Only three days after having her life ripped apart she sat there looking poised and beautiful once again. Through her immaculate make-up I could faintly distinguish the dark smudges of bruising on her face, but that was all. Otherwise she was as stunning, if not possibly even more so, than she ever had been before.

We sort-of shook hands. Not in the usual hi-how-are-you way, but in a respectful yet stilted manner, more of hands brushing than a shake. We didn't hug. We didn't blow fake air kisses across each other's cheeks. We both murmured wooden hellos.

Hopkins was about ten years my junior, somewhere around thirty, and boyishly handsome. He was tanned and wind-swept, looking like he spent a lot of his spare time on the water; sailing or surfing or similar. He looked fit and vital. I sucked in my stomach and wanted to hate him, but he struck me as a genuinely nice sort of bloke. Although he did try to hide it he was clearly quite entranced by Sharon's beauty. But then, she did have that effect on most men.

I joined them at a round table in the corner of his office. Clearly this was to be an amicable gathering of equals.

"Sharon, Adam. Thank you both for coming in at such short notice. I understand that this is a difficult time for all."

We both smiled grimly and nodded.

"Adam, I hope you will forgive me for the way I'm approaching this but, unfortunately, especially for Sharon's sake, we need to discuss a fairly delicate situation that Mr Barclay has unwittingly created."

I didn't know what to say and looked to Sharon. She met my gaze briefly and then looked away. The temperature in the room seemed to drop a little and I shivered involuntarily. Unable to read her expression I turned back to Hopkins.

"I don't understand," I said.

"I'm sorry, Adam. This must seem a little . . . mysterious, but, please, let me assure you that the issue we need to discuss is actually a very simple one." He paused to favour Sharon with a reassuring smile before he continued. "You see, Mr and Mrs Barclay came to me a while back to update their wills, as I'm sure you'll understand most newly married couples do."

I nodded and waited.

"The process is usually fairly straightforward in this sort of situation, with each partner naming their spouse as beneficiary of all assets should tragedy strike. And it was for exactly this that we were preparing documents to cover, however there was one rather odd bequest that Mr Barclay insisted upon that was complicating the, ahh . . . proceedings."

Sharon shifted in her chair uncomfortably.

"You see, while the essential elements of Mr Barclay's will were to leave, as you would expect, all of his property, his wealth and his business interests to his wife, Sharon, there was one element that demanded a variation of the beneficiary path. This particular variation was in regards to the proceeds of one of Mr Barclay's two life insurance policies."

He paused and I glanced across at Sharon. Her face was a mask staring fixedly at the desk before us. Hopkins continued.

"For all intents and purposes it appears that Mr Barclay was intending to leave the proceeds of this second policy to you. However, and this is most unfortunate, Mr Barclay was still in the process of finalising this particular bequest within his last will and testament when he passed on."

Sharon flinched slightly at his words causing Hopkins to pause momentarily. She continued to stare determinately at the desk rather than at me.

"I'm sorry," I said, "But I really don't understand."

Hopkins briefly made eye contact with Sharon who nodded slightly before he shifted to face me full on.

"Please appreciate, Adam, that this is a highly unusual situation. While there may be precedence in the courts there are many variables and this is why we are hoping to work with you to mediate an agreeable outcome."

Too many big words. I shook my head. "What?"

"Mr Barclay visited me earlier last week to complete the documentation of his will. But he found a couple of errors within the typing of the document and requested that these be tidied up. We could have hand-amended them but Mr Barclay was quite insistent. He wanted the document to be clean, without flaw."

I could just hear Brent, inside my head, brutally demanding that the documents be redrawn and refusing to pay any extra. He was a consummate nit-picker.

"Now this normally wouldn't have been a problem. We, in fact, had the documents available for signature the same day but Mr Barclay was very busy and . . . so, well . . . he never actually got around to completing the appropriate execution of this will. The new document remains unsigned today."

"So there is no will? No second insurance policy?"

"That's where this becomes a little complex. The second life insurance policy was actually completed a few weeks back. And there is, in fact, a prevailing will."

I waited. Hopkins looked uncomfortable.

"Mr Barclay had a last will and testament lodged with us prior to his marriage to Mrs Barclay. In fact he made this, ahh, old will quite a few years ago." Hopkins again looked at Sharon. She stiffened.

"And . . ." I prompted.

"Technically, when someone marries, any will made prior to the marriage falls void. It is automatically revoked. But, given that there is some similarity within the two documents, and the unfortunate timing of events, this situation is not so clear cut. To be frank; it opens the possibility of contestability." Hopkins leaned back in his chair. "The old will, the document that Mr Barclay was in the process of superseding, was also fairly straightforward. It had only one beneficiary . . ."

Suddenly I realised where this was going.

". . . and that person was you, Mr Holt."

I gave it no thought at all. "I don't want it."

Hopkins did a small double-take. Sharon turned to stare at me intently.

"I don't want it," I repeated. "Whatever the old will says I don't care. It's not what Brent wanted now, that's obvious." I locked eyes with Sharon. "Understand this, please. I knew Brent all my life and I never thought that he would marry, that he would find someone that he could truly love, that he would want to commit himself to. But he did . . . and I was very pleasantly surprised. I was also very, very happy for him. He chose you, Sharon. He loved you. He wanted to be with you. To grow old with you. He would want me to make sure that you're taken care of. And that's good enough for me. I don't want his money."

I could see the relief and gratitude blossom in her face. She must have been so worried. To have everything go so horribly wrong and then have to face losing everything else. It just wasn't fair. I wouldn't do that to the woman my best friend had loved. A small, uncertain smile touched her lips.

"Thank you, Adam," she said softly.

There was another awkward moment. I felt like she wanted to lean over and hug me but, because of her recent horrific experiences, I realised she couldn't bring herself to.

Hopkins intervened to break the silence. "That's very generous of you, Adam. I'm sure that Mr Barclay would have truly appreciated the way you're helping us to deal with this."

I almost laughed out loud. If Brent were here he would more likely have berated me as a little girl's blouse for so easily giving away a possible fortune. The phrase soft-cock reverberated around inside my head.

"So what do I have to do? Just sign something?" I said.

"Essentially, yes. But, given the circumstances –in that you are still grieving the loss of Mr Barclay– I think that there would be some benefit to holding fire on completing any documentation until you've had some time to really consider the implications. I'd like to propose that we allow, say, a thirty day period to elapse before we formalise things."

A look of surprise flashed fleetingly across Sharon's face, but disappeared quickly as she began to nod. "That's a great idea, Lance," she said, "but it won't complicate anything, will it?"

"Not really," he said. "It will restrict any large financial transactions during the period, but you'll still have access to sufficient funds to operate your day-to-day requirements as normal. And, to be frank, it serves to strengthen the final outcome. By providing Adam with a cooling-off period at this point, and not forcing him to make a snap decision, we are able to assure your position against contestability at a later date." He turned to me. "You understand this, Adam, don't you? By taking the thirty days to think things through and ensure you're happy with the outcome you effectively waive the possibility of changing your mind after the fact."

"I won't change my mind," I said.

"I hope that won't be the case, but this way we can all be more certain of avoiding any future disputes."

"I understand. It's fine with me."

We both turned to Sharon. She nodded. "Yes, that's fine with me too. It makes good sense," she said.

Hopkins smiled, nodding too. "Great. Fabulous. Then I propose that we move forward as if the new will had been signed and I will prepare a waiver that Adam can run past his own lawyer to essentially void the old will."

There was more nodding all around.

"Okay," I said, "So that's that? We're all good here?"

"Yes, we are, this is all —," Hopkins began, but suddenly stopped. "Actually . . . just a moment." He shuffled through some papers. "There is one little thing that I should share with you, in regards to the bequest of the second insurance policy." He found what he wanted and produced an envelope with a small flourish. "Mr Barclay left a note."

He held it out to me. Sharon leaned over to see it better. My full name was typed across the front along with words *'Private and Confidential. In conjunction with the last will and testament of Brent Maurice Barclay. Only to be opened in the event of my death.'*

It was sealed. It was signed with Brent's wild scrawling signature across the seal. I stared at it.

"Brent left me a note?"

Hopkins nodded. Sharon's eyebrows rose slowly.

"I don't understand," I said, not for the first time.

"It's not that unusual, really. I have a number of these sorts of note on file within peoples wills. Usually they are brief messages of farewell or good wishes to explain their bequest decisions. Here Mr Barclay has left you quite a sum from his insurance policy. I assume this note will have something to do with that."

I stared at the note. Brent had always been a controlling bastard. This was so like him. He always had to have the last word. If it hadn't been for a developing sense of trepidation I might have smiled. Hopkins proffered the note again.

For some reason I didn't reach out and take the note immediately. Something felt wrong about it. I looked across at Sharon who seemed oddly troubled, but she said nothing, shrugged slowly and then gestured that I should take it. A lump formed in my throat as I reached for the envelope.

Without speaking Hopkins produced a silver letter opener, shaped like a tiny medieval broadsword and held it out to me. Silently I took it from him too and stared at the envelope in my hand, a deep feeling of dread rippling through me.

Hours seemed to pass, but I couldn't do it. I turned to Hopkins. "When did Brent give you this?" I asked; mostly to distract myself.

"Just last week, when he dropped in to review the draft document. It was actually a replacement. He had included a sealed note for you within the old will as well."

Sharon watched on, frowning as the envelope weighed heavily in my hand. She was obviously perplexed but tried not to show it, as Hopkins waited with infinite patience. He was obviously being paid by the hour.

Slowly I nodded and then gently hefted the miniature Excalibur. It was solid, weighty. A potential weapon. It had warmed in my hand as I procrastinated. Another minute passed in silence before I finally drew a deep breath and turned the tiny sword to its task. Both Sharon and Hopkins stiffened in anticipation.

I pulled out a single slip of folded A4 paper. I recognised Brent's handwriting immediately. It read:

Adam,

We all made mistakes, but I made the worst.

I lied about that night onboard the Kestrel, I had to. You need to find Doug Masters. Let him tell you what really happened.

Money doesn't resolve things, but it's what I know best and I want to try and atone. It's too little, too late

but when you find Doug I know that you'll do the right thing. You always do.
And, for what it's worth . . . I am sorry.
Please forgive me.

Brent.

I could feel the colour draining from my face as I read it through three times. The words never changed but I still couldn't believe what I was reading. I felt light-headed. I wanted to tear the note up or burn it, but I couldn't move. I stared at it in disbelief, haunted by the scribbled lines.

Brent's message seemed clear. It was a confession.

"What does it say, Adam?" asked Sharon.

I looked up at her beautiful face and saw both concern and curiosity staring back at me. Hopkins was watching me also; clearly he had no idea what was in the note either. "I don't know," I said. "It doesn't make sense . . ."

Holding the note gave me an uncomfortable feeling. I folded it, slid it back into the envelope, placed it on the table and stared at it some more. I realised that I was shaking my head continuously and tried to stop, but found it impossible. I needed some air. Some time to think. I couldn't tell them what the note revealed. I had to get out. I picked up the note, shoved it into my pocket and stood up, surprising them both.

"I'm sorry, but I have to go," I said abruptly. But as I reached the door I stopped and turned. "You said there was a note with the old will also. Am I right?"

Hopkins hesitated. "Yes, there was . . ."

"Do you still have it . . . on file?"

He shook his head immediately. "I'm sorry, no. Mr Barclay took it with him. We exchanged envelopes last week. No copies were ever made."

I nodded. Sharon rose and moved towards me.

Hopkins looked worried. "Mr Holt," he said. "I do hope that Mr Barclay's note hasn't changed anything for you."

Suddenly I realised that my reaction must have been a major concern to them both, potentially casting some doubt over our earlier agreement. Sharon gently laid a hand on my forearm.

"Adam," she said. "Are you okay?"

Her hand felt warm and strangely comforting as it suddenly came to rest on mine. I wanted to pull away and run from the room but the consternation in her eyes made me pause. Hopkins eyed me watchfully.

"I don't want Brent's money, Sharon. I won't change my mind on that," I said.

She shook her head in frustration. "I'm not worried about that. I'm worried about you. You look like you've seen a ghost. Please . . . sit down."

Embarrassment trickled through me. God only knew what they must have thought of me. Neither of these people had any idea who Doug Masters was and I had absolutely no desire to explain him to them. I took a deep breath and gently removed Sharon's hand from my arm.

"I'm sorry, but I really have to go. Rest assured; nothing's changed. I will not contest the will. Please go ahead with all the paperwork as we've discussed."

I offered a weak smile and silently left the office.

EIGHT

More than anything else Donny was mystified. While his wrist was firmly secured to the couch he lay upon he honestly couldn't complain about being all that uncomfortable. It was frustrating, not being able to move his left hand around, but it could have been worse. Suzy had made that clear.

His wrist bore a solid, thick black cable tie. It was pulled tight and impossible to pull over his hand, but not so tight as to bite into his flesh. Attached to that was another matching cable tie which was secured more loosely to a third cable tie that had been punched right through the stuffing of the couch and wrapped around the sturdy wooden fame beneath. His other hand was free, but there wasn't much he could do with it.

Suzy had gone out for a run along the beach. He thought about trying to escape but wasn't too keen. He hadn't gotten far the first time he tried and the fresh bruises that Suzy had given him for his efforts still smarted.

And he had no idea why he was here. She wouldn't say.

He stood up as best he could. Being tethered to the couch meant he could only stand hunched over like a gorilla. Dragging the heavy couch a few feet away from the wall allowed him to see out the main front window of the holiday house she had brought him to. They were at a bach. Right by the beach. Suzy had been serious when she told him they were going away on holiday. He scanned the panoramic view beyond the deck and saw no one. No sign of Suzy or anyone else either. No one that might come and rescue him.

Donny sighed in frustration. When they'd arrived here last night he'd tried to do a runner as soon as the car stopped. It was a big mistake. Suzy was much smaller than he was, but she was bloody quick and deceptively strong. He barely reached the end of the driveway before his legs were taken out from beneath him and he was on the ground taking sharp, stinging blows to the ribs. She had led him back to the car with his arm in a powerful half-nelson. And she hadn't seemed bothered by his cries of pain, so obviously there were no neighbours about that might hear him.

He wasn't sure, but thought they were on the east coast somewhere along Pakiri beach. He'd been to Waipu Cove once, a few years before, with Bella and one of her previous boy-friends. But that was further north. Suzy had turned off before they reached Wellsford and they'd wound their way through dark countryside and finally onto unsealed roads to this isolated spot, by the beach, in the middle of nowhere. Donny thought that it had to be private land; there were no other dwellings around, at least not within sight. After he'd tried to escape, and been so quickly recaptured, Suzy had broken into the bach, he'd heard the window break, and forced him inside. It only took her a few minutes to choose the couch in the lounge for him and to cut it open to add her simple security system. She stopped talking to him then too, refusing to answer any questions, so he'd pretended to go to sleep. He waited about an hour and then, working in the soft moonlight that drifted in the windows, he tried to escape. This was his second big mistake. He'd barely managed to drag the heavy couch, as quietly as he could, into the middle of the room when Suzy emerged from the bedroom and laid a single precision kick into his leg. The pain was excruciating, he thought he might never walk again. She threw him back onto the couch and pushed them both back up against the wall. Donny's leg was still quite numb. He hadn't tried anything since.

Suddenly he heard soft footfalls on the deck outside. He leaned further forward, straining to see who it might be, desperately hopeful. He opened his mouth to call for help just as the sleek form of Suzy stepped into view. Springing back he threw his weight into moving the couch back to its rightful position and then flopped onto it in panic.

He heard her enter the bach through a French door that connected the deck to the bedroom she had slept in. In moments she breezed into the lounge to smile at him.

"Morning, Sunshine. Did you sleep well?" she said.

Donny wasn't certain how to respond. He stayed quiet and stared as she leaned her hip gracefully against the door frame. She was wearing nothing but form-hugging lycra bike pants, a tiny sports bra and sneakers. A sheen of sweat glowed from her perfectly proportioned body. Donny swallowed hard and decided to play along. He motioned to the couch beneath him. "It was a bit lumpy, but I've had worse. How 'bout you?"

She smiled, seeming pleased with his response. "Very well, thank you. I'm a light sleeper, so it was nice that I didn't have to get up and rearrange the furniture out here again . . ." she tailed off meaningfully. "Are you hungry?"

"Starving," he said. "Would you like me to run down to the shops and pick up a few things?"

She laughed. "Oh, you are sweet but, no. I packed enough to keep us going."

Donny shrugged. "Happy to help if you need it."

"I'm not much of a cook though. I do hope you like eggs. I make a mean scrambled eggs."

"Sound's great."

"Good," she said and spun gracefully on one toe, like a ballet dancer, to disappear back into the bedroom. "I just need to have a shower," she called out, "and then we'll have a bite to eat."

Donny listened to a bit of fumbling around next door before Suzy emerged again with a toilet bag, towel and fresh clothes. She glided through the lounge towards the bathroom. But just as she reached the door she suddenly stopped and spun back to stand in front of Donny's couch. She crouched down directly in front of him. She leaned in close. He could feel the warmth of her body and the sweetness of her breath. The perfect smile belied the coldness he saw in her eyes as she whispered to him. "You won't give me any trouble today, will you?"

Donny felt a knot clench deep within his stomach. There was something very disturbing in the way she appraised him. He leaned back slightly, away from her, and shook his head slowly.

"No," he whispered back. "Of course not."

Suzy paused meaningfully and leaned even closer, so their noses were almost touching. "Good," she said. "Because I would get quite annoyed if you were to try running away again. Last night's efforts were, shall we say, a little tiresome, you know. And I really don't think we'd continue to get on so well together if you got me truly annoyed." She paused. "Do you understand?"

Donny understood, so he nodded carefully.

* * *

"Mrs Coddington for you again, Adam. Line One"

"Oh Christ, no. Not again. Please, Julie. I can't deal with her right now. Tell her I'm out, would you," I said, pleading with my eyes like a deranged puppy.

Julie raised her eyebrows for a moment, challenging me, and then finally spun away, returning to the phone. As she smoothly lied to my most annoying customer I sighed and dropped my head into my hands once again.

Coming back into work was obviously a mistake. I couldn't concentrate; my mind was a million miles away. Or rather, it was lost in the past. Somewhere around twenty years ago. I simply couldn't get thoughts of Doug Masters out of my head.

I barely remembered driving back to the North Shore. I must have managed it on auto-pilot as my mind whirled, reliving yet again what little I remembered of that terrible night and trying to understand what on earth Brent's apparent confession truly meant.

I pulled the note from its envelope and read it through yet again, for what felt like the hundredth time. It still made very little sense.

The note proclaimed that Brent had lied about that night. That *'He had to'*. But why? And what exactly did he lie about? I was so hung over the next day I remembered nothing. He had said the same thing. Was that the lie? Did he remember? Then why didn't he just say what happened in the note? Why tell me to find Doug and get him to tell me? The directive was so frustrating, even for Brent's overbearing and controlling manner. Mainly because finding Doug Masters would be impossible. The guy had been in hiding for twenty years. I really couldn't see how I was supposed to find him. I'm not a detective. Why on earth would Brent think I could do that? It was just plain crazy.

"Mrs Coddington just wanted to double-check that you had confirmed them a window seat for their flight on to Bangkok tomorrow night," Julie said, interrupting my fruitless train of thought.

"Oh, thanks . . . Did I?"

"Yes."

"Fantastic."

"They're going to hate Bangkok, won't they?"

"Absolutely. They'll despise everything about it."

"Then why are they stopping over?"

"I tried to talk them out of it."

"It'll be too hot, too dirty, too noisy . . ."

"I know."

Julie paused and appraised me for a minute. "So what's up?" she asked.

"What?"

"With you? What's up? You're acting like you have to disprove gravity before afternoon tea or the world ends."

"Maybe I do."

"No, you don't. Gravity sucks just fine without you."

I said nothing, just rubbed my tired eyes.

"Come on, spill. Maybe we can help," Julie said.

I thought about it. Usually I tried not to bother Julie with my problems, which were mainly related to either Bella and/or

Donny or to my convoluted and sadly shallow love-life. But this was different, really quite different.

Julie tried again. "Did something happen at the lawyers earlier?"

I knew from her tone that she wasn't going to leave me alone. "No, that's all fine," I said, already feeling colour rising in my cheeks as I spoke. Brent told me once that I blush whenever I try to lie. He would laugh at me every time. "It's just . . . Brent's funeral is tomorrow and there was someone we used to both know, way back when, that I wanted to invite. But we fell out of touch. I don't know how to find her."

Julie has known me long enough to know I wasn't telling the whole truth and she rolled her eyes. "Seriously? Is that the best you can do . . .?"

But Kylie suddenly called out: "Facebook." It's a small office. We can't help but listen in to each other's conversations. Julie may not have believed me, but Kylie wasn't watching my face.

"Or Old Friends on Trademe," said Julie, obviously deciding to play along anyway. But I didn't know what she meant by Old Friends and she frowned as I looked at her quizzically. "You're kidding . . ." she muttered.

"You got a name?" Kylie asked, excited at the prospect of something to do.

I shrugged. "Really, you think that'd work?"

"Try it, you dinosaur," Julie said. "Give us a name."

I felt my shoulders slump. Why is it that the bloody internet is always the answer to any question these days? I hate the bloody internet. I mean sure, I have email, and I use Trademe.co.nz to buy and sell stuff now and then, but in general I don't go online unless I absolutely have to. Mainly because I hate what the internet has done to my business. It used to be that only travel agents could book airline flights on special computers. But now any idiot can do it on the airlines websites. So what was once my primary skill, the weaving together of travel itineraries in multiple airlines booking systems, is now so simple a monkey could do it.

It pissed me off.

I gave in with a sigh. "Okay, how about Deborah Masters."

"Can you tell me more?" Kylie said. "Date of birth? What school she went to? A middle name?"

I surprised myself by being able to provide two out of three. Debbie was Doug's twin sister. Doug's birthday was the 1st of April; we used to joke about it. April's Fool and all that. We were the same age so I could offer them a year. And I knew they'd both gone to Wanganui High School. Doug used to always wear his old WHS rugby jersey to footy training and we'd teased him about that too.

"Do you know if she's married?" asked Kylie.

"No idea."

"What does she look like?"

Bland, I immediately –and unkindly– thought. Like a female version of Doug. "Hard to say . . . it's been years."

"Come on, Adam . . . tall, short, dark, blonde?"

"Shortish, mousey-brown hair . . . pretty plain really."

"Not much to go on . . ."

"Nope, she was always somewhat . . . ordinary."

Both ladies turned their backs on me, tapping away on their keyboards, searching God-only-knows-where online. I had nothing else to offer so I stood up to make myself a cup of coffee when the front door opened.

For the first time ever Sharon Barclay entered my shop.

"I know this is going to sound strange, Adam. But I kind-of feel that I owe you an apology . . . as well as my thanks."

There was no way I was going to have any sort of private discussion with Sharon in my office so I had quickly guided her a few doors down the road to a café. I had probably been a bit rude to my staff, so hastily escorting this stunning woman out the door without introduction. I promised myself that I would apologise to them later.

"I don't understand," I said as I concentrated more than was necessary on stirring sugar crystals into my coffee. The café wasn't very busy and we were both having trouble making eye contact, yet again. As always I found the intensity of her beauty somehow made me nervous and, I suddenly realised, this was quite possibly the first time we had ever been alone together.

"I guess my thanks should be fairly obvious," she said, pushing over a copy of Brent's will that I had failed to take with me from Greenwood & Associates. I didn't pick it up and it lay there between us, glaring up at me like an angry ghost. "This whole situation with the wills could have become a dreadful mess. I appreciate what you're doing."

Our eyes met briefly and I looked away first. "There's no need for thanks, it's the right thing to do."

She nodded slightly. "It's funny though, isn't it? That in the last few months you've probably seen less of Brent than ever before in your lives . . . because of me."

I offered a feeble shrug, but said nothing.

"That's what I need to apologise to you for . . . for, well, monopolising him so. I was selfish. And the way you've been about all this," she waved a hand towards the will, "it just makes me realise that I should have tried harder. I should have made more of an effort to . . ." she tailed off, seeming unable to find the words anymore.

"You don't need to apologise," I said.

"But I do."

"It's okay, I understand." Our eyes met again and this time I managed to hold her gaze.

"Thank you . . ."

I shrugged again. There was silence for a moment.

"The funeral is all set for tomorrow morning," she said.

"Yes."

"I was hoping that you would speak. No one knew him like you did . . . not even me."

I hate public speaking. Loath it. "Of course," I said.

"Thank you."

Silence fell again. Normally I could chat easily with anyone, anytime, about almost anything. But, today, no words came and I sat there feeling awkward.

"I was just wondering . . ." Sharon said suddenly. "What can you tell me about Marguerite Dodd?"

The new topic was a welcome relief, but still left me befuddled for a few moments. "I'm sorry . . ." I managed.

"Marguerite Dodd, Brent's business partner at Barclay and Dodd. I've just been in to see her, you know, to talk about the funeral and other things. But I'm not sure what to make of her. How well do you know her?"

"Not all that well, really."

She was quiet for a moment. "Would you trust her?"

I felt myself frown. "Why? What's she done?"

"Nothing in particular. She just seemed, I don't know, evasive. I tried to ask about the business. How it's running. How she plans to replace Brent, you know."

I held back a wry smile. Evasive. I bet the poor woman was really scrambling. "She was pretty shaken up when I visited and gave her the news last Friday."

"But do you think she's trustworthy?"

I had to really consider that. I'd always believed Marguerite to be more of a simple socialite. Privileged and easygoing. But not someone who would rip you off. "I can't really say, Sharon. Brent used to talk about her being a bit lazy, but I'm pretty sure he trusted Marguerite." I shrugged. "And if Brent trusted someone, well . . . that's always been good enough for me."

She offered me a small smile, silently acknowledging that my words included her in Brent's circle of trust. She nodded. "Then why would she be so cagey with me? It was like she was trying to hide something. It was odd. She wouldn't even commit to coming to Brent's funeral."

That struck me as odd too, but I didn't know how to respond. Instinctively I felt that Marguerite must be really floundering without Brent and didn't want to admit her managerial limitations to Sharon. It seemed only fair to give the poor woman a chance to work things out so I simply shrugged again.

Sharon looked into my eyes then and something passed across her face. Anxiety; annoyance; desperation. I couldn't be sure but I immediately felt a warm shiver of guilt. Brent loved this woman. I should be helping her.

"Would you like me to visit her with you?" I said. "See if we can work out what you need to do?"

Her relief was palpable. "Would you? I really don't understand the travel industry. You must know it well."

I tried not to cringe at the comment. While I did know a fair bit about travel I was nowhere in the same league as Brent when it came to business.

We'd actually travelled around the world together in our early twenties and that's how we both fell into the industry. I simply loved being in different places, soaking up unusual cultures, observing the way other people chose to, or were forced to, live. Those experiences often remind me that I'm actually pretty lucky to live in this beautiful country. In fact I know I can get a bit preachy on the subject when I hear people moan about the little first-world problems they have to face.

But Brent, I think, saw it all differently and he definitely put in more effort when we returned home. He worked part-time and studied hard earning qualifications in business and commerce and marketing. It's no exaggeration to say that the way he ran his corporate travel business was light-years more advanced that my little shop. Still, I wanted to be positive.

"Sure, if you think it would help," I said.

"Thank you, Adam. I'll set up another meeting."

There was another awkward silence before Sharon spoke again. "I'm sorry about all this."

"It's not your fault, Sharon."

"I know . . . it's just . . . he was such a rock. And I don't know who's going to miss him more. You or me."

I had no answer for that.

After yet another agonising period of silence Sharon again shook me with a sharp change of subject. "The note he left you," she said. "I know I have absolutely no right to ask –it was obviously a private thing– but it's been gnawing away at me. I can't help wondering what he wrote to you. What he could possibly have shared with you like that . . ."

I picked up my coffee too quickly, in an effort to avoid immediately answering, and spilled some on the table. Sharon quickly scooped up a napkin and set about blotting it up. But my clumsiness gave me the chance to try and gather my thoughts. I wanted to simply refuse to talk about it, but that kind of response somehow didn't feel right. Brent had loved this woman, trusted her. Yet I doubted that he'd told her about the *Kestrel*, about Kieran. What should I tell her? I struggled to decide as my lack of reply dragged on.

"I'm sorry, Adam," she said eventually. "I've upset you. I shouldn't have asked. It was obviously private . . ."

Guilt flooded through me. The note was back on my desk. I had read it over and over, yet was still in two minds. Was it really a confession? I was no longer so sure. The wording was so vague. Was that deliberate? Brent had clearly said that he lied, but not what about.

"No, please. I'm not upset. It's just . . ." I said, but I didn't know where else to go. Our eyes met and this time they locked. I couldn't look away. Her expression was difficult to read, yet I'd swear she seemed to be in desperate pain. In that moment I suddenly understood what was tearing her apart.

I got a note.

She didn't.

Pity ran through me like warm treacle.

NINE

My heart sank as I realised I would have to tell her something. But it wouldn't be easy. I had spent my entire adult life avoiding this subject. Wishing things had been different. I sipped my coffee again to bide time.

"Perhaps . . . if I could just ask one thing," she said tentatively. "The note . . . was it about me?"

I closed my eyes and sighed deeply, shaking my head. "No," I said. "Absolutely not." Sharon became still, waiting. Now I was committed. I had to offer her something. Evidence that the note was not about her, not about the life they had shared. Finally I opened my eyes, staring into my coffee, and spoke.

"It was about something that happened . . . a very, very long time ago. When we were teenagers." She raised her eyebrows, encouraging me to go on. I hate lying so I told her the truth in the most abbreviated format I could manage.

"It was a request, sort-of. Brent asked me, in the note, to try and find someone. A guy who was with us when this thing happened. He, well . . . disappeared . . ."

Sharon made no effort to interrupt and I found myself staring into my coffee and telling her more than I have told anyone else in the last twenty-odd years. I thought for a moment that I would feel like a weight had been lifted but it didn't. I felt numb. Just like I had when it happened.

"One night, when we were both about eighteen, we went out for a big night on the booze. There were four of us. Brent and I, a guy called Doug Masters, and . . . another guy . . . Kieran Sandford. We were so young, just kids really. We were all friends. We played together in the same rugby team. Brent and

I, we were both loose forwards. Doug was our half-back. Kieran the first-five-eights."

I had to stop as a lump formed in my throat. Sharon waited patiently, saying nothing. I continued. "We'd just won a big game. We were celebrating. We went over to Auckland and pub crawled around downtown. We had fake ID . . . as you do. We went everywhere. We got drunk. Very, very drunk."

I had to stop again. The words weren't coming easily. This time the silence rang on for a while and Sharon had to eventually prompt me. "Adam, please . . ."

I nodded in apology. "I'm sorry; it's been such a long time. Anyway . . ." I paused to sigh deeply. "Kieran died that night. Somehow. And Doug ran away. I don't actually remember anything, and neither did Brent. We were both so damn drunk. Somehow Brent and I got ourselves home and woke up the next day with stinking hangovers. We didn't even know that something bad had happened until Kieran's body washed up on a beach later that day . . ."

Sharon somehow managed to remain composed, but I could sense her surprise and disgust. She sat back in her chair, folding her arms. The classic body language quietly displaying her repulsion. I didn't blame her. It was a horrible, shocking story and not one I am proud of in any way. I looked back down into my coffee, searching for some way of telling this that didn't make both Brent and I seem like completely useless morons. But there wasn't. When you remember absolutely nothing about such a terrible event like that there are no excuses. And nothing can make you feel good about your part in it ever again.

I continued in a flat voice. "Over time the police managed to piece together what they think may have happened, but it's really still a mystery. Apparently we got onboard the *Kestrel* – the ferry to Devonport back then– and something happened. Kieran went overboard. They found blood on the ferry. Doug disappeared. He's never been heard from since but the police seemed certain, back then, that he was still alive. They thought he did something, and ran away. I don't know what happened. Brent didn't know either."

It all sounded so very lame as I said it, yet again. In the following years I had struggled to explain that night many, many times and every time I got the same empty, sick feeling in my stomach that I was feeling now. It's been a long time since I last had to endure this feeling. I hate it. I hate myself. I wish I knew what happened, but I simply don't.

After a few moments Sharon broke the silence. There was no obvious recrimination in her voice and I was thankful of that. "And Brent wants you to find this man, Doug, who ran away and has been missing for over twenty years?"

"So it seems."

"But why?"

"He didn't really say."

"But that doesn't make sense," she paused and her eyes narrowed, "unless you already know where he is?"

I felt like I'd been slapped. I sat back in my chair and stared at her. She watched me cautiously. "I don't know where he is."

"Then why would Brent ask you to find him?"

"I don't know."

The ensuing silence was tense and heavy and drew out uncomfortably. She stared at me openly and then rearranged her expression so I couldn't be sure what she was thinking. "So what are you going to do?" she asked.

"What do you mean?"

"Will you look for him?"

"For Doug Masters?"

"Yes."

"I guess I'll probably try, but I'm not a detective."

"You could hire one, a private investigator."

"I wouldn't be the first to try . . . Kieran's parents did. They spent a lot of time and money chasing Doug."

"Oh."

I shrugged once again. I felt that I'd shared as much as necessary to confirm that the note wasn't about her, nor did it need to involve her. She had clearly been hoping that the note contained something magic from Brent that we could possibly share. But it did not. The note was not a gift, nor a pick-me-up from my oldest friend, but a damning reminder of a time I would have preferred to stay forgotten.

Another eternal silence descended as it became clear to us both that there was nothing Sharon could say or do to help with my dilemma.

"I'm sorry, Adam," she said after a while.

"It's not your fault," I replied once again.

"You are going to be so impressed with us," Julie announced as I returned.

Sharon and I had murmured pitiable farewells as we left the café. She would set up a meeting with Marguerite Dodd and call me. I would prepare some words for the funeral.

"Have you finally sold something?" I asked hopefully. "Will we actually make this month's sales target?"

"No, don't be silly. We found Deborah Masters."

I was shocked. "You're kidding."

"We kid you not."

"Where? How?"

"Don't act so surprised, it wasn't that hard."

"Do you want to see her Facebook page?" asked Kylie.

I shook my head in disbelief and moved to stand behind Kylie, at her desk, to see her computer screen. Julie jumped up, obviously full of pride, and joined us.

The screen showed the blue strip and white background of what I vaguely recognised as the now ubiquitous Facebook frame. To the left, near the top, was an image of a woman in her late thirties. The hair was darker, pulled back in a pony-tail and she was grinning sweetly but I recognised Deborah Masters immediately. Beside the image was a name, in bold font: 'Debbie Ngatai'.

"How did you find this?" I asked.

"Old Friends, firstly," Julie said. "She's registered with both names as part of the Wanganui High School old girls hockey team."

"And then I just searched the married name on Facebook," continued Kylie. She pointed at the screen. "She and her husband own the Bakers Delight in Albany. See there."

"Good grief . . ." I muttered.

"I think he means; *Thank You Ladies*," said Julie.

"Obviously," said Kylie, smiling broadly.

"That's incredible," I said. "Well done, Thank you . . . Does it tell you anything else?" I asked, scanning the screen.

"No, not really. You need to become her friend to see who she's friends with and read any updates. But she would need to accept you as a friend first and I don't know her."

It sounded complicated and I was already overawed by the information on the screen before me. Doug's sister lived here in Auckland, on the North Shore, only a few kilometres away. She and her brother had been very close when we were all teenagers. If anyone knew where Doug was hiding –and even if he was still alive– it would be Deb. Surely. Maybe finding him wouldn't be as impossible as I had thought? But what would I say to her? My mind was reeling with the implications when another image on the screen caught my eye. This one was smaller, but the face it depicted was immediately familiar. I leaned in, squinting to see it more clearly and to read the words. There was a heading above the image that said: *'People you may know'*. The face was at a three-quarter angle, like she had been caught turning away, but her eyes were still on the camera, looking straight at me.

I froze in disbelief.

It was Claire.

The words beside it read: *'Claire O'Driscoll. 1 mutual friend. +1. Add Friend.'*

I suddenly pointed at the screen, at the tiny image of Claire, surprising Kylie. "How did you find that?"

It took Kylie a few moments to react and then focus on the face I was pointing at. "That one . . . you mean Claire. I didn't find it. Facebook did."

I stared at her blankly.

"Those images come up all the time," she said. "Facebook looks through your list of friends and matches them up with other people who are friends with them and then it suggests that you might like to be friends with the other person."

I frowned, struggling to follow. "So that image isn't part of Debbie Masters' information?"

Julie leapt in, shaking her head at me. "No, that's from Kylie's profile. Don't tell us you know her?"

"Then how come she's on the same page as Debbie?" I said.

Kylie held one hand up in front of the screen blocking off the right hand column. Now I could only see Deb's picture, some header navigation links and a few words in the middle of the white page. "This bit," she said, "is Debbie's information – which is pretty minor because I'm not her friend." Then she moved her hand to cover what I had just been looking at to leave only the strip down the right-hand side. "All this stuff is just advertising from Facebook."

I could now see that the header below Claire's image read: '*Sponsored*', and had small, brief adverts for the latest iPhone, some bizarre looking sunglasses and something to do with the All Blacks.

"I don't get it," I said. "Facebook knows that Debbie knows Claire? How does it know that?"

Kylie just looked at me. Julie laughed. "You're not listening, Adam," she said. "The image of Claire O'Driscoll isn't there because she's got mutual friends with Deborah. It's there because Kylie is logged in and it's suggesting that she –Kylie– might like to be friends with Claire."

Finally the penny dropped. I stared at Kylie open-mouthed. "So you know Claire?"

"Sure, but not in the way that I'd want to be her friend, you know, on Facebook. I'm just friends with her daughter . . . because I baby-sit her sometimes."

I was almost lost for words.

I would have recognised the woman in the picture anywhere, anytime. I used to know her many, many years ago . . . in what may as well have been another life.

Only I had known her as Claire Sandford.
She was Kieran's little sister.

TEN

"Call for you on line one, Adam."

Julie was annoyed with me; that was obvious. Normally she would have screened the call and checked with me first before telling anyone I was available. But I understood. I owed her, and Kylie, apologies. I was behaving badly.

A barrage of questions had poured out of me as soon as I finally worked out that Kylie actually knew Claire Sandford – or O'Driscoll as she was now known. I simply needed to know everything and I had greedily absorbed every answer she provided, although some were only supplied quite grudgingly. Poor Kylie, she didn't really understand, and I have to admit that I'd made little effort to explain.

And for the last twenty minutes I had been sitting at my desk, stewing silently. Claire was a solo mum, with two children, and lived nearby in Glenfield. She worked in Takapuna, would you believe; only a few minutes' drive away.

I hadn't seen her in over twenty years but the feelings that tore through me felt fresh and raw. I sighed deeply and picked up the phone. "Adam Holt."

"Mr Holt, this is Harold Armitage."

A voice inside my head, which sounded an awful lot like Brent's, screamed out: *'Fuck off, Armitage'* but I managed to ignore the compulsion and respond appropriately. "Hello, Harry," I said tiredly.

There was an exhale down the line that sounded suspiciously like a huff, then: "Adam. I was so sorry to hear the news about Brent. I hope you'll accept my condolences."

I sighed again, more softly this time. "Thank you."

"I was actually hoping that we could get together, at your earliest convenience, with regards a proposition."

"A proposition? To do what?"

"Could I buy you a coffee, Adam? Are you able to spare me a few minutes this afternoon? I could come to your office or meet you locally."

He'd taken me by surprise. The thought of Harold Armitage anywhere near my shop made me shudder, yet I couldn't think of a good enough excuse not to meet with him. And I probably needed to leave the shop, get some fresh air.

"Sure, Harry," I said, and suggested a café I occasionally went to in nearby Takapuna rather than a more local one in Milford, "When?"

"I can be there in fifteen minutes," he said.

My cell-phone rang as I began to climb into my car. I pulled it out and answered. "Adam Holt."

"Donny didn't return the remote."

"Uh . . . hey, Bella. Nice to hear from you."

"He's not answering his phone and isn't returning my calls. I've left half a dozen messages. When you see him later, get him to call me will you."

I closed my eyes, softly shaking my head in wonder.

Bella wasn't taking Donny's move away from home well. I vaguely recall her initial response to his suggestion that he move in with me as something close to *'Over my dead body'*, but with a few more choice words. Yet, as I was assured by my son, she had slowly come around to it. And it did make sense. I live much closer to Massey University and I had a spare room. Donny wasn't getting on all that well with his latest 'step-father' and it was a great opportunity for him and me to really get to know each other better.

"I'm sure it's just some kind of misunderstanding, Bella. Maybe he's used up all his pre-pay phone credit. Maybe his battery has died. He'll call you soon, I feel certain."

There was silence down the line. I had learned long ago that Bella dealt with disappointment by lashing out. Usually harmlessly, but this time she seemed to be in real pain.

"Did you try calling him at home?" I asked.

"He's not at home. He's living at your place."

I sighed. "You know what I mean. Did you call there?"

"Of course I did, there's no answer."

"Then he's probably at Uni, where he should be."

There was silence for another moment. "Just tell him I want my damn remote back," she spat finally.

"Your remote . . .?"

"For my DVD player. He returned that yesterday, but he didn't bring the remote with him. I want it back."

I could hear the tears in her voice and I almost felt sorry for her. For so many years it had just been the two of them. Donny being the only constant in an ever-changing sea of men. Most of them drop-kicks or scum-bags. Yet the simple truth was that she missed him terribly and felt cheated and alone.

"I'll talk to him when I see him," I said.

"Fine," she snapped and the line went dead.

I stared at my cell-phone for a moment and shook my head in resignation. When Donny moved in with me he brought with him all the stuff from his old bedroom – as you do at his age. The only trouble was that, technically, he didn't own much of it. His mother did. So now she was taking every opportunity to make him suffer for his terrible betrayal. Every week she would call up and demand something back. First it was little things, like his pillows and bed-sheets and a towel. Then it escalated to a bedside table, and then his dresser. The old Playstation went soon after and she even made a play for his lap-top, but we managed to calm her down on that one and she let him hang onto it as he needs it for University. Then he had to buy the bed off her and now she seems to have recovered the DVD player. I guess the TV set will be next, and that will annoy him, and after that there's really only his clapped-out car. But she'll probably have to pay a tow-truck driver to get that back.

Poor Donny. We've talked about it and I think he understands that it's just her way of grieving for him. So far he's been playing along quite placidly, although I am concerned that he's stopped returning her calls. That's just not like him.

I started the engine and tried to remember what I was supposed to be doing.

"I do appreciate you meeting us like this, Adam."

Harold Armitage was dressed in a sharp, obviously tailored, suit –presenting a significantly more formal vision than the garish ensemble he wore to the gala dinner last week– and he'd bought along his faithful retainer, Cato, who sat at the table managing to both glower and look bored all at the same time.

I played nice. "My pleasure, Harry."

Armitage's offices are in downtown Auckland, along with almost all the other big corporate travel agencies in the country. Very prestigious being in downtown, apparently. Quite a few people, myself included, thought it was an odd move when Brent and Marguerite moved Barclay and Dodd's out of Auckland central a couple of years back and set up shop here in Takapuna. Brent had blathered on about cost-savings and other benefits but, honestly, at the time I tuned out most of his spiel. He wouldn't have done it if it hadn't put more money in his back pocket – and it was closer to both his home on the banks of Lake Pupuke and to Marguerite's which was nearby, with views over Black Rock and out to Rangitoto.

It took me a moment to realise that I had subconsciously chosen this café because it was where Brent and I occasionally met for a coffee when his busy schedule allowed. We were meeting here supposedly on neutral territory, but this was definitely more like my home turf.

Cato toyed with a straw in a tall iced tea while Armitage and I awaited the delivery of our barista-made coffees. "So, what is this all about?" I asked.

Armitage offered me what he probably thought was a warm smile, but it came across as more of a grimace. "I know we haven't always seen eye to eye, Adam, but I do want you to understand how sorry I was to hear about Brent's passing. It was a tragic thing. Unbelievable."

I said nothing.

"I will miss Brent as anyone would mourn the loss of a skilled adversary. Brent was an accomplished businessman and I admired that." He paused, obviously seeking my approval but I stayed silent. Then he nodded, as if agreeing with something positive I had said, and continued on. "I'm sure you understand, Adam, that I did not consider Brent an enemy, but a worthy opponent. A true competitor. And I enjoy competition, because it is a good thing, as you know. Competition allows us to sharpen our processes, to hone our efficiencies, to strive for perfection. You understand all this though, of course . . ." He drifted off provocatively, but I just raised my eyebrows, again saying nothing. He accepted my silence with a casual shrug and moved on. "I wanted to talk with you today about Barclay and Dodd," he said, finally making some sense. "As I understand that you are to be assisting Brent's widow in her efforts to move the business forward."

"Where did you hear that?" I asked.

He hesitated. "From Mrs Barclay."

I was astounded. "You've spoken with Sharon?"

"Briefly, yes. She referred me to you."

"Her husband hasn't even been buried yet."

"Adam, I understand that this is a sensitive time. But business is still business and time is our enemy."

I stared at him, outraged. Cato suddenly became interested in the conversation as he felt the atmosphere change. "What the hell do you want?" I said coldly.

"Adam, please. If you could put you emotions aside for a few moments . . . I assure you I have nothing but the best of intentions towards Mrs Barclay."

I began drumming my fingers on the table and said nothing. I could feel a throbbing start up in my temples. Cato sat forward, watching me as Armitage continued. "You obviously know that Brent and I have competed for many of the same corporate accounts over the last few years. He won some and I won some. That's okay, that's how it goes. We all do what we can to be successful." He paused meaningfully. I wanted to hit him. "But Brent's passing is a significant blow for the industry and especially for Barclay and Dodd Travel. I'm sure we can agree that Marguerite Dodd, although a lovely lady, is hardly likely to . . . shall we say, maintain the agency as Brent did."

"What do you want, Armitage?" I said.

He ignored me. "And that, I am afraid, is going to be an issue for the beautiful widow Barclay, don't you think?"

"What do you want, Armitage?" I repeated.

Cato's eyes narrowed in anticipation and he leaned forward a little more. After a moment Armitage responded. "I want to make Mrs Barclay a generous offer. I want to help her to move on with her life, as she now faces a difficult time without the man that she loved. I want to help her to avoid the undue torment of having to deal with the business woes and complex issues of her husband's agency as it slowly sinks into the mire."

"You want to buy her shares in Barclay and Dodd?"

"I would like to present her an offer for them, yes."

I couldn't believe it. Brent had been savagely murdered less than a week ago and this scum-sucking wretch was moving in to gnaw on his bones already. I felt sick, and very, very angry. "Fuck off, Armitage," I said sharply.

He blanched and Cato tensed, he seemed to be enjoying the increased hostility.

"I don't believe that's called for, Adam," Armitage said. "I come in peace. I honestly want nothing but the best for Mrs Barclay. Selling now, as soon as possible, will be by far and away the best possible outcome for her."

"And how do you figure that, Harry?"

He hesitated. I already knew what he meant but I wanted to hear him say it, I was starting to really boil. "We're in a competitive market, Adam. Surely it's obvious . . ." I stared at him blankly and he tiredly rolled his eyes. "Every account that Barclay and Dodd manage is going to soon become available for tender. The loss of a principal, especially one as dominant as

Brent Barclay, will be seen as a major concern. B&D will lose business; big accounts will drain out of there quickly." He was right, of course. But that didn't make me like him any more for what he wanted to do. He continued. "I can stop Barclay and Dodd from hemorrhaging. I can keep the accounts with the business, maintain momentum. But only if I have a controlling interest. Only if I am able to persuade Mrs Barclay to part with her shares. If she does I can help to keep Brent's business alive."

I stared at him. I couldn't believe what I was hearing. I couldn't believe that he actually sounded so sincere. Anyone who hadn't known first-hand of the intense hatred that existed between the two men could easily have been convinced that Armitage and Brent had been the best of buddies.

I'm not proud of this, but I snapped.

"You're a lying scumbag, Armitage," I spat angrily. "You have no interest in saving Brent's business. All you want is control of it so that you can siphon off all the best accounts and merge the staff into your own agency with the least amount of hassle. I mean, why tender for all those accounts individually when you can swoop in and snatch them all up for a song. And you want my help to do it, well . . . Fuck off, Armitage!"

I stood up as I finished speaking and suddenly everything went horribly wrong. Our coffees finally arrived just as I told Armitage what I thought of his bullshit and accidentally bumped into, quite forcibly, the poor girl delivering them.

The coffees flew through the air.

One went directly into Armitage's lap and the other straight at Cato's face. If I'd aimed and thrown them I couldn't have hit both men so perfectly. Armitage squealed like a girl as the hot liquid found his thigh. Cato roared in surprise and anger as scalding coffee splashed into his eyes. I tripped over the girl and stumbled backwards, falling onto the floor. As I tried to rise Cato was suddenly standing over me, rage seared across his blotchy face. He crouched and swung a fist at my head. I only just managed to react in time, twisting away, and the blow glanced off my forehead. As he drew back to strike again I instinctively lashed out with my foot, putting him off balance and toppling him. But he was very quick and bounced back up angrily as I too managed to get to my feet. Then one of the other customers screamed and I saw why.

My blood ran cold.

Cato had pulled a knife. It looked long and very sharp. He half-crouched, his arms spread wide and began to circle me, preparing to strike.

ELEVEN

Donny sat as still as a statue, terrified that any movement might end in disaster. Twice already Suzy had jabbed him with the scissors and he simply couldn't understand if she was doing it deliberately, and trying to provoke him, or if the jabs had been as accidental as she claimed. He closed his eyes again, trying not to breathe. Suzy jabbed him a third time. This supposed slip caught him behind the left ear. "Sorry," she mumbled, but it sounded more like a giggle than an apology.

He continued to say nothing and clenched his fists tighter. He was perched upright on a chair, in the middle of the lounge, both hands cable-tied to the seat of the chair. A sheet was wrapped around his neck, with only his head exposed. Suzy moved lightly on her feet, dancing around him. Her fingers worked feverishly around his head.

It had been a long day, so far. She'd let him watch TV for a while but, although the bach had a satellite dish, it only offered the basic Freeview channels and nothing worth watching had been on on a Monday morning. Donny had grazed between channels, flicking back and forth, desperate to find something of interest until Suzy suddenly became frustrated and snatched the remote control from him. With a cry of exasperation she'd thrown it across the room and bounced up to turn off the TV. After ten minutes of terrifying silence she'd produced the board game Monopoly and insisted that they play. Donny hated the game but agreed without argument. Then he let her win, choosing not to buy the better properties he landed on and failing to collect rent on the lesser ones he actually purchased. If she noticed she didn't say anything, and she seemed to prefer winning. He didn't want her becoming upset.

She'd fed him, as promised earlier, and Donny thought the scrambled eggs had actually been pretty good. And they had had baked beans for lunch so he couldn't complain that she was starving him. In fact –even though the menu was incredibly basic– she was proving a much, much better cook than his dad who tended to overcook everything. Even baked beans.

He had wondered earlier if Adam had even worked out yet that something had happened to him. His mother would have noticed, for sure, if he was still living with her. She used to track his every movement. Surely Adam must be wondering where he was, or would he not even be worried, figuring that Donny was an adult now and that he had to let him find his own way. Probably. His dad was so incredibly easy-going. The complete opposite of his mother. Damn it. If only Adam and his mum got on better and were able to communicate with each other more easily. Someone would definitely be looking for him by now.

But he very much doubted it. For as long as he could remember they disagreed about everything whenever they got together. At sports games when he was younger –he used to play soccer in winter and cricket in summer– they would always be there to watch and support him. But never side by side. Never together. The only times they spoke were to negotiate spending time with him. Adam would always ask if he could take him out for a while after the game but Bella always said they had other plans, even when they didn't. Donny had learned to stay quiet when these negotiations took place and he hated the ever-present tension between them.

But thoughts of his parents had been swept aside when, about twenty minutes ago, Suzy's cell-phone rang and she disappeared outside to take the call in private.

When she returned there had been a rather fanatical glint in her eye and a dangerous smile. She cut his binding to the couch and forced him to sit on the chair. He only considered resistance for a moment, quickly thinking better of it at the thought of how much Suzy seemed to enjoy inflicting pain upon him.

So he let her bind him to the chair placidly and only truly began to get worried when she produced the sheet and wrapped it over him.

"So, which ear are you most fond of," she asked as she produced what looked like a very sharp pair of scissors.

He'd almost fainted at her words.

This was it. She was going to cut off an ear, probably to send to someone to pay a ransom. He couldn't understand why though. His family wasn't rich, far from it. Sure, Adam owned the travel agency but, although it had never been openly discussed, Donny was pretty sure it wasn't doing all that well. He knew that both Adam's business and the small two-bedroom unit they lived in had been bought only with thanks to his dad's parent's financial support – but they weren't rich either. Maybe they were comfortable, but definitely not rich. So no one on Donny's dad's side of the family would be able to scrape up enough money for a serious ransom demand.

As for his mum, well that was a joke. She owned next-to-nothing, and never had. To the best of his knowledge she'd never had a job. Not once, ever. Donny's memories of growing up consisted almost entirely of his mum bouncing from one boyfriend to the next, making them move at least once a year, often more than that, as Bella seemed incapable of a long-term relationship –with anyone other than her son, that is– and had raised him entirely supported by her boyfriend's hand-outs and a pittance from the social welfare system. They never had any money, although things were going okay for her at the moment because Bella's current man –Grunter– seemed to be doing all right, even if he was a complete prick.

Donny simply couldn't fathom how anyone could benefit financially from his abduction. It made no sense at all. Why the hell was Suzy doing this?

He sat rigid and still, terrified that if he struggled she would do more than just remove one ear. Squeezing his eyes shut he clenched his teeth in dreadful anticipation, determined not to cry or call out when the blades sliced into him.

Then she laughed and produced a heavy comb and started to cut his hair.

She'd jabbed him a few times since, but it had become clear that all he was going to lose was his scruffy mane. Once that happened his relief was immense, but he was still no closer to understanding why he was there.

* * *

Cato danced lightly before me. I stepped back quickly, immediately terrified, and pulled a small coffee table between us.

Armitage screamed. "Jeremy, no! My God, put that away!"

But Cato kept circling, trying to outmaneuver me and my table. I couldn't believe what was happening. He seemed to float along effortlessly as he waved his other hand to try and draw my eye away from the knife. All the while he said nothing, just glared at me with wild eyes.

"Jeremy," Armitage shouted again. "Put it away!"

Cato continued to ignore him, his eyes locked on mine. I clutched the coffee table for all I was worth, keeping it in front of me, and played for time. Surely he wasn't that crazy. The café was full of customers. There had to be more than a dozen witnesses if he did lash out and stab me.

A voice from behind the counter called out: "I'm calling the police. They'll be here any minute."

Cato didn't blink. I backed away a little more, dragging the coffee table. It wasn't that heavy. I felt sure that I could, at worst, block him if he did decide to rush. At best I may even have been able to drive him back, disarm him.

Then Armitage whined, "Put it away, Jeremy. Please don't do this. I'd be so alone with you in jail . . ." and this time Cato reacted, just a momentary flicker of the eyes. Armitage tried again. "Please. I need you, Jeremy."

Finally Cato blanched, before suddenly releasing a howl of frustration. Without warning he waved his arm quickly and the knife disappeared. Whether it went up his sleeve or into a pocket I couldn't say, but it was no longer in his hand. A sense of relief surged through me but still I clung to my coffee table.

Armitage moved closer to him and whispered in his ear for a few moments. The café was otherwise silent, with all eyes on the bizarre entertainment. Cato continued to glare at me as Armitage murmured comforting sounds. It was unnerving, like trying to hold eye contact with a snake. Armitage rubbed Cato's shoulder for a minute before the younger man suddenly spun away, darting between the tables and out the front door to disappear from view.

I could barely breathe as a chill of relief stole through me.

Armitage said nothing for a few moments, staring forlornly out the café's doorway. Then he expelled a deep sigh and walked over to the counter, picking at his coffee-soaked trousers as he moved. I stayed where I was, keeping a watchful eye on the door to make sure Cato didn't suddenly reappear. I could hear Armitage appealing for the owner not to call the police, telling him that he would pay for any damage, sort everything out. But the owner was desperately trying to console the blubbering waitress who had tried to deliver our coffees – and he was furious. There was no way he was going to let it slide and anyway it was too late. The police were on their way. Armitage's shoulders were slumped as he returned to where I still stood clutching my defensive coffee table.

"I'm sorry, Adam," he said. "This got out of hand."

I was incredulous. "Out of hand? Out of bloody hand? That crazy son-of-a-bitch nearly stabbed me," I said, finally releasing the table to point towards the door that Cato disappeared through, ". . . over a spilled coffee. He's fucking crazy. He needs to be locked up."

"You don't understand. He sometimes overreacts–"

"Overreacts! For fuck's sake. He could have killed me."

"He would never . . ." But Armitage went white and could find no more words.

I looked down to see that my hands were shaking. It was only then that I abruptly remembered how Brent had died.

Stabbed to death. Eight times. A wash of fresh anxiety made my knees weaken to jelly.

Jesus Christ. How lucky had I just been?

Three hours later I got up from my desk at home and wandered through to the kitchen to retrieve another cold beer from the fridge. The cap popped off with that satisfying little snick and I took a long pull.

My home is pretty plain. It wouldn't be unfair to say that it lacks a woman's touch. I did go to a bit of an effort when Donny first moved in and bought a few indoor plants and even added a colourful throw rug in the lounge, but it's still pretty bleak. And the plants are now slowly dying.

I used to have an office here, so I could work from home if I wanted, but that is now Donny's bedroom so my PC is set-up in my bedroom, squeezed into a corner.

I took another pull of the ice cold beer. My thoughts were a mess. So much had been happening that I didn't really understand where I was at anymore. But above all else the short note that Brent had left for me, which I had now pretty well memorised, continued to gnaw furiously.

He lied. He was sorry. He wanted me to find Doug and talk with him, find out what really happened. It still didn't make any sense.

Sharon had phoned again too. Marguerite Dodd had agreed to meet with us, but not until Wednesday, the day after Brent's funeral. Sharon was upset as, apparently, Marguerite still wouldn't commit to attending the funeral either. I didn't understand that, not at all. Surely the pressure on her business wasn't so great that she couldn't leave her desk for a couple of hours. So I'd called her myself to try and confirm that she'd be coming. However, without thinking it through, I found myself telling her about the approach by Armitage and the incident with Cato. So I probably didn't help ease her mind. She was evasive with me too and remained non-committal.

And that mad bastard Cato was still out there somewhere, running around with a bloody knife. Did I think that he might have killed Brent? God only knows, but I didn't hold back on offering the possibility to the police when they arrived at the café. Armitage was well out of earshot when they interviewed me but I can almost guarantee he will have provided an alibi for his psychotic boy-toy for the hours after the gala dinner when Brent was murdered.

I drank some more beer. What a day.

Since getting home and talking with Sharon and Marguerite I'd achieved little and wasn't even succeeding in trying to drink away my woes.

After a fair bit of moping around I actually went to my computer and googled Doug Masters name. Sad really. And, no surprises, but it was a disappointing waste of effort. I honestly thought I'd find more than I did, but no. There was the ever-present LinkedIn listing; one obscure reference to an old movie character and a whole lot of unbelievable nonsense – including multiple pictures of a bloody stupid cat on one website where Doug the Cat was apparently Master of his own weird little Universe. I'd sat and stared at the screen in dismay. But, really, what had I expected to find? Some kind of blog outlining how Doug had disappeared and went to live in Eketahuna under an assumed name? Who was I kidding?

I took another long pull on the beer. I knew I needed to get my shit together and come up with some kind of plan. If I was actually going to try and go along with Brent's wishes, and find Doug Masters, it was clear that I had to make a more focused effort. But, so far, it simply wasn't happening.

I thought about the information I now had on Doug's twin sister, Debbie. I could try to go and see her. She was by far the most likely person that I could think of that may actually know where he was. That's why I'd asked Julie and Kylie to try and find her online – which they had managed so easily. Maybe Debbie would help me, or at the least help to provide a little direction. But I doubted it. Twenty years is a long time, it was possible she wouldn't even remember my name. And Debbie wasn't really someone I had ever counted as a friend.

Back then Debbie lived out west, in Henderson. I only really got to know her about a month before the night it all fell apart. We'd gone to a party in Te Atatu. Kieran, Brent and I, without Doug. I don't remember whose party it was, we probably crashed it. But we ran into Debbie there, having met her briefly a few times before, with a couple of her friends. We all got into some drinking games and, as these things tend to, it got very loose after that.

Kieran, being a good looking guy and a pretty smooth talker, hooked up with Debbie that night. But we all thought it an odd pairing as she was quite plain compared to most of the girls Kieran dated. Maybe he was just taking advantage of the drunken opportunity. Maybe he saw something I didn't. I don't know.

As it happened we all scored that night. Brent got lucky with a vacuous blonde girl while I somehow managed to convince one of Debbie's friends to accompany me to the back seat of Kieran's car. Later I passed out in the car alone and can still remember being awoken –just before dawn– by Kieran leaping in, starting the car up, and driving off with his foot flat to the floor, laughing. It wasn't till we were half-way back to the Shore that I remembered we'd left Brent behind. Kieran was blasé about that and I wasn't able to convince him to go back.

That evening caused definite friction between Kieran and both Brent and Doug for a few weeks afterwards, although it was never quite clear to me just what did happen between Kieran and Debbie. He wouldn't admit to anything but, whatever happened, Doug sure wasn't happy about it.

But the subject resurfaced again after Kieran died. The police picked up on the connection somehow and Doug's displeasure at the liaison became yet another black mark against him as a possible motive.

It was also another thing that I proved to be absolutely useless in providing information about. I was there, but I didn't know what really happened. Just like I was on the *Kestrel* that night and still couldn't tell the police anything helpful.

I took another pull on my beer and smiled, amused at the irony. That night had been a strange one but, as it turned out, a fateful one. My son Donny was conceived that night, completely unbeknownst to me with thanks to my back-seat hook-up with one of Debbie's friends . . . a feisty girl named Bella.

I suppose I could have called Bella and asked if she was still friendly with Debbie . . . if she knew where I could find her, but that hadn't occurred to me earlier and I doubted very much that Bella would tell me the truth anyway.

I looked at my watch. It was late and I suddenly realised that Donny wasn't home yet, once again. I tried to remember if I'd seen him this morning either, but couldn't recall. His absence wasn't that unusual though. In the three months we'd lived together he'd occasionally crashed at friends places without telling me, so I wasn't worried. He was probably giving me a bit of space to grieve in.

Donny was a big boy. He'd be fine.

TWELVE

"Brent Barclay was a tower of strength within the community that knew and loved him. A man dedicated to those who worked with him, a rock that others could cling to as the tides of change swept through . . ."

I listened to the chaplain expound positively about my oldest friend and wondered if the two men had ever actually met. I doubted it. Brent was never big on any form of religion, usually comparing them off-handedly to various mind-bending cults. I didn't even know where Sharon had found this man. Was it possible that she had been able to drag Brent out to actually visit his church? He'd never mentioned it. But then, a lot changed when Brent married Sharon. Perhaps he did find religion? I don't know.

The chapel at the North Shore Memorial Park –out the back of Albany on Schnapper Rock Road– was packed. There was quite a strong representation of faces from the travel industry. I recognised senior people from both Qantas and Air New Zealand, all the major wholesalers and suppliers, and quite a few of Brent's opponent corporate travel agents. There were a lot of suits, men and women, that I didn't recognise, who were probably his corporate customers. I was surprised to spot the local mayor and a couple of politicians. I had never fully realised just how connected Brent was. He used to name-drop all the time, but I would just nod and yawn whenever he tried to tell me who he had lunched with.

But there was little in the way of family gathered. Just Sharon and I. Sharon had a small circle of friends around her, Gemma and two other women I had never met, but she also had no family in the country. All together we didn't even fill one pew at the front of the chapel.

I had been expecting Donny but he hadn't shown up yet. He didn't sleep at home last night, which wasn't unusual in itself, but I had expected him to attend the funeral. Perhaps the old Mirage had finally given up and died on him? I tried not to let his nonappearance bother me.

I did recognise a few of Brent's staff from my irregular visits to Barclay and Dodd, but Marguerite Dodd herself was conspicuous in her absence and that was gnawing at me more than a little. They ran a business together for crying out loud. Why wasn't she here?

Bloody Armitage was, and that annoyed me particularly. Despite everything that happened yesterday I actually caught him presenting himself to Sharon. He didn't have Cato with him, and I wondered if the police were still looking for him or if he was safely locked-up in a cell by now. Regardless of that, here was Armitage, brazenly approaching Brent's widow at her husband's funeral. I saw him slip her his card just before I got there to move him along. He'd been angry with my intrusion but thankfully left her side with little more than a pout. I was feeling unnecessarily vindictive and briefly told Sharon who he was, what he really wanted and what had happened at the café last night. She was shocked and thankful and promised to keep a distance. But he was still here though. I'd seen him take a seat near the back as we'd all filed into the chapel.

Suddenly I realised the room had gone quiet and Gemma nudged me sharply. She nodded towards the lectern up front where the chaplain was standing silently, gazing meaningfully at me. Sharon and the other ladies along our pew were turned also, looking my way. My heart froze.

It was my turn to speak.

I hate public speaking, and I think most people do. But today I had little choice. Eulogies don't deliver themselves, someone has to actually stand up and utter the words. I had to get up. I owed it to Brent.

Hesitantly I rose on wobbly legs, my knees feeling like rubber, and made my way forward. As I reached the lectern the chaplain nodded and offered a warm smile of encouragement. My stomach knotted.

Turning to face the packed chapel I felt momentarily faint. My vision swam just a little as I pulled a few notes from my pocket that I'd scribbled out earlier. They immediately seemed inadequate. I took a deep breath and exhaled slowly, grimacing as I looked out into the audience. The faces stared back at me, solemn and still. My mouth was dry as sandpaper as I opened it to begin my speech.

Then I saw him.

There was an unshaven man standing near the back wearing a long grey overcoat which seemed out-of-place indoors on this warm day. His hair was a shock of black, almost Beatlesque. Something about it looked wrong. But those things didn't really register at first. His face did. Although his jowls were lightly bearded, and flecked with grey, the man looked remarkably like Doug Masters.

I stared at him. Our eyes met. His expression changed to what I took to be surprise and he quickly produced a pair of sunglasses and put them on. Almost immediately he realised that that was a very odd thing to do and took a step back. Without thinking I took a step forward from the lectern ...

... and as I did he suddenly bolted. He just turned and ran, darting out the chapel door.

The crowd erupted into a chatter of surprise when I instinctively followed, sprinting down the aisle and out the door after him. No one in the crowd moved or tried to stop me so I found myself on the chapel's landing in moments. A car park spread out immediately before me with the lush rolling grassland of the cemetery beyond. A flash of movement to my right made me turn and I sprinted after it. Reaching the end of the building I turned again, just in time to see the man in the grey coat racing through the overflow car park out the back of the chapel. He ducked between cars, one hand firmly on his head, obviously there to hold the black mop of a wig in place.

He glanced over his shoulder and saw me pursuing before darting across the rear driveway and dodging into the heavily wooded bush beyond. I gave chase, ducking between the parked cars and reaching the spot where he'd entered the bush in seconds. Then, rather stupidly, I followed.

I'd only taken three steps into the bush when I found myself flat on my back, struggling for air. Someone, I presume the man I was chasing, had stepped out from behind a tree and stiff-arm tackled me – right across the throat.

They used to call that sort of tackle a coat-hanger in my day. You just stuck your arm out straight and firm and drove it into the opposition ball-runners neck. It was dirty play, dangerous, and often left the ball-runner on the sideline.

I stayed down, dazed and fighting for breath. The arm had taken me right across my throat and it hurt like hell. I saw a pair of sneakers running away, deeper into the bush, and then he was gone.

As I lay there struggling for breath, I decided firmly that the man I had been chasing simply had to have been Doug Masters. Back when we were rugby playing teenagers, Doug –who was no saint– used to use the stiff-arm tackle as a regular feature of his game. He was our team's half-back, a short scrappy player who enjoyed a tussle. If an opposition player annoyed him, and the opportunity arose, he would deliberately use the dirty tactic to flatten the guy and then apologise profusely for the benefit of the referee. It usually worked too because he was almost always smaller than the player he'd fouled so he'd just get penalised but never once got sent off. I never approved, but I must admit that I never tried to talk him out of doing it. I wish I had now.

I was still lying prone when another man suddenly appeared and helped me to sit up with one hand while holding a cell-phone in the other.

"Who was that man, Mr Holt?" he asked with a South African accent. Then he flashed a badge in my face. He was a plain-clothes cop. "Which way did he go?"

I couldn't speak, my throat was too sore, my breathing still being dragged in desperately. I pointed into the bush.

"Stay here," he said and started to move cautiously deeper into the bush. He was talking into the cell-phone as he disappeared from sight.

Less than twenty minutes later I stepped down from the lectern at a much more leisurely pace than before. All eyes remained on me as I returned to my seat. I had told the gathered congregation nothing, deliberately made no effort to explain my sudden disappearance. Most of the crowd had remained in their seats and when I returned to the chapel a hush descended awkwardly. Without pausing I walked straight back up to the lectern and began my eulogy as if nothing had happened. My throat burned as I stuck determinably to my notes.

Afterwards the chaplain resumed the service. A couple of Brent's travel contemporaries stood and said a few kind words, hymns were sung and the service wrapped up as his coffin was slowly trundled through the doors to the waiting furnace.

I stayed in my seat as the chapel gradually emptied feeling numb and confused. The plain-clothes policeman appeared sooner than I'd expected.

"Mr Holt, I need to ask you a few questions."

I nodded. "Did you catch him?"

"Not at this stage," he said. That meant he got away. There was only one way in and out of this area and if they hadn't found him yet he would be miles away by now. "It looked like you recognised him, Mr Holt. Did you?"

"I don't know, but I think he was wearing a wig."

"I think you're probably right. Why did you chase him?"

"Because he ran . . ."

He waited, but I said no more. "With all due respect," he said, "that's really not much of an answer."

"I guess not," I said. "But tell me. Why are you here?"

"Standard procedure," he replied. "It's quite common for the perpetrator of a violent crime to attend their victim's funeral. I'm here to observe the attendee's."

I nodded. It made good sense. "Let me ask you another question, then," I said. "Does the name Kieran Sandford mean anything to you?"

He paused, considering the name. He shook his head.

"Then we really need a long chat. I probably need to talk with whoever is in charge of Brent's murder investigation."

He frowned, thought about it briefly, and then pulled out his cell-phone.

I checked my watch. It was well past lunch time, but I simply wasn't hungry having spent about two hours at the North Shore police station updating them on the mysterious death of Kieran Sandford and the subsequent disappearance of Doug Masters all those years ago.

The lead investigator, a dour man named Millward, had stared at me blankly throughout. He gave nothing away and left me feeling unsettled. We were accompanied by the plain-clothes cop from Brent's funeral service. His name was Rhodes and he did all the talking for them both. He probed and cajoled me, having to drag out much of the detail. I really do hate talking about this subject.

When I told them that I suspected the running man to have been Doug Masters, Millward actually raised one eyebrow. But that was all. We didn't talk about the incident with Cato and Armitage yesterday. I had already covered off my thoughts on the possibility of Cato being responsible for Brent's murder with the uniformed officers I'd spoken to at the café after that event. Millward and Rhodes either didn't know about it or didn't want to discuss it with me.

Eventually Rhodes thanked me for coming in and led me out of the station. Millward still never said a word.

I should have gone back to work, but my mind simply wasn't focused in that direction. The girls would be fine. I'm sure they weren't expecting me in.

The image of Doug Masters –unshaven and wearing what had to be a bad wig– filled my thoughts. He was here.

In Auckland. But why? Was it possible that he had murdered Brent? And if so, did that mean I was next?

I didn't know, but the memory of his coat-hanger cheap-shot left me with a bitter taste. I was angry. I wanted to find him.

I got in my car and pointed it north.

Albany Village used to be just that. A village. An obscure little settlement out in the middle of nowhere boasting nothing much but a pretty big car sales yard. But that was years ago, when I was much younger. Now it was more filled in, less of a village, more of a bustling township with its own university and a massive footy stadium. And the North Shore had grown to more or less catch up with it as it continued its ever expanding creep north.

I parked my car on the main road and looked around at the line of bland, low concrete shops that had recently sprung up near the intersection that marks the start of the village. Between a $2 Shop and a rather flash looking café the Bakers Delight signage greeted me cheerily. This was the bakery that Doug's sister Debbie co-owned and worked at. I got out of the car and was halfway across the road when a wave of doubt made me hesitate and almost got me run over.

What was I doing? What could I possibly say to Doug's sister that would convince her to tell me where he was now? What made me think she even knew?

I started to turn back but found myself stranded in heavy traffic in the middle of the road. The flow of cars forced me to carry on and I eventually crossed to safety. Pushing myself blithely on I made it to the row of shops where I stopped and stared at the bakery's entrance. They were promoting a delicious new style of pizza bread. I could smell the warm, comforting aroma of fresh baking which would normally have me salivating but, instead, made my stomach lurch.

I was procrastinating. I knew Doug was in Auckland. I'd seen him. Surely Debbie would know it too. In fact, it was quite possible that he could be staying with her. Assuming he didn't actually live in Auckland himself. I mean it's a big city, he could live anywhere. Why not Auckland? But doubt swept over me again. Trying to find him suddenly seemed crazy, fruitless. I should go home, or back to work. Chasing ghosts would get me nowhere. I couldn't do it.

I turned to walk away and stumbled headlong into a short, dark-haired woman. She would have fallen if I hadn't shot my hand out to catch her so quickly. We sort-of danced in an uncoordinated way for a moment as I apologised profusely. Then we regained our balance and I let her go.

The woman looked up at me angrily, obviously about to share her thoughts on what an idiot I was when she recognised me and stopped cold. Debbie Ngatai's mouth closed in a thin line and her eyes narrowed accusingly.

"You," she said. "I should have known."

"I'm sorry, that was my fault," I apologised again.

She glared at me as if I'd just bitten her deliberately and then abruptly turned on her heel and moved past me.

"Wait," I said, instinctively reaching out to lay a hand on her shoulder. She spun violently and smacked my hand away, fury in her eyes.

"Touch me again and you'll regret it," she spat.

"I'm sorry," I repeated. "I didn't mean . . ." My words drifted off as the look of unbridled hatred in her face unsettled me. She started to go into the bakery but suddenly stopped. I could see her shoulders shaking with rage as she turned back and stepped up in front of me.

"What the fuck do you want?" she snarled.

I wasn't prepared for her overt repugnance. For a moment I thought she might spit on me. I couldn't respond.

"He didn't do it," she said.

"What . . ."

"Barclay's dead, isn't he." It wasn't a question. "And all of a sudden here you are. You're looking for Doug, aren't you? You're going to try and pin this one on him too."

I was stung. "No, hang on . . ."

"Yes, you bloody are. You framed him for that prick Sandford and now you're going to try and set him up for that bastard Barclay."

"No, wait –"

"Well you can just piss off, do you hear me. Keep away from me! You and that son-of-a-bitch Barclay ruined my brother's life. You have no right coming here. I don't want to see your bloody face here ever again. Do you hear me? Fuck Off!"

Before I could respond she had spun away and entered the bakery. For a few moments I was speechless, too stunned to move. Finally I pulled myself together and decided rashly to follow her. I wanted to set things right somehow.

As I stepped into the shop I saw her behind the counter encircled in the arms of a short, but incredibly wide, man. They both looked over at me as I entered and a glance was exchanged. Obviously this was her husband and he didn't look happy either. Mister Ngatai's face soured further and Debbie ducked out of his arms to disappear out the back. There were no customers in the storefront and Ngatai glowered at me as he made his way around the counter to confront me.

I stood my ground. "I didn't mean to upset her," I said. "I just wanted to talk to her for a minute."

"I think you've said enough," he said.

I was getting a bit pissed off. Our encounter had been brief, but I was pretty sure that I hadn't actually said anything yet. "I'm not here to cause trouble. I was just hoping to have a quick word with Debbie."

He stepped up in front of me. I was a good six inches taller but he was around half a mile wider and, while he had clearly enjoyed far too much of his own baking, it wasn't all fat. His tone was flat and precise. "You've had all the words you're going to get. You should leave now."

We sized each other up for about twenty seconds before I decided to walk away. If Debbie actually knew where her brother was there was obviously no way she was going to tell me. I nodded at her husband. "I'm sorry for upsetting her," I said. "I saw Doug today. I thought she might like to know."

He didn't blink, but shook his head slowly. "I very much doubt that."

"Really?"

"You must have seen a ghost."

I frowned. "Why do you say that?"

He paused meaningfully, still without blinking. "Doug Masters is dead. Has been for a long time now."

I stared at him. "You don't know that."

He spoke menacingly, inching a half-step forward. "I know what I know . . . and I know that you need to leave my shop."

I nodded, raised my hands in surrender and walked away. Just before I crossed the road I turned back to see him still there, standing just inside the doorway, watching me like an overly-wide granite sentinel.

THIRTEEN

As I drove myself back towards work my cell-phone rang. I pulled over and picked it up, this time looking at the display before I answered. Bella, yet again. I put the phone down, not in the mood for another nonsensical ear-bashing, and let it ring out. She could leave a message.

But I didn't pull back out into the traffic flow. I quickly realised that I really couldn't face going back to work. And there was no need. I'd be useless to anyone anyway. Instead I just sat there trying to decide what to do next.

Doug Masters was here in Auckland, of that I felt almost certain. But what did that mean? Why was he here? His sister certainly wasn't going to tell me anything.

Could he have been responsible for Brent's death . . . as well as for Kieran's?

My mind reeled at the thought. This morning I was practically convinced that Armitage's boy-toy Cato was Brent's killer . . . but now . . . I was no longer so sure.

But why would he resurface now, after twenty long years? My insides turned to lead at the thought of Doug spending all that time simmering, stewing, waiting, intent on . . . on what, exactly?

On finishing the job he started on the *Kestrel*, perhaps? Surely, if he had wanted to kill Brent, he could have finished it then; we were both so damn drunk. And why kill him anyway? To silence him? That made no sense. Neither of us could remember what happened on board. What was the point?

I shook my head in frustration.

Doug was back, but I just couldn't imagine why.

Impulsively I made a snap decision. There was another way I could try to find him, a different source of information. Brent, for whatever reason, had asked me to locate Doug Masters and I was now determined to try and honour his request. I owed him that, at the very least.

I took a deep breath and, with a suddenly burning desire to know more, I pulled out into traffic again.

As I climbed out of my car in Takapuna waves of self-doubt once again washed over me. A small sensible voice inside my head screamed out *'BAD IDEA'* over and over again but, driven by an inexplicable urgency, I just couldn't stop myself.

The entrance to the Work and Income (WINZ) offices in Takapuna was slightly obscured behind a large bus stop area. As always, there was a transitory crowd of car-less folk milling around outside while they waited for their buses. I've never been all that keen on public transport and have been fortunate enough to own some form of car, and none quite as clapped out as *Milly*, ever since my teenage years. As I weaved my way through the cluster of waiting people I silently thanked my lucky stars for my moderately privileged upbringing.

Stepping inside the doors I was immediately struck by how quiet the WINZ office was, and how vast. The room was about half the size of a rugby field and bathed in the wash of fluorescent lighting. My eye was drawn to one bulb flickering and humming about half way down the room on the right. I turned back to take in the large, oval desk directly in front of me, with waiting areas to the left and right and lines and lines of open-plan desks stretched out before them. Each desk had two visitor chairs and a computer screen. Most were manned and almost every chair was occupied. Suddenly anxiety washed over me again and, feeling very out-of-place, I almost turned tail and left. But I steeled myself, shook it off, took a deep breath and stepped forward.

"Help you?" said the woman behind the oval reception desk without looking up. She was short and round with a brightly coloured blouse. She looked like a beach ball.

"Yes. Hi. I want to see Claire O'Driscoll, please."

"Appointment?"

"Ahh, no. I just need five minutes of her time."

Her eyes flicked up finally. She looked fed up. "Mrs O'Driscoll's very busy. You need an appointment."

"Okay," I said, offering her my best winning smile. "I can wait for a bit. When is she next available?"

She sighed and rotated to stretch pudgy fingers onto her keyboard. She tapped and stared at the screen, then tapped some more. Eventually she said: "Friday, next week, 2 pm."

"Oh," I said. "Nothing sooner? Today perhaps?"

She rolled her eyes languidly from the screen. "Nope."

My winning smile was failing me, yet again. "Look," I said, "I'm an old friend, just in town today, and I was simply hoping to catch up, you know, say gidday. Maybe you could just let her know I'm here . . ."

"You need an appointment."

"But I can't come back on Friday," I said.

"Next Friday, not this Friday."

"But that's no good–"

"She's very busy, seeing people with appointments."

This was going nowhere. "Okay, thanks anyway," I said as I stepped back, away from the counter. An anorexic woman immediately pushed past me and began to regale the brightly-clothed receptionist with a fresh tale of woe.

I pulled out my cell-phone and pretended to start texting someone while I took another, longer look around the big room. It didn't take long to spot Claire. It was easy, I'd recognise her anywhere. She was over to the right, a few desks in front of the flickering fluorescent. Her honey-blonde hair was pulled back in a pony-tail and she was talking into a phone while a scantily-dressed teenage girl lolled in her visitor's chair. I kept pretending to text and moved casually to the right, taking a seat in the waiting area. The beach ball behind reception took no notice of me. The people waiting ignored me. Everyone looked bored and frustrated.

It only took a few minutes to work out that each of the WINZ consultants operated their appointments much like a doctor's waiting room. As their clients left they would sit at their desk and organise themselves for a minute or two and then walk up to the waiting area and call out a name.

I sat and waited for over twenty minutes before the teenage girl Claire was dealing with finally dragged herself to her feet and started shuffling away from her desk. I didn't hesitate. The receptionist had a queue of people waiting and wasn't watching so I stood up and purposefully strode down the aisle, past the girl, and deposited myself in one of the chairs opposite her.

She had her head down making notes in a file and didn't look up immediately. I leaned forward and spoke softly. "I'm sorry to intrude like this . . ."

Her head came up slowly. Our eyes met. My heart froze.

In a sudden wash of memory, just like one of those awful flashback montages you see in the movies, distinct images of the teenage girl I had once loved –with every ounce of fiber in my being– came crashing into my mind's eye. We were walking on the beach; kissing in my car under a streetlamp; holding hands waiting in line for the movies; I saw her eyes holding mine, her smile; heard the whispered promises that have long since faded away . . . and I felt myself sway slightly.

Claire's face initially registered surprise but then changed to annoyance before quickly moving on to weary resignation. I had been hoping, praying no less, for very different emotions. Bitter disappointment washed over me.

She looked tired and wore very little make up but, while her eyes were hooded, they were still that incredible deep green colour that had so entranced me all those years ago. She glared at me and said nothing.

"Hello, Claire," I said finally, trying to offer my brightest smile. But she didn't smile back. "You look great." It wasn't a lie. Even though obviously tired and sitting beneath an unflattering, flickering fluorescent light see was still striking.

She frowned. "Why are you here?"

"It's been a long time, I just, well . . ."

"And how did you know I work here?"

"I'm sorry if I've surprised you . . ."

She was annoyed. "Look, Holt. I'm already behind schedule. There are people waiting. If you have something to say, let's just get to it."

For years I had dreamed of this moment, but it wasn't going anything like I'd imagined. My chest tightened so much I could barely breathe.

"I think I saw Doug Masters earlier today," I managed to blurt out. Her eye's widened. "He's here. In Auckland, but I don't know why." She frowned again and stared at me, hard. "I thought you should know." I added lamely.

She shook her head in obvious exasperation. "Why?"

Suddenly I felt like an idiot. "What?"

"Why would I want to know that?"

"I guess, so you could be on the alert . . ."

"You think Doug's come back to Auckland to stalk me?"

I faltered. "I don't know . . . it's possible."

"Why are you here, really?"

"I just told you–"

"That's bullshit. You don't believe that Doug would try to hurt me any more than I do."

She was right. I didn't know what to say. The reunion I had long dreamt of was imploding in my face. My chest hurt.

"Why are you here?" she demanded again.

I took a deep breath and exhaled slowly. "Brent's dead. You know that?"

She looked away briefly and pursed her lips. "Yes."

"I'm almost certain I saw Doug earlier today, at Brent's funeral . . . I want to try and find him."

"You want to find Doug?"

"Yes."

"Why?"

I shook my head, trying to dismiss the question. "I don't have enough information though. I know your parents hired a private investigator to try and find him. So they must have a file on him. On everything that happened after that night. I'd like to borrow it."

He eyes widened in disbelief. "You can't be serious."

I nodded and attempted a cute smile. But it didn't help.

She closed her eyes, probably wishing I had never materialised before her. Then shook her head and spoke bluntly, "You think Doug killed Brent."

I didn't know how to respond. I shrugged limply.

She shook her head again. "I think you should leave."

"Claire, please. I'm just asking for a little help."

She looked angry and frustrated. "Look here, Holt. My brother has been dead for a very long time, with no thanks to you and Brent Barclay. And since nothing is going to bring Kieran back I have no interest in helping you find Doug Masters. And I have no interest in anything that you might have to say about him, or about Barclay, or about anything else. Please just go away. Leave me alone."

There was a pain in her eyes that tore through my heart, making me deeply regret being there. "I'm sorry, Claire. I just thought . . ."

She fixed me with an angry glare. "You just thought what? That after twenty bloody years you could waltz in here, turn on the charm, and I would fall all over myself to help you find a man –who may or may not have murdered my brother– that you've shown no interest in finding all these years?"

I stumbled over my words. "But he's here . . ."

"Then tell the bloody police. Don't tell me!"

I gestured frantically, desperate that she calmed herself. "I have told them, it's just that I thought your fathers investigation . . ." The look on her face stopped me.

"Don't you dare," she snarled.

"I'm sorry. I didn't come here to upset you."

She stared at me, repugnance on her face. "He's dead."

"I don't think so," I said carefully. "I'm pretty sure I saw him earlier today."

Claire shook her head slowly. "Not Doug, you moron. My father."

I didn't know what to say, so said nothing.

She turned her gaze away from me and spoke evenly, her tone belying the pain that floated just beneath the surface. "My father is dead because of the way that Kieran died." She paused to look directly at me again. "You know he hired a private investigator. But you weren't there to watch as he became obsessed with finding Doug Masters. You have no appreciation just how completely his world fell apart that day. Kieran was his pride and joy, his only son, his everything. He spent every penny my family had on trying to track Doug down. But you know what he found? Nothing. Not a bloody thing."

Claire was breathing heavily, our eyes locked. I couldn't look away. I could offer nothing to ease her pain.

"He started drinking," she continued quietly, "and when mum finally left him he took his own life. My father was a good man who never hurt anyone – and he killed himself because he could never come to grips with losing Kieran like that. With never knowing what really happened. With never being able to face the murderer and see him punished for what he did."

After an eternal silence I finally found my voice. "I'm sorry, Claire," I said, feeling hollow. "I really am. I didn't know. I didn't mean to upset you . . ."

"My mother has cancer. She's in a hospice up in Whangaparoa. She's dying. There's nothing more they can do for her except make her comfortable. Do you want the address? You could go and see her too. Tell her about how you think you saw Doug Masters today. Ask her for all Dads' files. I'm sure she'd love to see you. I'm certain she'd just love to chat about old times. Don't you think?"

Her sarcasm tore through me like a scythe. I felt like dirt. Worse than that, lower than dirt. Like a worm that eats dirt. I stood up slowly. "I'm so sorry, Claire. I'll go now. I should never have bothered you like this . . ."

She wouldn't look at me.

I turned and walked away, my heart in fresh tatters.

* * *

Claire O'Driscoll was flustered. She stood, gathered her handbag, and headed for the ladies room, keeping her head down so as not to have to acknowledge or respond to any questioning looks from her colleagues. There were clients waiting.

Pushing through the doors she slipped quickly into a cubicle, locked it behind her and sat down on the toilet seat, hugging her handbag to her chest.

She couldn't understand why Holt would show up like that, barging right into her workplace, forcing her to lie. Was he really after her father's files?

She pulled out her cell-phone and began to scroll through its contact list, then hesitated. Tried to calm herself with a deep breath. Replayed the conversation in her mind. Wondered again why Holt would come to see her now, at a time like this.

She found the name on the list then paused. Perhaps Holt's visit was just a coincidence. Perhaps it really did mean nothing. She didn't want to overreact. Closing her eyes, she contemplated her options silently, and then decided.

Carefully placing the phone back in her handbag she took another deep breath to steady herself. Now wasn't the time. Face to face would be better.

Right now she needed to get back to work before anyone took notice of what had just happened.

* * *

Donny was on a leash, being walked along the beach like a dog. If he wasn't so damn scared he would have been humiliated.

Earlier he and Suzy had played every stupid board game the bach contained. But only one time each. He had quickly learned that Suzy didn't like to do the same thing twice. They'd also played cards. And they'd watched some TV. But Suzy got so very bored so very quickly. It was becoming more and more of a problem because, to put it simply, she didn't handle boredom well. Donny had never met anyone like her. She simply wasn't any good at sitting around. She fidgeted and wriggled just watching TV.

And so they had come outside for a walk. Suzy had decided that they had to get out, get some fresh air, move around a bit. But she wanted to ensure that Donny wouldn't try running away again so, fitting two cable ties together, she had fashioned a rudimentary dog collar and then tied a thin rope to it. Fortunately, when she pulled on the rope the collar did not automatically tighten, but it did cut into his neck and he was already feeling raw and bruised.

The beach was long, wide and utterly deserted. They had wandered about two hundred metres so far, Suzy actually skipping along beside him, and they hadn't seen another soul. Apparently late on a Tuesday afternoon was not a popular time for beachgoers. Although he wasn't all that certain he actually wanted to see anyone. God only knew how Suzy might react.

"Smell that gorgeous sea air, Big-boy. Isn't it fabulous?"

Donny had also learned that agreeing with Suzy was always the best course of action by far. He wasn't about to argue. "Yeah," he said. "It's great."

"It's better than great. It's the absolute business. It's friggin' awesome."

"Oh yeah," he tried to sound enthusiastic, "It's the business."

She danced around in front of him. "Do you have any idea just how lucky we are, to live in a country like this, with beautiful beaches like this? You should count your blessings every damn day. Breath in the air and simply rejoice."

Donny nodded. "Of course. Yeah. We're really lucky."

But, oddly, her words struck a chord with him. Adam was always saying things like that. Talking up the country. He railed endlessly about how many kiwis were so damn complacent about how they lived. How beautiful the country was, how abundant food and other basic necessities were. This made him think about his father and momentarily a desperate hope surged through him.

Adam must surely now know he'd been kidnapped and would be looking for him. Unless, of course, he was still lost in the black funk that had descended over him on Friday, when he found out that his old mate Brent had been killed.

Suddenly Donny realised that the funeral had been set for today, for this morning, and he'd missed it. Adam would be crushed, or furious, probably both. He stopped walking and faced up to his captor. "Why are we here, Suzy? Does this have anything to do with Brent Barclay's murder?"

She gave him a quizzical look then smiled benignly. "I thought we'd agreed that you weren't going to ask any more silly questions?" The words came out sweetly, but her eyes flashed with a coldness that reminded him why he was wearing a leash. He started to open his mouth to ask again before quickly thinking better of it. She wasn't going to tell him. There was no point in annoying her.

Abruptly she flashed a disarmingly stunning smile. "Want to head down and dip your toes in the surf?"

His feet were already bare. She'd whisked his shoes away yesterday although he was still wearing his jeans and short-sleeved uniform shirt from KFC. Normally Donny would have loved to paddle along the beach but the coldness that was still clear in Suzy's eyes made him worry about ending up getting drowned.

He wrinkled his nose. "I don't know," he said half-heartedly. "Maybe on the way back to the bach?"

She laughed, a sweet and lilting sound, not at all the maniacal laugh you would expect from an obviously psychotic person. "Oh, come on–", she started to say but suddenly cut herself off. Something behind him had caught her eye.

Donny tensed. Suzy's expression had become suddenly serious and that frightened him. Something was wrong. She looked around them quickly, clearly searching for somewhere to hide and finding nothing. They were practically in the middle of the open space, at least twenty metres to the water's edge and a similar distance to the grassy scrub area that fringed the golden sand.

With a sudden intensity she glared into his eyes. "Lie down. Don't try anything," she snapped as she pulled on his leash.

Donny dropped to his knees and, following her silent direction, rolled obediently onto his back. In a moment she was on top of him, straddling him, leaning in close. She was wearing very little, just cut-off jeans and a bikini top.

"Put your hands on my ass . . . quickly," she ordered.

Feeling he had no other choice he raised both hands and put one on each of her cheeks. With Suzy staring zealously into his eyes he dared not turn his head, but that was when he finally heard it.

A car.

The throaty purr was making its way up the beach towards them. Who the heck would it be? A forestry ranger? A lost tourist? His heart gave a small leap. Maybe it was the police?

Suzy cupped his face in one hand, forcing him to continue to look directly at her, not at the oncoming car. Then she moved her other hand to his leash. Onto the join between the two cable ties. She pulled it one click tighter, then a second click. He could still breathe comfortably but it would only take a few more clicks to severely restrict his airflow. To effectively suffocate him. His eyes flew wide.

Suzy smiled at him again, but this time the smile was neither stunning nor disarming. A chill stole over him. Her voice was edged with menace. "If you try anything I will pull this as tight as I can. Do you understand?"

Donny swallowed involuntarily and nodded. If Suzy pulled the cable tie tight he would die, it was that simple. He had no scissors, no knife, no clippers, no way of cutting through the strong plastic. He would have no way of removing it once it bit into his neck and he would suffocate within minutes. His heart began to beat a rapid tattoo as the horrifying possibility of his situation enveloped him.

She wriggled a little on top of him, assessing his response. There was a strange flash of excitement in her eyes that truly frightened him. It was almost like she was daring him to try and throw her off. To try and escape and run to the car.

Donny didn't dare move. The car was getting closer now. Its occupants would be able to see them. They were lying on the sand in the middle of the beach. There was no way they couldn't be seen. He listened as the engine note became louder.

Then Suzy pulled at his hair with her free hand and he opened his mouth in surprise. She kissed him, her lips diving onto his in a frenzy. Her tongue lashed his. He didn't know what was happening, how to respond, what to do. He didn't kiss her back but he didn't try to pull away, an image of his own face turning blue without oxygen focusing his mind on blind obedience.

She kept kissing him as the car pulled up near them. Donny could barely breathe. He heard a honk, a friendly peep-peep sound. Suzy didn't stop kissing him and she didn't sit up. From the corner of his eye Donny saw her raise one hand out to the side and extend her middle finger. He felt her wriggle her bum in the air. He thought he heard a laugh from the car and there was another honk. This one longer, encouraging and playful.

Suzy stayed where she was. Donny froze. After what felt like an eternity he heard the car accelerate, pulling away and leaving them to it.

He risked a glimpse. It was an old Toyota Surf, rusted and battered, stacked with fishing gear and other junk. Locals, probably out fishing. Suzy unlocked her lips from his and turned her head to watch it moving away also. She stayed where she was, perched on top of him until the car began to shrink into the distance. Then she turned back to face him and smiled wryly.

"You can take your hands off my ass now, Hot-stuff."

Donny dropped both hands to the sand instantly.

FOURTEEN

Lloyd would have liked to enjoy the gentle breeze on his face but the full-faced motorbike helmet he wore restricted him from that small pleasure.

He eased the little motor scooter around a bend, turning into the unsurprisingly named Beach Road, being the main thoroughfare running parallel to the beach. He took in the quiet streets. The houses were well spaced, neatly fenced and most had nearly new cars parked in the driveways or double garages. He was riding through a nice, moderately affluent neighborhood. And he was getting close. The shop he needed to visit was only half a kilometre ahead.

About a hundred metres from the shop he pulled into a side street and parked his tiny bike behind a shiny black BMW. He sat for a moment, casually surveying his surroundings. The street was quiet. No curtains twitched to observe him.

Satisfied, Lloyd stepped off the scooter. He was a little shorter than average height, in his late-thirties and had a slightly boyish, but otherwise rather bland, face that was, today, totally devoid of facial hair, allowing him to look younger.

Removing the bike helmet revealed his dull brown hair, cut short in a common style. He locked the helmet to his bike; put his sunglasses on; adjusted his sweatshirt and walked purposefully back out onto the main road. He was well prepared for his task, as always, and moved with a fluidity and precision that belied his physical appearance.

It was late afternoon, schools were out but it wasn't yet rush hour. As he ambled along Lloyd had to step out to the grass verge to avoid a scantily dressed woman who was washing her car in a driveway. While prepared to offer a benign smile as he passed this wasn't required as the woman ignored him, lost to whatever music flowed through the headphones buried in her ears. He ignored her in return and kept walking.

In less than a minute he reached his destination and double-checked the shops name with the one he had been provided. *Flower Power*. It matched.

The flower shop was painted a modern, tasteful grey tone with bright and colourful floral displays out front and visible through the windows which stood out sharply against the muted background. It stood at the left-hand end of a short row of three stores. Next along were a hairdresser and then a dairy. He smiled as he noted that the hairdresser was closed. A stroke of luck.

Lloyd looked through the flower shop window, pretending to survey the variety of multicoloured and vibrant blooms available. Inside a man in a suit was purchasing a bundle of roses. The man behind the counter, the florist, was wrapping them. Lloyd watched and waited patiently. The customer produced a credit card and repeatedly looked at his wristwatch while the transaction was being completed. Probably late home and feeling guilty about something.

Checking the road behind him he noted some traffic, but it was quiet enough. He waited patiently and shortly the customer hurried out, leapt into his car and drove away. Lloyd casually reviewed the road around him yet again. All was well. There was no one about to walk by. Hardly any cars. It was time to do his thing.

He deftly pulled the hood on his sweatshirt up and over his head before walking into the flower shop. He left his sunglasses on. The florist was no longer behind the counter having come out to rearrange a display. Lloyd walked straight up to him.

"Are you Anthony Davis?" he asked.

The man turned, raised an eyebrow, smiled. "Yes," he said. "How can I help you?"

Lloyd smiled back. "I have a message for you."

Without warning he let the crowbar he was carrying, previously hidden inside the sleeve of his sweatshirt, drop out into the open. He caught it and spun in one abrupt movement. Clutching it with both hands, he swung it like he was hitting a cover drive with a cricket bat. He stepped forward; driving the crowbar up and through, using his momentum to slam the weapon with massive force into the florist's lower left leg. There was a distinctly satisfying snap just before the man screamed, in both surprise and agony, as his shinbones broke.

The florist fell to the floor and moaned piteously.

Lloyd bent down so that his face was only inches from the other man's. He watched his eyes widen with fear. The florist began begging, pleading, trying to push himself away, inching back from the face before him.

"You need to pay your debts, Anthony," Lloyd told him sternly. "You have forty-eight hours or I'll come back."

He didn't wait for a response. He knew the florist would understand the message, having already received plenty of warnings from his employer. The man's gambling debt was out of hand. It needed to be sorted out . . . and fast.

Lloyd turned and pushed the crowbar back up the sleeve of his sweatshirt as he walked to the door. He left his hood up until he'd passed out of the florist's sight before pulling it down and walking with a casual, unhurried pace back to his motor scooter. The car-washing woman steadfastly ignored him again as he sauntered by, still intent only on her work and the music in her ears.

He was back on the scooter and riding quietly away within two minutes of the attack. No one had seen him, and even if they had they would never remember him. He worked on being bland, colourless. He could blend in at will and doubted if even the florist would be able to provide the police with a description. That's if he actually called them and Lloyd doubted he would. The florist would call an ambulance and give them some bullshit story about tripping and falling. Then he would find some money and pay his debt to Lloyd's employer.

That's how it worked.

He cruised away on his little scooter, meandering along, enjoying the late afternoon sun on his back. With his job done

–just a very small and simple one today, completed effectively and efficiently, as always– he was heading for home, thoughts turning to what he might choose for dinner, when one of his mobile phones rang. He pulled over, removed his helmet and answered the call.

"Yes."

"Is this Lawrence?" asked the voice.

"Yes," he said.

Lloyd wasn't his real name. Neither was Lawrence for that matter. He had many names, each one for a different purpose, for a different employer.

"I'm going to require your help again," said the voice.

Lloyd frowned. The last aid he had provided for this caller was a fairly substantial and carefully planned termination, but it had been less than a week ago. It was unusual for an employer such as this, a first time user of his services, to make contact again so soon. "Another one . . . like the last?"

There was a pause. "No, not like that. Less extreme. And this one needs to happen a lot faster. Tonight if you can manage it. I actually have an idea that might work well on a number of levels. Are you available?"

Lloyd was intrigued. He usually didn't take last-minute jobs; he preferred to plan well in advance. He had made a good living in his line of work, and that was because he was always cautious, always in control. He took a moment to consider the proposal, factoring in the way that the last job had gone so smoothly while consciously ratcheting up the price he would charge with each second he made this employer wait. "I'm available," he said finally. "But it won't be cheap. Moving this quickly raises the stakes. You understand that?"

"I understand. Money isn't an issue."

"Good. But I'll need to know more before I fully commit."

"Of course. He's another travel agent. His name is–"

"Wait. Right now isn't actually convenient. Can you call me back in twenty?"

"Yes, of course."

He ended the call. He would learn more once he was back home, not sitting on the side of the road on his scooter. Lloyd allowed himself a faint smile. Business was good. In fact, business was very good. Adding the fee for this job to his recent commissions he'd be able to take a very nice holiday this year. But where to, that was the question? Lloyd enjoyed visiting the world's more historic and monumental destinations. Among his travels he'd walked along The Great Wall of China, canoed on the Zambezi River and marveled at both the Taj Mahal and the Pyramids of Giza. But there were still so many more fabulous places to experience. Perhaps this was the year he'd make it to Peru and Machu Picchu?

He shook his head in wonder as he pulled out onto the road on his scooter. Who would have thought that he would end up in this line of work? And turn out to be so damn good at it. A long time ago he'd made a bad mistake and fallen into the murder business by accident. Back then, the first time he killed, he'd panicked and run from the scene. But he learned a lot from that experience and over the years he'd researched carefully and worked out how to make a damn fine living from it.

He was a skilled practitioner now, one of the best in his field. He had a portfolio of regular employers and not one of them had any idea who he actually was, where he lived, or who else he worked for.

Lloyd was a professional . . . and very good at what he did. Sometimes, when he was feeling a little reflective, he actually considered himself an artist.

FIFTEEN

If I hadn't changed my mind about going back into work –yes, I know that I do that a lot, but Julie really does have everything under control– I never would have spotted *Milly*.

As it was, instead of heading towards the Milford shops as I departed Takapuna, I changed course and aimed my car for home. This meant I had to drive right past the KFC where Donny works and it was as I waited nearby for the lights to change that I looked across and spotted his clapped-out car in the car park there.

The lights changed and I drove on, slowly trying to filter out all the other problems in my head and turning my focus to my son. When was the last time I'd seen him? Sunday, or was it even Saturday? No, it was definitely Sunday morning. He slipped out with barely a word just after I dragged myself out of bed, somewhere close to midday.

And we hadn't caught up since. That was actually a bit strange. We often came and went at different odd hours, but usually crossed paths either around dinner-time or later in the evenings, around bed-time. Today was now Wednesday. Should I be worried? Maybe I should. But my overriding emotion was more annoyance. I was actually quite pissed off at him. Donny hadn't come to Brent's funeral this morning. We'd talked on Saturday and he definitely knew when it was – and where. When I really thought about it; no-showing at your Dad's best mate's funeral was actually pretty damn rude.

I slowed the car and turned it around at the next intersection. Donny had obviously made it to work, but had not shown the decency to come and support me at Brent's funeral. Damn him. I wanted an explanation.

I parked in the KFC car park and strode purposefully in through the front door. The damningly seductive aroma of fried chicken swept over me and for a moment I realised how hungry I was. I'd missed lunch.

But there was no sign of Donny behind the counter or at the window that serves the drive-through customers. He must be out the back, preparing the secret recipe, I decided as I waited behind the only customer at the counter.

"Could I have a quick word with Donny, please," I said to the young Indian guy who was serving when I finally reached the counter.

He looked flustered. "He's not here," he said. "What would you like?"

I was taken aback. *Milly* was right outside. "Are you sure? I thought he was working today."

"So did I, but he hasn't turned up. What can I get you?"

I shook my head. "I don't want anything. I'm Donny's father. I only wanted a quick word with him."

He frowned at me, obviously not in a good mood. The badge on his chest told me his name was 'Johnno' and it had MANAGER inscribed below. "Well, he's not here and I haven't heard from him. So when you do see him, tell him he's fired."

"Oh, hey. I'm sure there's no need for that. Donny's usually very reliable. When was he supposed to start?"

"Hours ago, on day-shift. He's obviously not coming and he didn't call to say anything so he's out. Nothing to discuss."

I tried to appeal to him. Wherever Donny was I felt sure he wouldn't want to lose his job. "Something must have come up," I said. "Did you know that his car's outside . . . in the car park. Are you sure he didn't come in and then leave for some reason? Maybe he cut himself or something?"

Johnno looked perplexed for a moment. "Which is his car?" he asked as he came out from behind the counter.

I pointed. "The old Mirage there."

Johnno shook his head. "He hasn't been here. Not today. I had to open up on my own and call Estelle in."

"Then how do you explain his car?"

He stared at me incredulously. "I don't have to explain anything. He's not here. He hasn't been here today and he damn well won't be coming back here again. And if that piece-of-shit," he pointed an accusing finger at Donny's car, "is still rotting in my car park tomorrow I'll get it towed."

I started to see red and opened my mouth to let fly, but managed to regain self-control before making matters worse. As Johnno returned to his post behind the counter I took a deep breath and then exhaled slowly.

I approached him again. "Sorry to hassle you, but when was the last time Donny came in to work? Did he work yesterday?"

Johnno glared at me, clearly wanting to tell me to piss off, but managing to contain his feelings. He turned and called out to the girl manning the drive-through till. "Estelle. When was Donny last on?"

She wandered over. "Sorry, what?"

"When was Donny last here, do you know?" he said.

"I worked with him on Sunday night. He said he wasn't due back in until today."

"So he was definitely here on Sunday night?" I said.

"Yeah, sure."

"And he definitely hasn't worked since then?"

She looked at Johnno. He shook his head. She shrugged.

I addressed the girl as Johnno rolled his eyes and walked away. "On Sunday, did you see how he got home? Because his car's out back. Did it break down? Did he get a lift?"

"He didn't say anything about his car. But his mate in the old Mini was here when he left."

"Slouch?" I said, immediately recognising the vehicle.

"I don't know his name . . . but he's kind of long haired and anemic. You know, looks like he's always out-of-it."

Definitely Slouch. I didn't even know his real name. "And you haven't seen Donny since Sunday night?"

She shook her head. "Is he in some kind of trouble?"

"I don't know," I told her truthfully. I was starting to get worried. No one seemed to have seen Donny since Sunday night, I certainly hadn't, and he wasn't returning his mother's calls. Something wasn't right.

I thanked her and left. Outside the KFC I peered in through *Milly's* windows, searching for clues. Not surprisingly the inside of Donny's car was exactly what you would expect after looking at it from the outside. A garbage-filled flea-pit. I cringed. My God, was I ever that dirty and careless? Probably.

The car was locked, although it didn't look like it would be hard to break into. I spotted Donny's day-bag, a smallish black Adidas backpack, in the passenger's side foot-well. That worried me. He almost always dragged that bag around with him. Everything else inside was either rubbish or discarded clothing. The car needed to be tipped on its side and shaken clean. I was glad I couldn't smell the interior through the window.

I went back to my car and drove home, hoping to find a note or some other simple explanation for Donny's absence. I found nothing out of the ordinary at all . . . and no Donny.

Fortunately, finding Slouch's phone number was easy. I keep a list of important numbers on a board near the phone including casual friends, neighbours, my preferred plumber and electrician, etc. Most of my business contacts and close friends I have stored in my cell-phone, but there is never enough phone memory available for everyone you need to call. I made no comment when Donny added a few of his own without prompting when he moved in. At the time I just thought that it was nice that he felt comfortable enough to do that. That he felt at home here.

Slouch's name only had a mobile number next to it so I used my cell-phone to make the call, so that Milford Trips and Travel paid the exorbitant mobile connection charges. After six rings it went to voicemail. Slouch's voice lazily suggested that I should say my piece at the tone, Dude. I left a simple message asking him to call me and left my number.

To be honest, I felt a bit silly doing it. Donny was a big boy; he'd be twenty years old soon, this coming weekend in fact.

What if Donny was just crashing with a friend to give me a bit of space while I grieved?

I checked my watch; the day had practically flown by. I needed to eat, and fast, I realised. I was due to go out again pretty soon. I went to the kitchen and peered hopefully into the fridge. I should have bought some KFC. Frozen vege and some bacon stared back at me. A quick stir-fry would have to do.

"Come on, Holt. Get your bloody head in the game. You're hopping around like a bloody one-legged toad. Wake up!"

Brent Barclay wasn't the only one of my friends with a charming turn of phrase. Lurch knew me well enough to ignore the fact that I had been at Brent's funeral this morning and offered me clear and sage advice.

"Bite me, Dip-shit," I responded. "I've taken more intercepts that you've made actual baskets tonight." He gave me the fingers and shuffled back up court. I turned my attention to the ferocious blonde who was trying to elbow me in the ribs to get her pass away.

Indoor netball is supposed to be a social game, but don't believe a thing. It's not. It's highly competitive and the action within those netted walls can easily get as fierce as any full international test match. My team, the '*Evergreens*', may have had some of the oldest players in the league, but we played to win. I played defense, mainly because I'm fairly tall and can handle a fair bit of bump and thrust. But mostly because I can't shoot a basket to save my life.

I tried to block the ferocious blonde and succeeded in knocking her on her ass. I got called for contact and had to stand down. The look she gave me made it clear she wasn't going to be slipping me her number after the game. I put my hands up in surrender and muttered a lame apology that we both knew I didn't mean.

The big clock on the wall indicated only thirty seconds to go in the match. We were up eighteen to six. The *Evergreens* would be happy tonight, we were going to win comfortably.

I relaxed a little as the ball travelled away down court again and cast another sneak peak at our reserves bench. Linda DeWalt was still red in the face from her efforts for the *Evergreens* in the previous two quarters. I still couldn't work out how she managed to talk her way into the team without me knowing. I'd arrived a bit late and there she was, warming up and looking pretty damn sexy in skimpy leggings and a fitted tee. All I was told was that our usual centre, Glenda, wasn't available and that this was Linda. Then I had to rush on court having barely said 'Hey' to her. She played well too, I have to admit. I was pretty impressed.

Moments later the final buzzer went and the sweaty handshakes all round were performed. Good game, good game, thanks a lot, good game. You know how it goes.

"You played like crap tonight," Lurch told me bluntly afterwards, with a broad smile on his face. His real name is Luke Andrews and he's a tall, rangy lawyer.

"Kiss my ass," I retorted. "You must have missed over half your shots. Is your eyesight failing, old man?" Lurch is at least six months younger than me. He gave me the fingers again and slugged back on his water bottle. "I need a beer," someone said. It might have been me. We all shuffled through to the basic bar area to sort out who owes who money for the game – and to enjoy a quiet, cold one.

Lurch got the beers. Small amounts of cash were exchanged. The banter eased to normal, more civilised conversation. The game was discussed, the weather, some stupid cooking show that was on TV yesterday, but, even though I'm almost certain they all knew, no mention was made of Brent Barclay. He had played for the *Evergreens* occasionally, if we were short, but wasn't a regular. And even less so since he'd been married. Lurch and one of the other guys also played with Brent and I in an indoor football league on Sunday evenings. I already knew we'd defaulted last weekend, but no one mentioned it. And neither of the guys seemed to want to talk about our next game and the issue of finding a replacement for Brent. I was actually quite relieved. I wasn't ready to move on like that quite yet.

One by one they all filtered away until I found myself with just Linda and Rose, who was apparently the person who had invited Linda along to fill in. I was a bit worried that Linda might be angry with me for disappearing on her the other night at the gala dinner, but she seemed okay.

"You're actually pretty fit, for an old guy," Linda teased.

"Don't be deceived, my age is really an advantage."

"Really? I'll bite . . . In what way?"

"Less hair to worry about getting in my eyes."

Both ladies laughed.

"Another drink, anyone," I offered.

"Not for me," said Rose. "Driving."

"Not for me either," said Linda. "Also driving."

"I guess that makes three of us."

"And I've got to get going," said Rose. "I'll talk to you guys later." She stood up to leave and hesitated, probably expecting Linda to follow her out. When neither of us moved she nodded knowingly to herself and departed.

After a moments silence Linda broke the ice. "I was very sorry to hear about Brent . . . the last few days must have been awful for you."

I nodded. "It hasn't been all that much fun."

"It's horrible, isn't it? When you think that you and I must have been the last people to see him alive."

Oh, God. That's right. I'd forgotten that I had left Brent with Linda at the dinner. I met her eye. She seemed genuinely troubled. "I'm sorry about that," I said. "I hope he didn't come on to you too hard. He was a bit of a rogue."

She shook her head. "Oh, Adam. Don't think that. He was definitely a tease, but he never tried to hit on me."

I was surprised. "Really, then what did you talk about?"

She smiled. It was like a breath of fresh air. "I sort-of tried to talk him into adding Picarso to his preferred rental-car list, but he just laughed. Then we spent some time talking about you."

"About me. Really? What about me?"

She couldn't meet my gaze for a moment and tried to stifle another smile. "He told me you were worth the chase."

"What?"

"He said that you were a fussy bastard, but that you had a good heart. That you were worth chasing a bit."

I didn't know what to say, so I just blushed.

"He told me you were one of the last true romantics, just that you didn't realise it yourself. I thought it was sweet, how he was defending you and encouraging me to not give up on you. He really seemed to care about you."

A huge lump grew in my throat. I couldn't speak. She wouldn't meet my eyes, but she kept on talking.

"He went on about how you'd let a few bad experiences cloud the way you handle dating, and how you were still hung up on some girl you used to see when you were teenagers. He made me laugh about that, the way he rolled his eyes . . . and he said that you just needed a good slap around the head, to get you to stop looking back and to start looking forward . . . He seemed really worried that life was going to pass you by."

Still I couldn't speak and when she looked up I turned away.

"I'm sorry, Adam . . . I just thought, well, it would have been nice if you'd been able to hear him talk about you."

I tried to force the tear that was welling up in my eye to bugger off and strained out a smile. "Thank you," I managed. She merely nodded.

Initially I couldn't believe that Brent had told Linda so much about me. Did he do this with every woman I dated? Probably not, because he didn't get to meet many of them. Especially not since he got married. But what upset me the most was that Brent was right. Ever since that night on the *Kestrel*, and probably even before then, I somehow managed to continually self-sabotage my relationships with women – and I knew it. I would find fault where there was none or unfairly compare them to the girl who I always thought about as '*The One*'. The one I should be with. The one that got away.

I've been such a fool.

"And so, on that note, I should be off too," she said and stood up before pausing to smile down at me meaningfully. "You've still got my number . . ."

This time I nodded, suddenly noticing how blue her eyes were. "I have, yes. Thanks, Linda. I mean it . . ."

With a final smile she turned and left.

As I watched her go –and Brent had been right, she really did have a nice ass– I thought a bit about what I knew of Linda. We'd been out on two dates. I could tell you that she was thirty-five, had no children and had never been married. And she wasn't what you'd call a dedicated career woman either as she'd only recently re-entered the workforce with her role at Picarso. On our first date it was those simple facts that had initially raised a few cautionary flags. She was an attractive and obviously intelligent woman. So why no kids? Why not married?

But it wasn't until our second date, which I almost didn't go on, that she reluctantly admitted that she had spent eight of the last nine years caring full-time for her already widowed father as he slowly gave in to a debilitating, and ultimately fatal, case of early-onset Alzheimer's. I can only imagine how hard that would have been on her, as it would be on anybody. Developing a career had clearly been impossible during that time and boyfriends were few and far between. Certainly none, as she succinctly put it, that were able to understand the incredible demands on both her time and her fragile morale.

But now that her father was gone, while still coming to grips with her own emotional well-being, Linda was trying to re-start her life. I admired her courage. My parents were both still fit and well and reasonably active. I simply couldn't imagine the type of heartache she had spent all those years going through.

It made me embarrassed to think of the pathetic efforts I went to last week at the dinner to try and avoid her as I gradually considered that Linda DeWalt might actually be someone I should try a little harder to get to know better.

I sat there for a few moments before attempting to stand and leave. My muscles had cooled and now ached as my almost forty year-old body pointedly reminded me that I was getting too old for these stupid netball games.

Then I thought more about Linda's struggle and about what Brent had told her and decided that my heart was probably getting too old for stupid games too.

As I shuffled out into the dimly lit car park I immediately became confused. Was I getting that senile? Where the hell did I park my car? I thought back to my late arrival. I got lucky and managed a spot quite close to the door. My car should have been just over there. But it wasn't. I walked slowly over to where I'd last seen it then walked up and down, spinning as I moved, searching every corner of the car park. The damn thing wasn't there. I checked in my pocket for keys. Yes, I had them.

A brightly-painted little Honda pulled up before me, its headlights dazzlingly bright. The window hummed on its way down and Linda's voice floated out.

"Are you all right, Adam?"

I walked over to her window, frowning angrily. "I think my damn car's been stolen."

She sighed. "You're not having a good week, are you? Need a lift?"

* * *

The sun was only just breaking through the tree spattered skyline as Lloyd's patience finally paid its dividend.

He couldn't believe his luck. This was going to work out nicely, he thought, allowing himself a bemused smile. He had initially considered his employers latest plan to be hastily sketched out. Too simple. Too obvious. But, he now had to concede, this looked like it was actually going to come together.

Lloyd started the car. He watched his targets, waiting for the right moment. Having already surveyed their premises he had decided that an external hit would be best. It could almost look like an accident, but that wasn't entirely necessary.

He had already planned another course of action. Something that would definitely incapacitate one of the targets, if not kill him outright. Either outcome was within his employer's guidelines. And he had it all planned out after that too. A man of his experience knew to have an exit strategy and Lloyd wasn't prone to making mistakes.

He had spent hours, as he waited overnight in the car, running scenarios in his head. His targets would pull out of the driveway in their silver Audi and drive away from him. He would wait a few seconds and then follow. After that it was just timing. He would accelerate as they started to pull out and into the right-hand turn at the top of this very street. He would aim to the extreme right of the road and felt certain he could put the left-hand headlight of his car smack into the targets driver's door doing at least seventy km's. Then he would simply bail out and run. His scooter was parked two streets away. He would be long gone before anyone even called an ambulance, let alone the police.

It was a simple plan. And simple plans were always best.

But now a new opportunity had emerged and this one might actually be better. If he performed to his usual high standards he could hospitalise both targets and probably still drive away and return for the scooter later, at his leisure. This new way would be excellent. He felt sure his employer would be very pleased.

Lloyd checked for other traffic and, seeing none, he pulled out into the quiet street to complete his task.

SIXTEEN

"I'm sorry, but I don't understand your concerns, Marguerite. I'm only here to offer Sharon a bit of morale support," I said. "Look, if it's going to be an issue I'll just go."

Marguerite Dodd wasn't keen on me being included in the meeting. The two women had been eyeing each other up in a way that had made me uncomfortable, like a couple of beauty queen's about to go to war over a title and crown. She opened her mouth to respond but Sharon intervened firmly.

"Marguerite, I appreciate your concerns, but I really would be more comfortable with Adam joining us. There is so much about the travel industry that I don't understand and I truly value his independent advice. I must insist . . ."

The reception area at Barclay and Dodd Travel was quiet for a few moments; I couldn't even hear that annoying muzak this time, before Marguerite finally gave in. Without another word she nodded in assent and gestured us forward.

I wasn't looking forward to this meeting and continued to have ill feelings towards Marguerite for not having turned up at Brent's funeral. And, honestly, I wasn't really sure what value Sharon thought I could possibly add. But I had promised to support her and I wanted to keep my word.

Getting there had proved quite a mission too, given that my car was still missing. I was lucky that Linda was still around last night, and she'd been great; running me to the police station, waiting around while I filed a stolen car report and then dropping me home. She was the only bright point in my whole evening. Being with Linda had almost made the whole thing fun. I even think she may have felt similarly. In fact, I was starting to hope that she had.

But it bothered me that Donny wasn't at home when I got in and he still hadn't made an appearance when I awoke this morning. I'd called his cell-phone about a dozen times now and left messages. I was getting quite worried, something definitely wasn't right.

Without transport I almost decided not to come to the meeting, but Sharon had sounded so disappointed when I called that, once again, I promised her I'd be there. So I dug out the spare key for *Milly* and jogged down to KFC. At least this way I could be certain that it wouldn't get towed away by Donny's ex-boss.

Inside the damn car it smelled even worse than I anticipated, but that's life. I brushed most of the crap aside and drove it home. Donny hadn't been kidding, it truly ran like shit. The whole way I felt like it was going to just stop and never start up again. But, somehow, it got me home to shower and change and then back into Takapuna for the meeting, only just on time.

Sharon and I followed Marguerite through to a well appointed boardroom where we found two men awaiting us. They both rose and introductions were made rather stiffly. A grey-haired man in an expensive suit with a hawk-like gaze turned out to be Marguerite's father; Gerald Dodd. Something about him, possibly his air of outright authority, or just knowing that the guy had bags of money, made me feel immediately inadequate. He barely acknowledged my handshake and only greeted Sharon with an unreadable expression and a tiny nod. He was the first man I ever met that didn't seem to be affected by her incredible beauty.

The other man was more amiable. Tall, thin, balding with a neatly trimmed grey beard, Walter Pickering was older that Dodd, also impeccably suited, and offered us both a lukewarm smile while allowing his gaze to slip momentarily to Sharon's cleavage. She pretended not to notice, as did I.

We took seats at the table, immediately delineating a clear division between parties. Dodd and Pickering moved away, around the table, leaving Sharon and I across the great divide. Marguerite sat to one side, but nearest to her father.

I thought it was odd that no one offered us tea or coffee and started to become apprehensive.

There was silence before Pickering opened the meeting. "Mrs Barclay, on behalf of everyone present I would like to begin by offering our sincere condolences for your loss."

Marguerite nodded half-heartedly and stared at the wall. Dodd didn't move; his rock-steady gaze trained impassively on Sharon who murmured her thanks softly. Pickering continued.

"With this in mind, I do regret that our discussion today may be somewhat difficult and I must ask if we could reconsider the presence of Mr Holt . . . given that these discussions should be considered, at the very least, highly confidential."

Sharon frowned. "We've already been through this. Adam and I merely wish to discuss the best ways for Barclay and Dodd to move forward, given the loss of my husband. I value Adam's knowledge of the travel industry. I would like him to be here. Why would that be of concern to you?"

"I appreciate that, Mrs Barclay, however there are certain factors here that the Dodd's are not entirely comfortable sharing with a wider audience than necessary, and with–"

"I'm sorry," Sharon interrupted, "But if a wider audience is not desired, then may I ask your involvement?"

Pickering was taken aback for a moment, but he quickly composed himself and was about to respond when Gerald Dodd sat forward and spoke bluntly.

"Pickering is our legal counsel. He's doing his job. Mr Holt has no business here. He needs to leave."

You could have knocked me down with a feather. I glanced over at Marguerite who had closed her eyes. She looked like she was wishing to be absolutely anywhere else. I started to rise. "Perhaps I should just go, Sharon."

Her hand landed on my arm with some force and I looked over to see an expression of grim determination in her eyes that I hadn't expected. "Sit down please, Adam," she said to me before turning back to Dodd. "Mr Holt will be staying. Whatever you have to say I think I would be more comfortable with a witness present. Perhaps I should have bought my lawyer with me too."

Dodd and Sharon eyeballed each other fiercely. The room was silent. The exchange seemed unnecessary and made me so uncomfortable that I froze, half-standing. Eventually Dodd turned to Pickering and gave a small nod and then leaned back in his chair, once again glowering at Sharon. I sat down.

Pickering produced a legal looking document and addressed Sharon evenly. "I will need Mr Holt to sign this confidentiality agreement if he is to remain with us here today." He slid the document and a pen over the desk and spoke to me. "Mr Holt. Would you mind, please?"

I didn't want to cause any further fuss and picked up the document, scanning it quickly. It already had my name and other details typed in. They were clearly prepared for this. I looked at Sharon who appeared annoyed, but shrugged in resignation. I signed the document.

Pickering's tone was still agreeable, but now carried an undercurrent of ruthlessness. "Mr Holt, I must be absolutely clear that we consider this matter to be of the greatest confidentiality. Any negligence on your part in relation to this confidentiality will be intolerable to all parties and will lead to prosecution."

"I understand," I said, still reeling slightly.

He nodded benignly and moved on. "Mrs Barclay, you are aware that your late husband was the majority shareholder in this business; Barclay and Dodd Travel Limited. To the tune of sixty percent of all shares."

"I am aware. Yes," she said.

"And you are also aware that the remaining forty percent of the shares are held by the holding company Dodd Travel, which is fully owned by Mr Gerald Dodd."

"I am."

"And it is my understanding that you are to be the sole beneficiary of the full complement of Mr Barclay's shares in Barclay and Todd Travel Limited."

She sighed heavily. "Yes, Mr Picking. That is the case."

"Are you able to substantiate this claim, Mrs Barclay?"

I think my mouth fell open. Was he serious? Sharon began to look angry again but said nothing. She dipped into her handbag and withdrew a copy of Brent's will. Opening it she flipped through to find the relevant clause. She slid it across the desk and pointed. Pickering leaned forward and quickly scanned the page without touching it. He glanced briefly at Dodd and nodded. "Thank you, Mrs Barclay," he said. She retrieved the will and returned it to her handbag.

"I am afraid, Mrs Barclay, that there are currently some financial concerns in relation to Barclay and Dodd Travel . . . and in particular to your late husband's administration of the company's financial affairs."

A sick feeling began to burrow its way into my stomach. I looked across at Marguerite who was still staring fixedly at the wall. Dodd continued to glare at Sharon. Unease was edging its way onto her face. Pickering continued.

"Over the last few weeks a number of accounting concerns have been discovered. After these were bought to Mr Dodd's attention an investigation into the companies accounting practices was considered necessary and has been quietly under-way." Pickering paused to take a deep breath. "Unfortunately there appears to have been quite a substantial misappropriation of funds, Mrs Barclay. Mainly in terms of income from certain sources not being correctly accounted for and being diverted away from the business."

Sharon became pale. "What are you saying?"

Dodd sat forward and cut in bluntly. "Brent Barclay was stealing from Barclay and Dodd Travel. Your husband was ripping me off."

Sharon immediately shook her head in what may have been either denial or disbelief. "No, that's not possible . . ."

Marguerite had closed her eyes again. I wanted to run from the room. The colour had almost completely drained from Sharon's face. Gerald Dodd was not happy. He leaned further forward and practically snarled at Sharon.

"Your son-of-a-bitch husband has bled off tens of thousands of dollars from this business. From my business. From me! And I won't bloody stand for it."

Pickering gently laid a hand on Dodd's arm and the man eased back, openly seething, into his chair. "The exact figure is yet to be determined, Mrs Barclay. The forensic accountant we bought in is still digging through the companies records to confirm everything. But it is clear that substantial funds have been diverted from the business by Mr Barclay."

"How do you know it was Brent," I leapt in. "How do you know it wasn't Marguerite, or someone else here?"

Pickering looked over at Marguerite, whose face was ashen, "Perhaps you could outline the airline commission's diversion for us?"

Marguerite looked like she wanted nothing more than to crawl under the boardroom table and hide but she nodded wearily and turned to face Sharon and I. She had trouble meeting our eyes as she spoke flatly.

"So far we've found ancillary contracts with two airlines providing bonus overrides, paid quarterly, that Barclay and Dodd never received. We did get the normal commission overrides, and the supplementary commissions for volume and market share, but the bonus payments were paid to separate accounts. Accounts that do not belong to Barclay and Dodd Travel. We've traced these accounts through various holding companies and they all, eventually, lead to Brent. And the contracts themselves, which I had never seen before, were only signed by Brent. We usually require two signatures.

"There are other, lesser anomalies – such as fake invoices from suppliers that don't exist, but . . ." she tailed off with a sigh. "I'm sorry if this is a shock to you, but Brent was definitely screwing the scrum here. There's no mistake. And the losses are really adding up."

There was silence for a full minute. I didn't know what to say. The airline bonus payments set-up was quite plausible and it made me feel even sicker . . . mainly because I immediately felt certain it was true. I'm sure she may have had reason to lie but, and I felt awful about this, I believed Marguerite. It was exactly the sort of egotistical thing that Brent would do. He always believed that he knew best, that he was smarter than everyone else, that he deserved more than others. Brent's self-confidence had always bordered on vain arrogance.

You stupid bastard, Barclay, I thought to myself.

What have you done?

SEVENTEEN

Donny shuffled around on the couch some more, fed up and uncomfortable. His left wrist was sore. It was his third morning at the bach and he was desperately sick of being there. And boredom was setting in . . . once again.

Boredom and Suzy did not mix well so Donny was dreading whatever plans she might have for him. She had been for a run again this morning and that seemed to relieve some of the pressure, but only for a little while. About an hour later she was moving around restlessly again, desperately craving anything that might hold her attention.

Since returning from the ill-fated beach walk yesterday, where she removed the leash and reattached him to the couch, Suzy had resumed searching the bach over and over, from top to bottom, each time returning to the lounge grinning from ear to ear whenever she found something amusing. In the last twenty-four hours there had been soccer, rugby and tennis balls from the garage which she'd tossed about inside carelessly. There had also been children's plastic toys, figurines and books. She had even dragged out a bucket of cleaning products after dinner last night and cleaned and polished every surface in the tiny, ramshackle house.

Anything to ward off boredom.

At one point she had appeared with a small bucket full of Lego. Donny used to love the stuff. He enjoyed creating things. Cars, houses, planes, anything you could possibly imagine he had built in one form or another. Lego was a big reason he was now studying engineering as he liked to pull things apart and put them back together again.

The bucket-full had reminded him of his first Lego set. Adam had introduced him to it on the first day they ever met – a historic day on two counts. He was seven. Bella had been unusually distracted, between boyfriends and not coping well. They were living in a tiny one-bedroom flat the welfare people had provided and Adam had turned up at the door, wide-eyed and pale, carrying a huge package under his arm. A gift. A simply huge set of Lego pieces. Enough to build half a town, with little Lego people and lots of wheels for cars and other fascinating stuff. Donny had been entranced and he and Adam had sat on the floor in the tiny room, with Bella balefully watching every moment from the sidelines.

Adam had been funny too, making him laugh often. It had been a magical day, one that Donny would never forget. He suddenly had a father, a real one, not yet another disinterested uncle. As Donny stared silently at the bucket of Lego that Suzy had found he wondered, not for the first time, why his mother had hugged him so tightly after Adam left that day and cried and cried and cried.

Sadly, and unsurprisingly, Suzy had quickly become bored with the Lego and began fidgeting again. What was worrying him now was that, not long ago, Suzy had been talking about tattoos and Donny was becoming extremely worried. What if she decided to try her hand at tattooing him? She'd already given him an awful haircut –which he had obviously thanked her for profusely– and she was now prowling around the place, desperately searching once again, the boredom gnawing through her.

Donny decided to try the TV, yet again. God willing there would be something on that might catch her interest. He doubted it, but he had to do something.

He sat up and looked around for the remote. Where had he left it? It wasn't visible on the coffee table, or on the floor nearby. He reached behind himself and felt under the couches cushions. Yuck. Lint, stale potato chips, a button –there's always a button, isn't there– a clothes peg, a muesli bar wrapper, an . . . oww.

What the hell was that? He reached in again, more carefully and suddenly felt excited. He froze, looking around, listening intently. Suzy was out in the garage, he felt sure. He slowly drew his find out into the light.

Oh. My. God.

In his hand he held a lightly rusted steak knife. Just a standard serrated-blade knife that you would use on your dinner, but a bloody steak knife all the same. It was easily sharp enough to slice through the cable tie that bound him.

Freedom called loudly.

He twisted around, bringing the knife down onto the cable tie around his wrist. Elation coursed through him. With just one swift cut he would be liberated. He could get out of there. Escape from Suzy's lunacy. His arm muscle tensed as he prepared to sever his restraint.

Yet he hesitated, holding his breath and listening carefully. Where was Suzy? He heard nothing. He wouldn't have long to think things through.

Once he cut the cable tie, then what? How was he going to get out of there? He was pretty sure that Suzy was just outside in the garage. What if she heard him? He doubted he could outrun her, she was bloody fit. He'd need to take her car. But where was the key? He tried to think back. Where had she put it when she first dragged him in, late on Sunday night? Her leather jacket, probably. That's where she'd left his cell-phone. Did he recall this correctly? Had she put the key in the same zip-up pocket of her leather jacket? He thought so. But where was the jacket now? He looked around frantically, couldn't see it. She hadn't worn it since they arrived, so it was probably in the bedroom where she slept. But what if it wasn't? That would be quite a risk. He couldn't afford to bungle an escape attempt. Suzy would not be happy.

Donny gazed at the knife in his hand, now uncertain. What should he do? Suddenly there was a noise from the kitchen. Suzy was returning.

He quickly pushed the knife back under the couch cushion, hiding it again. She sprang into the room, all smiles, just as he removed his hand.

Suzy was excited, she'd found something to do.

Clutched in her hand was a small bottle of bright red nail polish. "How are those toes of yours looking?" she said gleefully.

* * *

"What does this mean?" Sharon asked.

Pickering and Dodd exchanged a look before Pickering responded in a careful tone. "What it means, Mrs Barclay, is entirely dependent on how, together, we choose to handle the situation." He paused meaningfully. "But, unfortunately we do not have a lot of time to discuss options."

She gave him a hard look. "Go on," she said.

"I am not sure you yet appreciate the gravity of the situation we find ourselves in. Please understand that we are not here to discuss how Barclay and Dodd moves forward but, in fact, whether Barclay and Dodd continues to survive as a business."

Sharon's expression didn't change. She said nothing.

"You see, this is why absolute confidentiality must be maintained by all present today. If word gets out that Mr Barclay has been siphoning off funds from this business it would destroy the existing premise of the companies travel accounting model . . . thereby alienating it from all its current corporate accounts and destroying its reputation."

"I don't see how that would be possible," said Sharon.

"Actually, I think I do," I said, joining the conversation for the first time and feeling the knot of sickness in my stomach tighten. Pickering raised an eyebrow, questioning me silently. Then he gestured for me to continue, so I did. "To attract the big accounts this type of travel agency operates an open-book policy." I looked over at Marguerite and she nodded. "In effect they declare openly all the commissions and discounts they receive from all the airlines and suppliers they deal with. This is all then passed back to the customer as a combined discount and Barclay and Dodd then charge the customer structured service fees for their efforts. If Barclay and Dodd were receiving additional payments from, for instance, a customers preferred airline –and it wasn't declared– the customer would be the one losing out."

"Oh," she said, seeming to quickly grasp the concept. She looked over at Marguerite. "How many accounts would be affected by the airline bonus?"

She looked grim. "Most of them. That example was two major airlines."

"And that was just one . . . issue?"

"Yes. It's my feeling that almost every client we have would be affected in some way by Brent's . . . tinkering."

Gerald Dodd exploded. "It's not bloody tinkering, and these aren't bloody issues. This is God-damn theft. I have a hell of a lot of money invested in this fucking business and that bastard Barclay has gone and fucked it all up!"

"Gerald, please . . ." Pickering tried to calm him.

"Oh, for fuck's sake," he spat, leaning back into his chair and resuming the glowering vigil. "Just get on with it."

Pickering took a moment to let the tension ease and then addressed Sharon once again. "Mrs Barclay, after much serious consideration we can see only one practical solution to the situation in which we are all now faced.

"On one hand we can allow this information to become public. If that happens then the Dodd family will be forced to move against the estate of Brent Barclay to recover the funds that have been stolen. If this were to occur though it would effectively spell the end of Barclay and Dodd Travel as its corporate accounts would inevitably lose faith in the company and quickly depart, removing all income streams from the business.

"Please remember that there are almost sixty employees here that would be affected and your husband's reputation would be inexorably sullied. In short, no one wins. It is a most disagreeable outcome.

"The only alternative we can sensibly suggest is one where Mr Barclay's theft remains confidential and the business is allowed to continue to trade with an untarnished reputation. However, to achieve this, the Dodd family would obviously need to be reimbursed for its losses."

Sharon's face was now reddening. After a few moments silence she murmured. "What do you suggest?"

"We will need to finish tallying up the total amount that has been stolen and, of course, you will want to review our findings with your own accountants and legal counsel. But, once this is completed, we feel that it would be best if you stepped away from the business entirely. And to achieve that we would suggest that the Dodd family acquire your total share of the business as a starting point for recompense."

"You want all my shares in Barclay and Dodd and you would still pursue me for more?"

"I think you will need to remember that any alternative solution is likely to leave you with even less. And we should be clear that, as having received benefit in regards to your lifestyle with Mr Barclay, you would have to be considered a co-conspirator in any legal action that was undertaken. Given the extreme level of fraud that has occurred I tend to feel that a custodial sentence would have to be sought."

Sharon shook her head slowly. "You bastard . . ."

"You can't be serious," I suddenly blurted. "You can't possibly think that Sharon knew about all of Brent's finances. For God's sake, have a little heart. She's just lost her husband. She didn't know about any of this."

Dodd leaned forward. "How about you, Holt? Did you know about it? Were you also a co-conspirator?"

I froze, incredulous. The son-of-a-bitch was serious. I began to sputter. "How dare you–"

"How dare I?" he roared. "Your mate, Barclay was a thief. A common, low-life thief. So how do I know that you weren't involved? How do I know that you aren't sitting on a fucking pile of my money and laughing at me? I don't even know what the fuck you're doing here, so don't–"

"Gerald, please. Calm yourself," Pickering interjected.

Dodd stopped in mid-flight, his face an angry red mask. "Fucking low-life, piece of . . ." he muttered, tailing off. I found myself unable to respond and slowly sank back into my chair, shaking my head in absolute disbelief.

Suddenly Sharon was on her feet. "I think we've heard enough," she said. "My lawyer will be in touch."

"Mrs Barclay, before you go . . ." Pickering spoke as she began to leave. She stopped; her back to him. "I do need to remind you that containing this matter in an absolutely confidential manner is imperative to any agreeable outcome for all involved. We must be clear. If any word of your husband's fraudulent activity reaches the public arena then there will be no easy way out for either party. This business will be destroyed and everyone will suffer."

He paused, awaiting acknowledgement. Sharon didn't turn, her face burned with sorrow and pain. "I understand, Mr Pickering," she said tonelessly and made for the door. The room remained silent. I stood too and followed Sharon out of the boardroom. No one bade us farewell.

Outside, on the street, I tried to gather my wits and find something positive and helpful to say, but nothing came. "I'm so sorry, Sharon. I had no idea, none at all. I honestly can't believe that anything they just said could be true."

But she didn't hear me. Her eyes were glazed, her expression blank. She looked lost.

"Maybe we should grab a coffee?" I said. "Give this some thought. See what we can work out?"

I'm not sure she heard that either, but she suddenly seemed to snap out of it and her focus returned to me. For a moment I saw a flash of fire in her eyes and then it was gone.

"I'm sorry, Adam," she said flatly. "I was a million miles away. What did you say?"

"Would you like to go grab a coffee, talk this through?"

She shook her head immediately. "No. But thank you. I think I need a bit of space to give this some serious thought. I'm obviously going to need a lawyer . . ."

After a moments silence, for want of anything more useful, I said, "If there's anything I can do to help. Anything at all." But she just shook her head. I felt useless. "I'm so sorry, Sharon."

She frowned at me. "It's not your fault, Adam."

But I couldn't help feeling that, somehow, it was.

I checked my cell-phone for messages as I returned to *Milly*. There was a text from Julie. I'm not a big fan of texting, mainly because of the way it's destroying the way people write to each other, ruining the simple use of good English. But Julie knew this and always made an effort to type text messages to me in full. I loved her for that. Her text read: *Call me. Police have been here. They found your car.* Thank heaven, some good news for once. I quickly found the office number in my contact list and hit dial as I sat down in Donny's filthy car.

"Hey, it's me. They found my car already?" I said as Julie answered the phone.

I could hear the smile in her voice. "Yes, they have. And Kylie is still getting goose-bumps thinking about the cute young copper they sent in to tell you."

"Tell her I'm thrilled to have made her day."

Julie laughed.

"So where is it," I asked. "What do I have to do?"

"They want you to call them. The nice young man left a number – which Kylie wants me to give her. But I think you need to go into the station, you know, up on Parkway."

"Really? Well that's okay. I'm just in Takapuna now."

Julie gave me the number which I managed to scrawl on an old McDonald's wrapper that I unearthed from the cars piles of garbage. I would be very glad to have my own car back. The number was a North Shore land-line. I dialed it and waited while it rang twice and then clicked and changed tone to begin ringing again. My guess was a diversion to a cell-phone and I was right. I could hear traffic noises in the background when the voice answered.

"Detective Boyd."

"Uhh, Hi. This is Adam Holt. I was given this number to call in regards to my car, which was stolen. I understand it's been found. Are you the right person to talk to?"

Boyd's voice was cordial, but somehow guarded. "Mr Holt, thank you for calling. May I ask where you are at the moment?"

It seemed an odd question. "Where I am? Ahh, I'm in Takapuna. Is my car near here somewhere?"

He ignored me. "Mr Holt, we're probably not too far away. Can I offer you a lift to the station?"

"That's okay; I've borrowed my son's car."

"Actually, it may be best if we picked you up. Would you mind telling me exactly where you are, please?"

Somehow the question sounded more like a directive. "I'm happy to drive to the station–"

"This would be more convenient for us, Mr Holt. Your location, please? We shouldn't be too far away."

I saw no point in arguing with a police detective so gave in and told him exactly where I was. He told me to stay put. I climbed back out of Donny's car, locked her up and waited. I'd parked in the metered zone along The Strand, behind the Hurstmere Road shops, as I normally did, and found myself staring across the grassy reserve to the beach, the harbour and Rangitoto Island. It was a magnificent view. The tide was out and people were walking the beach happily.

Before it all went wrong, all those years ago, Claire and I used to come here to talk and swim and generally laze about. Knowing now that she worked only two minutes' walk from this beach I found myself wondering if she sometimes came here during her lunch hour to soak up the view and reminisce about me.

My God, am I really that stupid? After yesterday's reunion I should have known better. Surely it was obvious to a blind man that Claire hadn't thought about me like that in years . . . if, in fact, she ever had.

Moments later a nearly new Holden Commodore pulled up alongside and drove me from my pathetic daydream. A solid looking man in a navy suit stepped out. His square jaw reminded me of a younger Daniel Craig and I understood immediately why Kylie had been so entranced.

"Mr Holt?" he asked, offering me his hand.

"Detective Boyd?" I said, accepting a firm handshake.

"Would you mind?" He opened the back door of the Commodore and guided me in before stepping back into the passenger seat. The driver didn't turn or speak and immediately the car pulled back out into traffic.

"So where did you find my car," I asked.

"If it's all the same, Mr Holt, I think it would be best if we reserved any questions until we reach the station."

"What? Why? You've found my car haven't you?"

"Yes, we have found your car."

"Then why the mystery? What's going on?"

Boyd turned in the seat and eyed me suspiciously. He said nothing though.

"What the hell is this?" I demanded.

"We'll talk at the station," he said, turning away.

EIGHTEEN

Although the interview room at the North Shore police station was still relatively new a faint odour of curry permeated the air while the stiff plastic chair I was perched on made me uncomfortable. Not just because it was obviously designed that way, but because it bought back a flood of memories from twenty years ago.

After Kieran's body was found the police came knocking and both Brent and I had found ourselves at Auckland Central Police Headquarters. We stayed for two full days, way back then. Two long, scary and humbling days. I think the laws have changed now and they can only hold you for twenty-four hours before they have to charge you, but I could be wrong.

I seem to recall, back when we got picked up, that my world-beating hangover was beginning to ease but the deep, torturous feelings of guilt were only just starting. I was in there –in a room very similar to this one– for most of the first day, and had been interviewed by three different men before they actually told me that Kieran was dead. Only then did I realise just how serious my situation was. The walls closed in and I became physically sick. Then, as I was only a teenager, I asked for my parents.

It's funny how your mind works. As I gazed around the incredibly bland interview room –four walls, one door with a tiny window, a table with one plastic chair on either side of it– the desire to call my mum and dad was strong. But I didn't need their help; I was only there to talk about my car. Wasn't I?

Finally the door opened.

Boyd entered, accompanied by Millward, the lead invest-igator on Brent's murder. But why was he here? Perhaps something new had come up. Had they caught Brent's killer? I straightened in my seat as Boyd strode over and sat down opposite me. Millward leaned against the wall.

Boyd initially ignored me and looked up at an obvious camera attached to the wall above the door. Twenty years ago at Auckland Central they had a simple tape recorder to keep a record of events. Technology has moved on. He pointed a remote at it and a red light came on, then he turned to face me.

"Mr Holt, this conversation is being recorded, do you understand?"

"Why?" I asked. "What the hell is going on?"

"Mr Holt, I need you to confirm that you understand."

I sighed. "Yes, I understand."

"Thank you," he paused. "Would you please describe for us your movements since 7.00 am this morning."

"My movements? Why?"

"I need you to tell us what you have done, where you've been, who you have seen today . . . starting at 7.00 am."

"Why on earth would you want to–"

"Please, Mr Holt. We'd appreciate your cooperation."

I stared at him, completely befuddled. Something bad must have happened. My thoughts suddenly turned to my missing son. "Is this about Donny? Has something happened to him?"

Boyd raised an eyebrow. "Donny?"

"My son, Donny. He's been missing for a day or two. Has something happened to him?"

Boyd glanced at Millward who shrugged. "Your son, Mr Holt, is missing. Correct? Have you reported this?"

"Yes, he's missing. But, no, I haven't reported it . . . yet."

Boyd stiffened and gave me a hard look. "Your child is missing and you haven't reported it?"

"Well, yes . . . no . . . he's not really a child anymore."

"How old is your son?"

"Almost twenty. His birthday is this weekend."

I could see Boyd visibly relax. He must have thought he was about to be hit with a kidnapping, but Donny was no child. He was old enough to legally disappear for as long as he liked.

146

Boyd nodded. "I see, Mr Holt. However, at this point, I don't believe this to be about your son."

Sometime I can be a bit slow. "So, Donny's okay?"

He gestured with open palms. "We don't know. We're not here today to discuss your son."

"All right, so why are we here today?"

He didn't answer, instead pausing before returning to his original question. "Mr Holt, would you please tell us what you have been up to this morning, since 7.00 am."

"Oh, good grief," I said, frustrated. I took a deep breath and ran him through my morning, starting with dragging myself out of bed at around 7.30 am, then jogging to retrieve Donny's car, eating a quick breakfast, showering and finally arriving at the meeting at Barclay and Dodd.

"Was anyone at home with you this morning that can verify your rising at 0730?" he asked.

"No. Donny's normally around, but he wasn't home."

"There's no girlfriend or partner?"

I briefly thought of Linda, but shook my head.

"I'm sorry, Mr Holt. I need you to answer verbally."

"No. No girlfriend at present."

"And did you encounter anyone whilst jogging or when you picked up the car that can confirm these activities?"

I had to think about it. I'm sure someone must have seen me, there were definitely other runners out and about –and a couple of people walking their dogs– but no one I actually knew or stopped to chat with that might recall seeing me. I shared my thoughts with Boyd who looked unimpressed.

"You reported your car stolen last night at the North Shore stationhouse. When did you last see your car, Mr Holt?"

"It would have been about 7.15 pm. I parked it outside the Indoor Sports Centre in Glenfield. I just made it inside in time for my team's 7.15 pm tip-off."

"And did anyone else see you park the car?"

"I don't think so, but possibly. People come and go all the time. There would have been someone leaving."

"And you claim that it was no longer where you parked it when you returned to the vehicle later?"

I was starting to get frustrated. "I went over this in detail with your people last night. What the hell is going on? Why are we even discussing this?"

He ignored my questions again. "Am I correct in understanding that you were involved in an incident at the Malacca Café in Takapuna on Tuesday afternoon with a Harold Armitage and one Jeremy Sung?"

The sudden change of direction confounded me. "What? What has that got to do with anything?"

"The incident, Mr Holt. You remember it?"

"Of course I bloody do. That mad bastard, Jeremy Soo-ng or Whatever, pulled a knife on me. He threatened me."

"Did that bother you, Mr Holt?"

I couldn't believe what I was hearing. "Are you serious? Of course it bothered me. The prick could have killed me."

"How angry were you?"

"I was furious. Wouldn't you be if someone pulled a knife on you? Is that what this is about? Have you caught him? Has he attacked someone else?"

"Would it be fair to say that you'd like to have seen Mr Sung punished for what he did to you?"

"Yes, of course. That's why I reported it."

"Enough to take the law into your own hands?"

That stopped me cold. "What?"

"Have you ever sought retribution when you've felt that someone else has done you wrong?

"Retribution? I don't understand."

Boyd paused again before suddenly careening off on another path altogether. "I understand you may have had some involvement in a murder investigation once before?"

I closed my eyes and shook my head. Here we go.

"Mr Holt? Do you recall an investigation some years ago into the unexplained death of one Kieran Sandford?"

"That was a very long time ago."

"The case is still open, however."

"So?"

"You do recall the investigation?"

"Of course I do."

"Why is that?"

I started to get angry. "Why is what?"

His face remained impassive. "Why do you recall it?"

I hesitated, completely unsure where this was heading.

"Mr Holt?" Boyd prompted.

I shut my eyes again. "Because I was a suspect," I snapped, wishing he would leave it alone.

"But you were never charged."

I shook my head. "No."

"Do you have a problem with your temper, Mr Holt?"

"What?"

"Do you sometimes lose your temper, you know, lash out at people when provoked?"

"No," I said angrily, although at that moment I wanted to hit him. "Never."

"I'm not convinced. You look pretty angry now."

"But I'm not lashing out, am I?"

"I think you'd like to."

He was obviously goading me, I just didn't know why. I drew a deep breath and tried to relax. "Wanting to lash out and actually doing so are two very different things. Perhaps you should be talking to Jeremy what's-his-name about this. He has a pretty loose temper."

"We're pretty sure Mr Sung isn't responsible . . . in this instance," said Boyd.

I frowned. "Responsible for what? And why not him?"

Boyd hesitated, clearly considering his words. "We're pretty confident that Mr Sung isn't the man we're looking for today. You see . . . he was one of the victims."

"A victim? I'm here because something has happened to that prick. And you think I did it?" Boyd didn't answer; he just stared at me watchfully. "Oh, come on . . . please. What happened to him? What am I supposed to have done?"

Boyd glanced over at Millward, who shrugged. He returned his gaze to me thoughtfully. I could see him weighing up his options, carefully considering what to say next. When he finally spoke his voice was flat and his stare intent.

"At approximately 0705 this morning Messer's Armitage and Sung were the victims of a car versus pedestrian's incident. Whilst they were walking their dog together a car mounted the sidewalk and appears to have deliberately targeted them. The driver fled the scene."

He stopped meaningfully and waited. This time I saw instantly where he was going. As I shook my head in silent denial he spoke again.

"The car used in this hit and run incident has been positively identified as your car, Mr Holt."

* * *

Donny stared at his bare toes again in horror. The gleaming, bright red nail polish glared back at him, oblivious to his discomfort . . . as was Suzy. She sat on the floor, leaning against the couch, liberally dabbing a second coat to her own exposed toenails. She hummed happily.

He tried to convince himself that there were worse things in life, but he was struggling to think of one. Thank heaven none of his mates could see this. And at least Suzy was occupied. Hopefully this exercise in degradation would entertain her for at least another hour. Donny sighed.

Then Suzy's demeanour suddenly changed. She sat up abruptly, twitching like a bird, and tilted her head, her eyes far away. She'd heard something. In a second she was on her feet and had switched off the radio. She stood like a statue, only her eyes flickering towards the window.

Donny sat motionless and listened. At first he could hear only the dull roar of the waves rolling endlessly onto the beach outside and the faint cawing of seabirds nearby. Then he heard it too. A car was approaching on the gravel road outside. Suzy slipped silently to the window. He watched as her expression changed from curiosity to annoyance in a terrifying flash. Was the car coming here? Until then the gravel road outside had been completely silent the entire time. Donny wasn't sure but felt it likely that the road outside led only to this bach.

Then Suzy was gone. She swept gracefully past him and out to the kitchen area that faced the driveway.

Donny found himself paralyzed. If the car was coming here, was that a good thing or bad? He still had no idea why he was being held against his will. Suzy had been in sporadic communication with someone over the last few days. What if this was her conspirator? What if he was coming to tell them that whatever they wanted had been achieved . . . or had not? Would they set him free? Or dispose of him? A chill ran through his bones as he tapped his painted toes nervously.

He listened intently. Suzy made no sound from the kitchen. The car crunched softly along the metal road and began to slow. The note of the engine changed, as did the sound of the tyres as the car began to turn into the driveway.

Donny could hear faint music. The driver must have the radio up loud and window open. He heard the car stop momentarily before it continued down the drive. Why? Was the driver surprised to see Suzy's bright yellow Falcon or was he checking for something else? Was the driver even a man?

Suzy cursed softly from the kitchen. Something was wrong. She wasn't happy. This car wasn't expected? Or had the driver signaled her with bad news?

Trying not to panic, Donny contemplated his options. If the car was unexpected it may present an opportunity to escape. But if it was here with bad news then he was in big trouble. Getting away from Suzy alone was one thing, but if she had friends now he would be outnumbered. There could be four or five people in the car. He'd have no chance.

Donny pushed his free hand into the couch cushions, searching for the rusted steak knife. When his fingers brushed the blade he wasn't sure whether to be relieved or terrified. If he cut his bonds then Suzy would be pissed off. Very pissed off.

But if he didn't he could end up in worse trouble, especially if the people in the car were bringing bad news. Donny gripped the handle of the knife but left it within the cushions and waited, listening, desperately unsure.

Suzy was suddenly in the doorway, fixing him with an icy glare. "Don't move. Don't speak," she said and then disappeared again, back into the kitchen.

Maybe it was the cops? Maybe someone had reported people at the bach when there shouldn't have been. Maybe if he simply called out they could arrest Suzy and set him free.

He listened and waited.

The door opened and Suzy called out, "Hey there, how you doing? Isn't it a beautiful day . . ." The rest blurred through the sound of the door closing behind her as she stepped outside. Then only the murmur of voices outside reached him, but he couldn't make out the words.

What to do? Wait and see what happens next, or make a move? It could be the cops out there, but Suzy was obviously now laying out some kind of bull-shit story to whoever it was. What if they believed her? Suzy was very attractive. Most men would yield to her lies. Donny held his breath, strained his ears, but couldn't hear the conversation.

He looked down at his bright red toenails, then tightened his grip on the steak knife and made a decision.

The knife appeared without hesitation and sliced quickly through the middle of the three cable ties leaving one on his wrist and one on the frame of the couch.

Donny was free.

NINETEEN

"So I guess I won't be getting my car back today then?" The question was intended rhetorically, meant as a joke, but no one laughed. I immediately regretted the poor effort.

It was nearly 2.00 pm. I was finally being released from the North Shore police station and was literally starving. Boyd had patiently run through all his questions twice more. Both times I think I responded in exactly the same way, but it's hard to be certain of anything in these situations. I was just glad to be finally leaving. My day wasn't going well.

No one offered to run me back to my car. I guess if it had been nighttime and I had been female I would have warranted a lift, but a middle-aged man –especially one suspected of a hit-and-run crime– didn't need to be mollycoddled. It was only about six or seven kilometres back to Takapuna. I could walk or take a taxi. I was too hungry to walk so called the taxi.

My head was spinning as I sat in the back and ignored the driver. Donny was missing; my car was impounded; my oldest friend had been skimming from his own business; Doug Masters had turned up out-of-the-blue; and now someone had tried to mow down Armitage and Cato – using my car!

Why would anyone do that? The police thought it was me. That I was so damn clever I'd faked the theft of my own car and lain in wait for them to hit the pavement. I told them I didn't even know where Armitage lived, but that didn't seem to help any. They thought I wanted revenge for the knife incident the other night. It was a struggle to convince them that I'm just not that crazy.

They told me little, but I managed to work out that Armitage was quite badly hurt while Cato was barely even bruised. Yet it seems that Armitage would live. There was no suggestion that his injuries would prove fatal and their case would become a murder investigation. And that seemed to be the main reason they agreed to release me.

Soon they would be talking with Linda DeWalt, who would at least support my claim to the car having been stolen. However this probably wouldn't help much as the car had been found this morning at the Smales Farm car park, only a couple of kilometres from my home. If I had somehow tricked Linda about my car being stolen I could easily have done the deed, ditched the car there and been home before 8.00 am. So I had no real alibi.

The taxi dropped me off on Hurstmere Road and I wandered piteously between the buildings, around to the parking zone, deep in thought, trying to work out how my life had suddenly got so complicated.

I didn't run down Armitage and Cato. I knew that. So who did? And why?

And where the hell was Donny? Was he involved in this somehow? Nauseous feelings gripped me at the thought of Donny's unexplained disappearance somehow being connected to all the shit that was going on around me. By God I hoped that wasn't the case.

Milly was exactly where I'd parked her, I was pleased to discover, but now adorned with a little white note beneath the windscreen wiper. A bloody parking ticket. I snatched it up and groaned. $40 down the drain. Could this day get any worse?

Once I finally got inside Donny's wreck-of-a-car a wave of utter bewilderment washed over me. Closing my eyes I put my head in my hands and tried to decide what the hell I should do next. Brent would have known what to do. Brent always had a plan. Always took control of the situation. I sat back and stared vacantly out of the window. Even the beautiful beach scene didn't help.

I made a decision. Armitage and Cato would have to wait. Doug Masters could wait too. My son had to be my first priority. I needed to find him. Pulling my cell-phone out of my pocket I turned it back on. It had been switched off since I went into the meeting at Barclay and Dodd. I waited while it ran through its warm-up sequence and got its act together. Hopefully there would be a message from Donny explaining everything. Eventually the phone chirped; I had a text message. I clicked and the message appeared. It was from Slouch.

Low crdt, call agn.

I had to read it three times before I worked it out. Stupid, lazy, abbreviated text messages. Slouch was low on credit on his pre-pay phone and wanted me to call him. I rolled my eyes and hit the dial button. After six rings he answered.

"H'lo?" He sounded half asleep.

"Slouch?"

"Yup."

"It's Donny's dad, Adam."

"Mr H, Hey."

"Hey, Slouch," I said. Adam Holt, hip dude.

"Wazzup?"

"I was actually trying to catch up with Donny. He hasn't been home for a couple of days. You wouldn't know where he is, would you?"

"He hasn't been home, woah. That's freaky."

Freaky. Really? Who says that anymore? "Have you seen him in the last few days, Slouch?"

"Uhh, no, Mr H. I haven't seen Big D since . . . uhh. Hmm. Probably not since Sunday night."

"He was working Sunday night."

"Yeah, that's where I saw him. At KFC."

"Did you give him a ride? I found his car there."

"*Milly* is at KFC?"

"It was, but I have it now."

"You're driving *Milly*?"

I closed my eyes in frustration. "Slouch, did you give Donny a ride after work?"

"No, man. Not me. He went with the hot chick."

"The hot chick?"

"Oh, Mr H. You shoulda seen her. She was smokin'."

"He left KFC with a girl?"

"Did he ever. And she was the hottest babe I've seen since . . . well, actually . . . since ever!"

"Donny left KFC on Sunday night with a really hot girl?"

"Yep. And he hasn't been home since? Woah. They must be really going at it. I mean . . . lucky bastard!"

I didn't know what to say. Part of me was relieved that Donny's disappearance no longer seemed so suspicious. And part of me was, just quietly, quite proud of the boy. But there was still some niggling doubt. Why hadn't he checked in to let us know all was well? Why did he skip work without even phoning in sick?

"So you haven't heard from him since then?" I asked.

"No, Mr H. Not a dicky-bird since he took off with the babe on Sunday."

"And they went in her car?"

"Yep. Hot babe with a hot car. A nearly new Falcon XR6. Bright Yellow. Mags. Spoiler. A sweet ride."

"Sounds expensive."

"You know it. Hot car. Smokin' hot babe."

"So he's not been at class at uni?"

"Uhh, I dunno. I sorta missed some classes myself."

Big surprise. "And you haven't heard from him since Sunday. No calls, no texts, nothing?"

"Uhh . . . no, I guess. No. Not a thing."

"Okay, Slouch. Thanks. Look, if you hear from him will you ask him to make contact with me?"

"Sure, man. Will do."

I thanked him again and rang off, then sat and stared at my phone for a while. On Sunday night Donny left work and disappeared with a really hot girl. That was three days ago. Surely he must have been able to come up for air at some stage during the last three days? I couldn't decide how I should feel about this news but, if I'm honest, I was a little relieved. Hopefully he would turn up soon with a swagger and a slight limp and a massive smile on his face.

My cell-phone suddenly started to ring in my hand. I frowned at the screen. Bella, yet again. I answered. "Hey, Bella. How are you?"

She sounded very annoyed. "Have you seen him?"

"I have not, but I think he may be with a girl."

"What?"

"I just spoke with his mate, Slouch, and he last saw Donny driving off with a very pretty girl. I'm sure he's fine."

"What girl?"

I explained the pick-up from KFC.

She still sounded annoyed. "Who was this girl?"

"I don't know, but I'm sure he's okay."

"You don't know that. Have you spoken to him?"

"Uhh, no."

"So this girl could have driven them over a cliff or off the road into a river. They could be lying in her car somewhere, dying, right now. They could have driven headlong into a bloody great truck. It's been three days, Holt. Why hasn't he called anyone?"

I didn't know what to say. All of a sudden my anxiety levels were peaking again. I'm an idiot. I hadn't considered any of those things, but all were reasonably possible.

Where the hell was that boy?

* * *

Donny had thought a lot about what he was now about to do, even to the point of visualising himself stepping through the plan calmly and precisely. But all that went out of his head as soon as the steak knife's blade cut through his binding. He managed only to stand before freezing in horror at his own recklessness. Suddenly all he could think about was Suzy tearing off one of his arms and beating him to death with it. He stared forlornly at the broken cable tie that lay on the floor at his feet and silently willed it back together.

Then a raised voice from outside snapped him out of it. There was definitely a man out there with Suzy and he was far from happy. Her voice remained low, as if she were trying to calm him.

Donny tried to focus himself. He needed to move and to move fast. Padding softly through to the little bedroom he discovered it practically filled with a queen-sized bed. To its right was a low table, to its left a narrow walkway that led to French doors. He'd been expecting something like this as Suzy had been coming and going from the room to take her runs along the beach. The French doors had deadbolts top and bottom, but both had keys protruding. Getting out would be no problem but getting away would still be.

Donny wanted just three things. His shoes, his cell-phone and the keys to the big Ford Falcon outside. He knew where his shoes were, he'd seen them outside on the back steps yesterday when they had gone out for their beach-walk, but Suzy was probably standing right next to them at this moment. He'd have to go without. He considered the cell-phone next. The last time he'd seen it was when Suzy took it off him in the car. At the time she'd pushed it into a zip-up pocket of her black leather jacket. He had been hoping the jacket would be lying on top of the bed, or hanging from a rack somewhere open and obvious, but it wasn't. He couldn't see it anywhere and desperately tried to slow his frantically beating heart. The jacket must be in the bedroom. It just had to be. The bach was so tiny. There was only the one bedroom, one main living area –where Donny had been resident for the last few days– while the bathroom was off the kitchen. And Donny knew he couldn't enter the kitchen without being spotted by Suzy. The jacket simply had to be in the bedroom.

More raised voices from outside. The visitor was clearly angry about something. Suzy's efforts to calm him seemed to be having little effect.

Donny needed to get a move on. He searched in a panic. There was no cupboard or even a wardrobe. Did no one wear clothes while they were at this bach? He dropped to the floor and looked under the bed to find two roll-away drawers, but both were empty. As he pushed the second one back in he spotted Suzy's sports bag beneath the small table on the other side of the bed. He darted over, dragged it out and almost cried in relief. The leather jacket was there, jammed in with a jumbled selection of other clothing. Ripping it out quickly he squeezed the pockets to feel in one what had to be his cell-phone. The other felt like it contained a car key with a plastic fob. Perfect.

With his heart hammering and the jacket clasped in his hand Donny unlocked the two dead-bolts on the French doors and turned the clasp to step outside. He barely noticed the gentle sea-breeze or the warm sun on his face as he pushed through the door and slipped off the deck beach-side. For a moment he could hear the voices more clearly, but moved away from them, circling around the little bach to approach the Falcon from behind the garage. Cobblestones ran around the exterior to lead him around the garage to a point where he was able to peek through some bushes at the scene playing out at the kitchen entrance. He held his breath as he tried to take it in.

Suzy was on the steps that led up to the kitchen doorway, the main entrance to the bach. His shoes were right there on the step beside her, airing in the sun in exactly the same place he'd seen them yesterday. He would definitely be staying barefoot. She was trying to calm a man standing near the foot of the steps. The guy was probably about his dad's age, balding with short cropped hair and a pot-belly. His face was red with anger, his arms folded across his chest.

"Look, I'm really sorry about this," Suzy was saying soothingly, "it's all just a misunderstanding–"

"But you broke my bloody window. Why would you do that, for crying out loud? What else have you broken?"

Donny looked about as the man waved his arms around. There was a dark blue SUV parked in the driveway with a trailer attached. A wooden picnic table filled the small trailer. This guy was most probably the baches owner.

"I thought I was given the wrong key, but I must have got the directions wrong–"

"So you just broke in? You just smashed a window?"

"How many times do you want me to apologise? I'll pay for the damage. If you'd just calm down–"

It seemed clear that Suzy was trying to convince the guy that they had come to his bach by mistake, probably hopeful of pacifying him enough so that he didn't call the police. In exasperation the man held up his hands in surrender.

"Don't bother, I've heard enough. I'm not stupid; I don't care who you are or what you've done . . . I just want you the hell off my property. Just get your stuff and go."

Suzy stopped trying to pacify him and frowned. "Really? Are you sure? I'm happy to pay . . ."

The guy wouldn't look at her anymore. He was obviously fed up. "I don't care, all right. Just get out."

She opened her mouth to say something else but hesitated, thinking better of it. Then she nodded and turned, opening the door to the kitchen. As she stepped inside Donny heard her call out, "Grab your gear, Lover. We gotta get going . . ."

He knew he had to move quickly. Suzy would discover him missing immediately. There was no time for thought. Donny leapt up and pushed through the bushes, startling the unhappy man. He had the Falcon's key out and pushed the little button on the remote. There was a peep, the car's lights flashed and he heard a satisfying thunk. In three steps he had turned the key in his hand, ready to slide into the ignition, and was at the drivers-side door grabbing the handle. One quick heave and the door should have opened, but with a rigid solidity the door remained firmly closed.

Suzy hadn't locked the car. Donny just had.

Suddenly Suzy's face was at the bach door, and she looked thunderous. Donny forgot to breathe. His hand shook in panic, but he hurriedly managed to adjust his grip on the remote and push the button again. The Falcon once again peeped at him, lights flaring and a slightly different thunking sound filled his ears.

Suzy was through the door in a heartbeat. Donny pulled on the handle and the car's door popped open. Suzy had to dodge the bach owner before she could reach him. As the man blocked her way momentarily Donny was granted just enough time to throw himself into the seat, pull the door closed behind him and push the button one more time. The thunking sound of the doors re-locking was a beautiful noise, reaching his ears a split second before Suzy grasped the handle. She wailed in frustration and slammed an open fist onto the window.

Donny tried to right himself and dropped the keys. Suzy smacked the window again, screaming at him, her rage intense and terrify-ing. He leaned away from the window, fumbling for the fallen keys. His fingers found a pen, and then an old muesli bar wrapper beneath the seat before he finally managed to pull the key into view again.

"Don't do it, Donny," Suzy roared. "Don't you do it!"

Still leaning away from the window as she smacked it once more Donny reached around and slipped the key into the ignition. The big car roared into life.

"Damn you, you little shit. Get the fuck out of my car!"

He slipped the shifter into reverse, grabbed the wheel firmly and planted his bare foot. The Falcon revved noisily, gravel spat from beneath the wheels and the cars nose swiped Suzy's thigh as it tore away from its parking spot. Suzy leapt aside, howling in frustration.

Donny turned the wheel to aim the car away from the bach owner's vehicle and point its tail up the driveway. Keeping his foot flat to the floor the Falcon spun wildly as it careered along the narrow drive towards the road. He felt a bump and turned to find Suzy riding the bonnet, clinging to the wind-screen wiper with one foot braced on the wing mirror. She screamed at him through the windshield.

"Stop this fucking car, Donny. Don't make things worse for yourself . . ."

He couldn't believe what he was seeing. Even after all he'd been through in the last few days he didn't think Suzy was all that crazy, but it seemed that she probably was. He turned away, eyes fixed on getting the car safely away from the bach. If he could get out onto the road he could get away.

"You can't escape, Donny. I can find you anywhere!"

The Falcon's rear wheels passed from the driveway to the road and Donny spun the wheel violently, slamming on the brakes. The nose whipped around too quickly for Suzy and she tumbled through the air, right across the thin gravel road. But she landed on her feet, like a cat, spinning in the air with poise and grace. He grabbed at the shifter and pushed it into drive, once again kicking the accelerator to the carpet as if his life depended on it. The Falcon's wheels spun again and then bit and the car leapt forward in a cloud of dust and flying gravel. For only a few seconds Suzy ran alongside the vehicle.

"You're dead, little man. Dead! You hear me . . ."

Then she was gone. Left behind in a haze of dust. Donny was so frightened he kept his foot flat to the floor until he reached the first bend and almost lost control. Once he managed to haul the car out of its slide and point the nose back onto the gravel he slowed a little, constantly checking his rear view mirror to ensure Suzy wasn't following. But she wasn't.

He'd escaped.

* * *

Suzy watched the car flying away up the gravel road and prayed for it to crash. It was weaving and sliding drunkenly but quickly came right after slowing down a little. She was out of luck. The son-of-a-bitch was going to get away.

She couldn't understand how the hell the damn kid had managed to escape. She'd had him secured, tethered firmly to the couch. Yet somehow he got himself free. Got away from her.

Damn it.

The job she had been given was a simple one . . . and, for the first time ever, she'd failed her assignment. This wasn't acceptable. There would be consequences.

She swore out loud again before turning her attention back to the bach. It would take too long to remove the trailer from the bloody SUV before she could pursue Donny. And she'd never catch up with him towing the damn thing. He was probably going to get back to Auckland.

She swore loudly again.

As she stalked angrily up the driveway the owner of the bach was staring at her, mystified, exactly where she had left him standing. He was a problem. She would need to resolve that problem before she could set about reacquiring the boy, not to mention her car.

She slowed her pace while considering her options carefully. First she would need to tidy up here, and then she would need to make a call. Tracking down the boy wouldn't be all that hard, but she needed to do it quickly to ensure her failure did not become a problem. But first things first . . .

As she strolled up to the unfortunate bach owner she quickly assessed her opponent. The guy was older, paunchy. He wouldn't trouble her in the slightest. And even though her obvious charms had had little effect on the angry man before she went with what she knew best, offering a seductive smile as a brief distraction.

Then she took him down.

TWENTY

Donny's crappy car finally started on my third attempt and then proceeded to idle as if someone had poured treacle into the gas tank. What a piece of shit.

I maneuvered *Milly* up the road and turned through the lights at Halls Corner to head past Shore City. I had decided to head home and check for signs of Donny again. Hopefully he'd be there or at least there might be some sign of a visit.

But as I meandered along Lake Road I found my eye wandering towards the WINZ office that Claire O'Driscoll worked in which was coming up on my left. I was never going to walk through those doors again but my pathetic subconscious seemed in hope of receiving a brief view of Claire out front or through the frosted glass windows. I know how sad that sounds, but there you go. I'm not proud.

Only this time I was jolted by the sight of a different, but also familiar, figure in my peripheral vision.

I couldn't believe my eyes.

He was now clean shaven and wearing a baseball cap –rather than the stupid wig I'd last seen him in– but I was almost certain I'd spotted Doug Masters again. There was something I recognized in the way he moved, in the way he walked, that I would characterise as a lazy, self-indulgent gait – if that makes any sense.

He was ambling his way along the front window of the WINZ office. As I drove along he looked about, possibly a little cautiously, before returning his gaze to the window. Was he trying to spot Claire too? The bastard.

I searched frantically for a parking space, but the stretch of road in front of Claire's workplace and then Shore City is a mess of bus-stops. But I didn't pause to think. I pulled over recklessly and ditched *Milly* into the first gap I could find, and then leapt out, barely taking time to remove the keys.

With a stumbling pirouette I dodged a car that came out of a side-street as I somehow managed to cross the busy intersection without getting run over. My instincts drove me to call out but I resisted the urge. The bus stop in front of Claire's work was again busy, crowded with people and provided good cover as I shimmied my way towards my quarry. Doug had his back to me and as I closed in he seemed to hesitate for a moment before suddenly standing more erect, pulling his shoulders back and taking a deep breath.

Then he stepped forward and entered the WINZ office.

Doug was going in to see Claire.

I was surprised but not shocked. Twenty years ago Doug had just started dating Claire . . . only a few months after she and I had broken up. At the time he'd actually asked me if that *'was cool'* and, although I clearly didn't mean it, I had told him *'no worries'*. I would never forgive him for that betrayal.

As I brushed my way through the crowds waiting for their buses I wondered if this would be the first time they'd met since Doug disappeared. He'd been in hiding for twenty years. Was he now, all of a sudden, going to visit his old girlfriend –the girl that I had secretly loved and pined for since our lives were torn apart all those years ago– or, my stomach clenched at the thought, had they actually been in contact all this time?

I stopped at the entrance, distracted by this thought and a sudden burst of sanity. What the hell was I trying to do? Why was I following him? Surely I should call the police instead? Let them sit him down in one of their bloody interview rooms and try to work out what really happened that night on the *Kestrel*. Have him explain why he had been lurking at Brent's funeral. Let them work out where he had been the night that Brent was murdered.

Then I remembered Brent's note. How did he put it again? *Find Doug . . . let him tell you what happened.* What the hell did that mean?

Then I remembered the stiff-arm tackle out at the cemetery and started to get angry. This little bastard was not only the cause of the worst thing that ever happened in my messed-up life, but he'd had the nerve to foul me with a cheap shot less than twenty-four hours ago.

The moment of sanity left me. I balled my fist and stepped forward.

As I entered the WINZ office I discovered Doug at the reception counter. He seemed to be encountering the same issues that I had when I tried to visit Claire yesterday without an appointment. The same receptionist, today dressed all in black (and looking like a bowling ball), was giving him the dead-eyed stare and pretending to listen to whatever story he was telling to try to see Claire.

I walked up behind and tapped him on the shoulder.

He turned quickly, his eyes widening in surprise as recognition shook him. He took a half-step away from me.

"Jesus Christ . . ." he said.

I said nothing and punched him in the face. Just once, a quick right jab. He stumbled back, pressing up against the reception desk. His hand flew to his cheek where my fist had landed. The bowling ball woman's mouth formed an 'O' as she pushed herself off her seat and stepped away from us both.

"That was for the stiff-arm, you little prick," I said as I stepped forward to grab his shirt in my left fist and press him up against the desk while drawing my right back for another jab. "You've got some fucking nerve, turning up here."

"Adam, wait," he sputtered, his hands now raised to defend his face. "This isn't what it looks like. I can explain."

Suddenly the big, round receptionist was shouting at us. "Stop that. You can't fight it here. Take it outside. I'm calling the cops!" She picked up the phone.

I glanced around the room. Everyone had stopped whatever they were doing and all eyes were on Doug and I. Claire was at her desk, standing up, staring over at us, a look of total incomprehension on her face. The damn fluorescent light was still flickering; someone should have fixed that by now. I looked back at Doug. He stared back at me, anxious, his eyes began darting around.

"Adam, I'm sorry . . ." he started to say and then I felt a searing pain erupt in my groin and everything else faded into the background. I immediately released him and dropped to my knees in agony. I lost focus for a few moments and then dragged myself as quickly as I could back to my feet.

The little bastard had kneed me in the crotch. I have never known anything more crippling.

The receptionist was still shouting. Tears blurred my vision but I could see well enough to know that Doug was gone.

Embarrassed and hurting I shuffled as quickly as I could out the door and through to the bus stop before I spotted him running through the car-park opposite. I staggered out to the road, bent over and limping like a poor imitation of Gollum from Lord of the Rings, intent on dashing across, but had to give way to a bus coming in to stop. Once it had passed I shuffled out behind it and limped tentatively over the road. Doug had disappeared, but I kept moving. As I reached the sidewalk I heard a squeal of tires at the far end of the parking area. A people-mover was ducking and diving rapidly between the other vehicles. I could see its driver glancing around frantically, desperate to exit the car-park.

I started to run, as best as I could with my temporary incapacitation. Maybe I could catch him if he got held up at the check-out booth. But I was still in significant discomfort and didn't feel confident of getting there in time. The people-mover reached the bright yellow booth and I watched as Doug's arm came out the window to push his parking ticket into the little slot. I tried to speed up. Maybe he would drop it, or not have the right coins for payment or something . . .

But the ticket slid smoothly into the slot and the barrier arm instantly began to rise. I was still thirty metres away. I stopped chasing and leaned against the nearest car, bending over in an effort to somehow reduce the burning from my groin. Doug was going to get away again. But this time all was not lost. This time I thought I might be able to find him again, on my own terms.

I looked up again as Doug, in his garishly painted people-mover, sped away. Then I closed my eyes as I committed the vehicles registration to memory.

* * *

Donny kept his eyes on the road as he motored along SH1, heading south, back towards Auckland, while he fished in the jacket's pocket for his cell-phone.

Suzy would be following; he had no doubt about that. He had really pissed her off. She had made that abundantly clear. He was in big trouble.

The cell-phone finally popped out of the jacket's pocket and he felt a wave of relief. Who should he call first? His mum? She would be incredibly worried. Or his dad? Would the kidnappers have been in contact? And if they had, who would they have called? What would their demands have been? Maybe he should call the police first. Donny was pretty worried about the poor guy that owned the bach. What would Suzy do to him? He assumed she would take his car. That was pretty obvious. But would she hurt him? He hoped not. He felt guilty about leaving the guy behind, but he hadn't had much of a choice, had he?

Donny glanced down at the phone. The screen was blank. Suzy must have switched it off. He pushed the button and waited, keeping his eyes on the road. When he looked back down again he almost cried. The icon showed nil battery life and the phone began to shut down again, the screen quickly going blank. Suzy hadn't switched it off. It had been sitting in the jacket's pocket for three days without charging. It was dead.

He looked quickly around the car, wishing another cell-phone would miraculously appear out of thin air. It didn't happen and he saw nothing else helpful. He considered pulling over and searching the glove box and under the seats, but decided quickly that he couldn't risk it. Suzy was probably following already in the guy's SUV. Donny wasn't prepared to risk getting caught.

He drove on towards Auckland. Once he was within the city limits he could pull over almost anywhere and be more comfortable that Suzy wouldn't find him. He could find a payphone and call someone then.

* * *

"I suppose you think that was Doug Masters?"

I saw no point in denying it. "Yes. It was."

We were standing on the footpath, just a few metres from where I had so carelessly abandoned Donny's wreck-on-wheels. Claire had caught up with me as I hobbled self-consciously back across the road to make my getaway. Giving chase wasn't really an option. Doug would be miles away before I could get my keys into the ignition.

She raised an eyebrow. "What just happened?" she said.

I shook my head. "I don't know."

"But you came in with him."

"No. I saw him on the street. I followed him in."

"So you haven't spoken to him?"

"No."

She hesitated, thought for a moment. "Why didn't you call the police?"

I shrugged. Even if the receptionist at WINZ hadn't called the police it was quite likely that someone else would have summonsed a tow-truck to remove *Milly* from where she was blocking the bus stop. I didn't have time for this. I needed to go and look for my son.

"I probably should have," I eventually replied.

She glared at me, trying to figure out what was going on. Her expression told me that she didn't believe a word I had said. I didn't know what else to say, I wasn't so sure myself. I probably could have handled the situation better.

169

"Whatever you two are up to," she said finally, "you need to keep the hell away from me and my family. Stay out of my life, Holt."

I wanted to protest, to make her understand that I was looking out for her, that I was on her side. But her words cut through me like ice.

I stared deeply into those beautiful green eyes. Desperately searching for the sporty girl who loved to read Stephen King and sing loudly and out-of-tune, the girl who once loved me with all her heart . . . but I couldn't see her.

And I knew that it was my fault she was no longer there. My fault that she and I never got to build the life I still dreamed about. I'd been so young, so damn stupid.

As teenagers Claire and I were a couple for over a year. We lost our virginity together during that year and my life was never more perfect. I thought it would last forever . . . wished it would last forever. But, quite simply, I blew it and we broke up. Another party, more binge drinking, and I went and passed out in the bathroom. It was at one of Claire's friend's homes. Her parents had to break down the bathroom door to get me out. They even called an ambulance. It was horribly embarrassing, especially once I sobered up later. Claire dumped me the next day. Apparently I'd been flirting with other girls before collapsing in the bathroom. I don't remember any of that either . . . no surprises there. So I spent the next few months trying to win her back. I sent flowers, poems I'd written, I even tried to serenade her one time –these days I might have been labelled a stalker, I tried so damn hard– but nothing worked. Then I found out she had started going out with Doug and we'd had that one, all-to-brief discussion about it. *'Is that cool . . . no worries.'* I couldn't believe it; he was supposed to be my friend. I think the fact that I never challenged him made things worse. Maybe if we'd talked things might have turned out different. Or maybe not. A month or so later Kieran was dead and Doug on the run. And after that night my many efforts to contact Claire were all rebuffed bluntly until finally, desperate to escape the intensely negative glare of a community in turmoil, Brent and I left town for our big overseas excursion.

Yet I never gave up on her. I always thought that one day Claire and I would be together again, as we should have been before my drunken mistake.

But, as I faced her on the busy sidewalk in Takapuna, I finally realised that my feelings were horribly misplaced. There was no love in Claire's eyes. There was no longing, no yearning for what might have been.

I had to look away as fresh sorrow pummeled my heart . . .

And there was *Milly*, parked askew, so obviously out of place. Buses were surrounding her. I slowly came to my senses. I had to move the car before it landed me in even more trouble.

And I could no longer face her. My eyes stayed on the footpath as I spoke. "I have to go, I'm sorry. I would never hurt you, you must know that. And if I understood all this myself I would explain, but . . ." I tailed off and walked slowly away, head still down, spirit hopelessly crushed. I hesitated for a moment as I reached the car but she didn't call out or follow.

Dozens of sets of eyes glared at me as I climbed into *Milly* and turned the key.

Nothing happened; the ignition just made a clicking sound.

I swore under my breath and turned the key again. More clicking; nothing else. Damn it. I looked in the rear-view mirror. Claire was standing where I'd left her, watching. I cursed again, louder. I know nothing about cars and really didn't want to have to pop the bonnet and stand there staring at an engine I had no comprehension of. I glanced briefly at the audience of bus-people that had gathered. Some rolled their eyes. Others shook their heads. I felt exactly like the idiot I was. I took a deep breath, closed my eyes and turned the key again.

Like some kind of miracle the old Mirage's engine turned over, coughed and reluctantly burst into life.

I silently thanked the Gods of internal combustion, slipped her into gear and drove away.

* * *

171

Claire O'Driscoll apologised to Jasmine, the receptionist at her work, for the unsightly incident, but it was too late. The police had already been called. There would be questions to answer, and not just from her employer. After doing all she could to placate her colleagues she was eventually able to return to the relative calm of her open-plan work-space.

She sat down at her desk and sighed heavily, with a deep sense of foreboding. Things weren't working out as they should have. They had thought that Holt was too useless to be of any concern, but here he was stumbling around, causing trouble, drawing attention to her, dragging her name into the police inquiries. That was bad, unacceptable. Things were unraveling. Whether he knew it or not Holt appeared to be getting close. Claire couldn't afford for the police to find the link between the deaths. That simply wasn't an option.

She pulled her cell-phone from her handbag, scrolled her contacts and dialed quickly. After three rings a voice answered, sounding a little breathless.

"Hello."

"We have to do something about Holt," Claire said in hushed tones. "This is starting to get out of hand."

* * *

As I rounded the first corner to take me away from central Takapuna my cell-phone started to ring again. Fishing it from my pocket I glanced down, instantly recognising the number I had been calling repeatedly for the last two days. Donny was calling me. I thanked a different God this time and answered.

"Donny, is that you?"

"Dad. Oh, thank Christ. Yes, it's me. It's Donny."

"Where the hell are you? Where have you been? Why haven't you called?" I fought the wheel and turned down a side street as I frantically questioned my son.

"You're not gonna believe me. It's been really crazy."

"Slouch told me you met a girl."

I could picture him nodding. "You could say that, but its way weirder. Where are you, Dad? I don't think I can go home. Are you at work?"

I pulled over and parked. "No, I'm in Takapuna. Why can't you go home?"

"You're out in your car. That's good."

"Uhh, no. I'm actually in *Milly*, but I'm mobile. Where are you?"

"You're in my car?"

"Forget it. Where are you? Why can't you go home?"

"I'm at Albany Mall. I had to buy a car battery charger for my cell-phone. Can we meet somewhere? I can explain then."

"What the hell is going on, Donny?"

"I don't know, Dad. I really don't know . . ."

We agreed to meet at Smales Farm, in the car-park near Columbus Café (where my car had been found by the police), as it would take us both about the same time to get there – but it didn't work out that way. After hanging up I tried to start *Milly* again and, you guessed it . . . click, nothing, click. The bloody thing wouldn't start again. I shouted at it, I thumped the steering wheel, I fiddled with the key and I even tried praying again. But it got me nowhere. *Milly* had had enough for today. Possibly forever. I climbed out and kicked the door closed, cursing the clapped-out good-for-nothing piece-of-shit fluidly. I called Donny back and told him to keep driving and to meet me at Takapuna, describing to him the side road that I was parked in. He understood and I rang off. I stood by the useless car, frustrated, my mind reeling once again but hugely relieved.

Donny was all right. He wasn't dead in a ditch.

I looked around. I could hear a lot of activity at the school across the street but could see nothing but the back of a block of classrooms. Behind me an old man was pottering in his garden. I started to walk up the main road I had turned off to check the street signs and work out if leaving *Milly* there was going to be a problem. I'd barely taken six steps when something hit me, hard, in the back of my left knee and I immediately lost balance and toppled. As I fell something hit me in the kidney, on my right. Searing pain tore through me. I went down in a heap, clutching my side, cursing loudly. A voice I vaguely recognised sneered at me, "You're a worthless piece of shit, Holt," and I looked up just in time to raise my arm and block a kick aimed directly at my face. Fortunately the swinging foot was contained in a sneaker, not a steel-capped boot, and I managed to deflect it without breaking my arm. I rolled quickly with the motion, putting myself just out of his reach as the next kick came flying in.

"Hey," someone shouted from nearby. I rolled again and tried to bounce to my feet but my left leg felt dead and wouldn't hold my weight. I crouched warily, trying to defend myself, ready to block another kick or punch.

But, thankfully, my attacker paused. The voice shouted out again, "Hey, cut that out." The man standing over me frowned. He could easily have lain into me again, his face was a mask of anger, but he somehow managed to restrain himself, perhaps deciding not to kill me in front of a witness.

"This isn't finished," Cato said in a harsh whisper. Then he turned quickly to dart away up the street, around the corner.

I limped back to *Milly* as the old man who had been in his garden reached me. He was wrinkled, bald and toothless. I could have kissed him.

"Are you okay?" he asked.

"Yes, yes," I managed to assure him. "I'm fine, thanks. No real damage done. Just a bit of a tweak here . . ." I said as I stretched out my tingling left leg and massaged my side.

"That guy was out of order," the old guy said, "I saw him. Bloody chink. Attacking you from behind. That's not right."

I chose to ignore the racist slur. The guy was very old. He probably fought in the war. "You saw the whole thing?"

"Yes." He pointed to a shadowed driveway behind us. "He came out of there. Looked to me like he was just waiting for you to turn your back, the bloody coward."

I shuffled over and looked into the driveway. Cato had run right past it so he must have a car parked around the corner. But how did he find me here? Could he have followed me? But how? From outside WINZ? That was unlikely. Or from the beach-side car-park near Barclay and Dodd? Possibly, if he'd known I was going there today. But probably, much more likely, he'd been following me since I left the police station. The police would probably have told him they had someone in custody. He could have trailed me easily from there.

I shook my head in disbelief.

Cato seemed to be stalking me . . . with intent.

I thanked the old guy again and got his contact details. I felt sure the police would be in touch with me again and wanted to have a witness available if I needed one.

As I shuffled back to the car I counted my aches and pains. I could use a nice cold shower, but I would live.

I only had to wait two more minutes before a big, flash, bright yellow Ford Falcon XR6 pulled up in front.

Donny had arrived in style.

* * *

Lloyd was relaxing at home, perusing travel websites online, considering options for this years monumental holiday when his mobile phone rang. Sadly, Peru was looking a bit too expensive so he was considering another trip into Asia.

He answered the call on the third ring. "Yes."

"Is this Lawrence?" asked the voice once again.

"Yes," he said, surprised to hear from this employer again so soon. He usually waited a few days before making contact to arrange payment. The last job had only been completed earlier that morning. "Is there a problem?"

The caller hesitated. "No. No problem. But, perhaps, a new opportunity."

"I'm listening."

"Firstly, I should congratulate you on your work earlier today. I was very impressed. You make this sort of thing seem easy."

"It's what I do."

"And you do it very well."

Lloyd waited a beat. He had received praise before, that wasn't a problem, but he sensed something . . . off . . . in the words. "What's the opportunity?"

There was another hesitation down the line and then, "There's been a slightly unexpected turn of events. I need you to take care of the owner of the car you borrowed last night."

Lloyd had long ago learned never to ask 'Why?', that was always more information than he needed. Nor did he need clarification as to the meaning of the phrase 'take care of'. Instead he said, "Is this another urgent job?"

"I think that sooner would be for the better."

"You understand, of course, that urgency increases the price significantly?"

"Of course. As before, money isn't an issue."

"Okay. Do you have any suggestions for method this time?"

"Actually, I do. I think your actions this morning will have helped to create quite a plausible cover opportunity. But it will only work if we move quickly."

Lloyd listened as the caller outlined a rather odd, yet very simple, plan. There was risk, as always, but nothing he couldn't handle.

However he did have concerns which he did not raise during the discussion. This employer was now calling with a second urgent job. That was bad. Lloyd was very experienced in what he did and he wasn't stupid; it was obvious that this employer was not as firmly in control of events as he would usually expect. Lack of control and urgency usually led to mistakes – and mistakes were what the police needed to catch someone like Lloyd. Being caught was not a consideration. Mistakes were unacceptable.

Lloyd resolved that he would have to be even more cautious than usual. Clearly this employer had misjudged something and he needed to make sure that, if things did go wrong, he wouldn't get dragged down too.

TWENTY-ONE

"That's quite a story . . ." I said, tailing off, not sure what to make of it or what to even believe. If it wasn't for the big yellow car sitting before us I don't know if I would have believed my son's wild tale at all. I mean, seriously: A beautiful, psychotic woman called Suzy. An isolated bach somewhere out near Pakiri beach. My son, all six foot of him, lean and strong, cowed and cable-tied to a couch. Then a desperate escape, a stolen car and an enduring death threat from the pretty girl.

Sure. What's not to believe?

I shook my head and held back from asking him for a third time why he hadn't just called her bluff and walked away. We sat for a minute and stared at each other. Something was really eating him. He seemed genuinely scared of this girl, Suzy, catching up with him again. I was confused. His hair was trimmed neatly and, to be honest, I thought he looked much better. But my eyes kept getting drawn back to his bare feet and the red nail polish on his toes. Wow, those toes. I was having a lot of trouble getting my head around them. I turned to face the dusty yellow Falcon again to distract myself, but it just reinforced the strange story and I had to look away.

If what Donny had told me was true then it seemed fair to assume that this Suzy would be pretty damn pissed about him stealing her car. I know I would be if he'd stolen mine. But, seriously, did he really think she was going to track him down and hurt him. I was more worried about being arrested if we drove off in it after she had called the police.

I took a deep breath. "So . . . Now what?" I said.

"She knows who I am, and where I work, so she must know where I live. So we can't go there. I don't know. Should we go to the police?"

I hadn't yet told him about no longer being employed at KFC. That could wait until we had him calmed down and this mess sorted out. But I really didn't want to go to the police. They weren't my favorite people at the moment. And Donny's story was simply too crazy. My instincts told me that going to the police would just complicate matters even more. I shook my head again. I was about to suggest that we leave both cars where we were and simply walk home when a phone started to ring inside the Falcon. Donny jumped nervously.

"That'll be her," he said.

"What, she's got your number?"

"Of course she has. She seems to know everything."

I rolled my eyes and climbed into the Falcon's passenger seat. Soft leather. Very nice. The car had more buttons than a Jumbo jet. Donny's phone was in a small tray between the seats, charging via a plug from the cigarette lighter. I picked it up and looked for the number calling but its ID was blocked. I pressed answer and put the phone to my ear without speaking.

"Where's my car, Donny? I want my fucking car back." The girl's voice was almost grating –a little 'Lynn of Tawa'– and didn't reconcile at all with the smoking hot image of near-perfection that Donny and Slouch had described, yet the menace in her tone sent a strange chill through me.

I said nothing and waited. Donny climbed into the driver's seat beside me.

"I know you're there, Donny. I can hear you breathing."

Still I said nothing. The voice's tone hardened.

"All right you little shit-bag, this is your last chance. Tell me where my fucking car is and I will leave you unharmed. But if I have to track you down I will hurt you when I find you, just as a reminder, and believe me – I will find you. You can't hide from me. And if you go to the police I will do a lot worse than a little hurt. So this is your last, and only, chance to–"

"You really have a charming way with people," I said, interrupting her tirade. "Have you ever considered a career in international diplomacy, or perhaps telesales? You have such a lovely phone manner."

Silence hissed back down the line for a few moments.

"Who is this?" she said.

I hung up on her and put the phone down. "Well, I think that was your friend, Suzy. She seemed quite delightful," I said to Donny. He looked terrified.

"You shouldn't have said that, Dad. She's a nutter."

"It would appear so."

"Now she's going to be even more pissed at me."

"Yes," I said. "I think you could be right." I looked about the car. "Have you searched it yet?" He shook his head. "We should search it, try and find anything that might help us understand just who this psychotic bitch might really be."

I opened the glove box. It was empty. Not even an owner's manual. The phone rang again. I picked it up and the screen displayed the same blocked number message. I hit the reject button to send Suzy's call to voice-mail and then held it out to Donny. "But first, I need you to call your mother. She's been bloody worried."

Donny was still trying to placate Bella when I finished searching the Falcon, having found nothing useful. The car was a void. There wasn't a thing in it of a personal nature. No business cards or old letters or scribbled shopping lists. Aside from a small amount of generic litter it was as if it had just rolled off the production line. I wasn't sure what to make of that, but it made me wonder if Suzy actually owned the car. She certainly did want it back though, and badly. Or was that just a ruse to find Donny again? It was a weird situation. What on earth had Donny done to bring this sort of madness upon himself . . . or was this all my fault somehow?

While Donny continued to take a brow-beating from his mother I suddenly remembered Doug Masters and his recent escape in the garishly painted people-mover. Outside the car I dragged out my cell-phone and made a call. But after four rings the call went to voice-mail. I thought quickly and left a fairly detailed message.

Then I had another brain-wave and made another call. Lurch answered on the second ring.

"Don't tell me," he said. "You never call just to say hello, so either you've injured yourself and can't make it to indoor footy on Sunday or the police have finally caught up with you and you desperately need legal advice?"

"None of the above," I said. "I need your wife's work number so I can seduce her into a torrid affair."

"Huh," he grunted. "Good luck with that. So what do you really want?"

"Your wife's work number. Seriously."

"Why? Also seriously."

"She still works for Land Transport NZ, doesn't she?"

"Yeah. Why? What do you need?"

"I need to know who owns a car, but I only have the registration."

"You don't need Clara's help for that. It's public record."

"What?"

"It's public record. Anyone with a drivers licence on them can get basic car ownership information either online or at any Post Office, anytime, for just a few dollars. Just fill in a form."

"You're kidding me?"

"Welcome to the real world, Holt. Where have you been?"

"But that's outrageous. What about the Privacy Act?"

"In this case the Privacy Act is trumped."

"I'll be damned."

He sighed. "Go to the Post Office, Holt. Pay a few dollars. Are we done here?"

"What time is footy on Sunday?"

"Early game. 6.35pm. Don't be late . . . again."

"Thanks, Lurch."

"My bill's in the post." The line went dead.

I turned around. Donny was out of the car too, waiting.

"How'd you go with your Mum?" I said.

"She wants me to go to her place. She's pretty upset."

"I'm shocked. You said you would?"

"I said I'd try, but I don't think it would be safe there either."

"I reckon your Mum could deal to this girl, Suzy. Don't you think?"

He pretended to think about it. "It'd be quite a fight."

I laughed. "I have an idea. I think we can find out who this Suzy is."

"Yeah, how?"

"We need to find a Post Office."

My good friend Lurch was right, as always. For the very reasonable price of $15.00, including GST, the Post Office in Takapuna was happy to provide us with a short printed note outlining the ownership basics of the Ford Falcon XR6.

But it was no help.

MacDoe Enterprises Limited was listed as the owner while the only address details were for a PO Box number in Wellesley St, in downtown Auckland. None of this led us any closer to finding out who Suzy actually was. I checked a phone book at the Post Office and wasn't surprised to not find either a number for *MacDoe Enterprises* or a Suzy MacDoe listed.

We needed to know more about this company.

Back in the Falcon –we'd ditched *Milly* as she still wouldn't start, even for Donny– we had some big decisions to make. We needed a computer so we could look up the Company Office's website and try to work out more about MacDoe. But where to go? The easiest internet access would be at home or at my travel agency in Milford, but it seemed quite likely that Suzy would be staking one of them out. Obviously I wasn't afraid of this girl, but avoiding her would keep Donny a little more relaxed. Alternatively we could go to the library or find an internet café, but the thought of hiding out like that made me feel like a criminal, or worse –as Brent would have put it– a big girl's blouse.

I was about to suggest just going home to Donny when his phone started ringing. The blocked caller ID suggested that Suzy wanted to chat again. Donny looked horrified as I picked it up and answered the call without speaking.

"Is this Donny?" Suzy's voice asked.

"I'm sorry, but Donny isn't able to take your call at the moment. May I be of assistance?"

I could hear the smile in her voice. "This must be Donny's dad, then? May I call you Adam or shall we just go with Big Daddy?"

I tried not to sound unnerved. She really did know all about us. "And you must be the delightful Suzy that I've heard so much about."

"You got it in one, Big Daddy. Thank you for taking my call."

"What do you want, Suzy?"

"I would have thought that was obvious. You have my car. I want it back."

"Let's put the car aside for now. Let's park that issue, as they say. Assume you can have it back anytime. What do you really want, Suzy?"

She was quiet for moment. "Nothing, anymore. Just the car."

"Why did you take Donny?"

"I don't know what you mean? We went on a little holiday together, that's all. Why? What's he been saying?"

"You held him against his will for three days. That's not a holiday."

"I guess that's a matter of opinion."

I sighed. Debating it seemed pointless. "So if we return your car this all ends. Is that what you're saying? It's all over, no repercussions?"

"Repercussions, hmm. I like that word. Very fancy. Yes, I think we can say that the return of my vehicle, in good condition, would end our current situation and that no . . ." she sniggered, ". . . repercussions would be required."

I paused. "Okay. Then we'll leave it right here and catch a taxi home."

"Fantastic. Everyone's happy. Where will I find it?"

I thought hard. I wanted to tell her we had driven it to Hamilton and get her out of our hair for a longer time, but I had to be reasonable. She knew where we lived, where I worked. She knew we would be somewhere on the North Shore.

"We're in Birkenhead. We'll leave the car half way down Hinemoa St, okay?"

"Keys?"

"On top of the right front wheel."

There was silence for a moment. "Thank you, Adam. Please don't do anything now that you may regret later. Neither of us wants any . . . repercussions. Do we?"

"Have a nice day, Suzy," I said as I hung up on her. Donny stared at me, relief in his eyes. "Come on then, let's get moving."

He nodded and started the car. "Birkenhead?"

I shook my head. I didn't believe a word she had said. There was no way she was going to leave us alone once she got the car back. Not after having gone to all the trouble of kidnapping Donny – for whatever reason. This woman struck me as being quite seriously disturbed and I didn't think she would just let things slide. We needed to understand why she kidnapped him. We had to find her first. Catch her off-guard. We needed to take some control over the situation.

"Absolutely not. Milford, and quickly. Let's find out who this crazy bitch is."

It was after 5.00 pm when we arrived at Milford Trips and Travel. Kylie had already left and Julie was straightening up, preparing to head off home herself.

"Oh my, the wandering spirit returns," she said as I walked in the door.

"I'm sorry, Jules. Things have been hectic."

She looked past me and smiled as she saw Donny. "Hey, Donny. Looking good. I like the haircut."

"Thanks," he managed uneasily.

Julie caught the mood. "Everything okay?" she asked.

He looked to me, unsure what else to say. Obviously concerned about whether to involve Julie in all our worries, or not. Instinctively I decided to keep her out of it.

"He's fine," I said. "He's had a hard day. *Milly* has given up the ghost."

Julie pursed her lips, mocking surprise. "Oh no, really? I'm shocked."

Donny shrugged and took a seat in the shops tiny waiting area. He said nothing more and looked at me again for guidance. I took Julie by the arm and turned her away, back towards the business end of the shop.

"Anything important happening here I should know about?" I said. "Did you sell any cruise packages or round-the-world tickets?"

"Oh, yeah, sure. Kylie sold a group of five hundred geriatrics to Disneyland and I booked a dozen business class tickets to Paris on Concorde. It's been quite a day."

I raised my eyebrows. "Sarcasm doesn't become you," I said.

She rolled her eyes and asked, "Did you get your car back?"

I shook my head. "Not yet."

"Why not?"

"Complications."

"Complications? Really?"

"I've had quite a day too, Julie. Like you wouldn't believe."

"And . . .?"

I took a deep breath and sighed. "Can I catch you up tomorrow? There are still a few things Donny and I need to do to sort some stuff out . . ."

She stared at me hard for a minute, trying to guess what on earth I was on about. Then she glanced over at Donny's troubled expression and back to me. She frowned and finally nodded. "You'll be in in the morning?"

I screwed my face up and shrugged. "Maybe, maybe not."

She sighed in acceptance and picked up her handbag. "Don't forget to lock up," she said as she slipped out with a puzzled look on her face.

I locked the door behind her, turned the 'Open/Closed' sign over to 'Closed' and went to Julie's desk. Her computer was still on and it would save me time in warming mine up. Donny got up and moved to sit behind me so he could also see the screen.

I went through Google and found the NZ Companies Office website. A quick search for *MacDoe Enterprises Limited* revealed that the company was wholly owned by another company called *Toroa Investments*. There were no directors listed. We searched Toroa and found much the same. It was also owned wholly by another company and no directors were listed. Odd. We searched the third company, with the unusual name of *Albatross Securities* and I started to get really frustrated when the screen revealed a fifty/fifty shared ownership between a fourth company, *Yokovich Consultants*, and, would you believe, *MacDoe Enterprises*. We'd gone full circle.

Who the hell actually owned the Falcon?

I was just about to search for Yokovich when there was a furious banging on the shops front door. Working in a goldfish bowl has plenty of downsides, especially as it gets dark because you become as visible to the world as if you were being watched on television. But it also lets you see whoever is pounding on your door at the same time.

I felt Donny tense behind me.

A small, dark-haired woman with anger in her eyes was demanding entry.

TWENTY-TWO

Lloyd had been waiting at the bus stop for less than an hour. It was an excellent place for surveillance. People came and went and he just sat there, in plain sight, bothering no one. He had a small knapsack and a bag of groceries and looked just like anyone else waiting for the right bus to come along and take him home. No one took any notice of him.

His bench was almost directly opposite the front door of Milford Trips and Travel which, as it had slowly become darker, was all lit up like a stage. Even with a few travel posters in the window –none promoting destinations exotic enough for him though– he could see everyone inside and, if he'd been better at reading lips, he could have followed their conversations with ease.

Finally it was starting to get interesting. About fifteen minutes ago his new target had arrived with a young man in tow, probably his son given the distinct resemblance. They had quickly sent the frumpy red-head on her way and had briefly been banging away on the computer before the arrival of an attractive little dark-haired woman. And boy, that had changed things. The little woman first hugged the young man with a passion and fury he had rarely observed and then started laying in to them both. Hands gesturing wildly, she fired off questions like bullets, demanding answers and quite obviously unhappy with whatever she was hearing. It looked like a bloodbath in there. Lloyd wondered idly as he watched if she might complete his job for him as she seemed to spend a lot of time pointing her finger accusingly at the man called Holt. That would have been ironic.

He was enjoying himself, watching the live theatre across the road, when a surreptitious movement caught his eye. Off to his right, twenty metres away, there was an alley between two shops which he'd considered using earlier that was now becoming quite gloomy. The dark shape of a man leaned against the corner of the building. Lloyd smiled. Someone else was watching the show in the little travel agency. He stood up and stretched, making a show of it. Carrying his knapsack and shopping he sauntered down towards the other voyeur. He pretended to look in shop windows along the way and then stopped when he was directly outside the alley.

"Hey," he said to the man leaning on the corner. "You got the time?"

"No. Piss off," was the blunt response.

Lloyd feigned surprise. "Woah, sorry . . . whatever," he said and turned away to amble back to the bus stop. He'd seen what he needed to see. The dark shape on the corner of the alley was definitely the Asian bloke from this morning. No doubt about it. He didn't know the man's name, but he recognised him. And the guy appeared severely aggrieved, clearly focused on Lloyd's target, Holt, for the hit-and-run that severely injured his boyfriend earlier. He smiled appreciatively, his employer's information was good.

He fished about in his knapsack and found what he needed then primed it ready for use. Once he was ready he re-checked the scene over in the travel agency. They were still going at it hard. The little woman was firing both barrels every time. He had time. They weren't going anywhere for the minute.

He stood and slipped away, down a little side road and out behind the shops to where he had left his scooter. There was a small public parking area there and he found the car he wanted almost immediately. The man's silver Audi. Or his boyfriend's. Lloyd didn't know and didn't care who actually owned it. All he knew was that it was definitely the car he had been planning on broad-siding much earlier this very morning. He quickly attached the GPS tracking unit to the vehicle and went back to his seat on the bus bench to join a little old lady there. He offered her a meaningless smile and quickly pulled out his smart-phone. A few taps and he would be able to follow Lover-boy anywhere he went.

The plan was simple.

His employer had told him that this man had pulled a knife on Holt earlier this week, in a café, and nearly stabbed him in front of dozens of witnesses. So the guy was obviously a loose cannon. And therefore it seemed highly likely that this unhinged guy would pursue Holt, believing that he was responsible for his lover's injuries, and seek revenge. Once the Asian man got Holt alone all Lloyd had to do was be there to ensure that Holt definitely ended up dead and then Lover-boy would either be allowed to run away or he'd die with Holt in the struggle. Either way the man would take the blame for Holt's death.

It was a reasonable plan for such a hastily pulled together operation, and Lloyd was fairly relaxed. It could work out nicely, just as long as the guy was successfully able to get Holt alone.

He leaned back on the seat, stretched out his feet and resumed viewing the entertainment through the window of the travel agency across the road.

* * *

"Don't you answer that, Holt. Don't you bloody dare," Bella snarled.

My cell-phone was ringing and I welcomed the opportunity to interrupt her steaming vitriol. There was no way we could have avoided letting her in, although Donny had made me laugh when I asked him to open the door.

"We could just turn off the lights and hide," he whispered as he'd risen reluctantly and shuffled towards the door.

I turned my back on Bella, bringing the cell-phone to my ear. "Adam Holt."

"I think I know where your mysterious mate is."

Linda DeWalt's voice had never sounded sweeter in my ear. I stepped further from Donny and Bella and spoke quietly into my cell-phone. "Are you sure?"

"About as sure as I can be, given the minimal information you provided. But it's only him if he changed his name since you last saw him."

I hesitated for only a moment. I hadn't told her everything. In fact I'd barely told her anything at all. I was surprised, and more than a little grateful, that she was even considering helping me out with such an obscure request.

"That's possible," I said.

"Seriously? You tell me that you've seen an old mate from school driving around in one of Picarso's cars and now you think it's possible that this guy has changed his name since you last saw him. Really?" Her tone was dripping in sarcasm, but she hadn't yet refused to help.

I took a deep breath and edged even further away from Bella who had now stopped castigating Donny so that she could listen in to my conversation.

"It's a long story . . ."

"I've got time," she said.

I tried to move the subject back. "So where is he then?"

There was a moment's silence. "I could get in trouble for this, Adam."

"I know. Honestly, I know. But it's really important."

"You could try telling me why."

This time I was silent for a moment. "I want to, but now's not a great time."

"So you don't want to track him down today?"

"Yes, yes, I do. As soon as possible."

"But you won't tell me why I might be putting my job on the line for you."

I was silent again, for too long this time.

"Maybe this is a bad idea," she said.

"No, wait. I will tell you. I promise. I'll tell you everything, but right now I just need to find him and sort a few things out with him."

"So this isn't just a catch-up with an old mate?"

"Would a yes and no answer be good enough?"

She sighed deeply, her resignation reverberating in my ear. "He's downtown. Not far from my office here. Come and pick me up and I'll take you to him."

"I don't know, Linda. Can't you just tell me where he is?"

"I could, but he might move. I can track him. You can't."

It was my turn to sigh deeply. She had a point. "Okay. I'm on my way."

She sounded unsure then. "Uhh, okay, great. I'll wait out front."

"I really appreciate what you're doing here, Linda."

"Yeah. Okay. Well . . . See you soon."

"On my way," I said, hanging up. Both Bella and Donny were staring at me silently. "I have to go," I said. "I think I can end this."

"You're going to give the car back?" said Donny.

I looked at him and shrugged. I didn't want to say too much, at least not in front of Bella. I won't pretend that I really thought I knew what was going on but I felt pretty sure that –from what Donny had told me about the phone calls she occasionally made– whatever Suzy had been up to someone else was in on it with her. And it made the most sense to me that that someone was probably Doug Masters. Think about it. Everything started after Brent died and Doug Masters suddenly turned up. There had to be some link there and the only thing that made sense was that Suzy was working either for, or with, Doug, for whatever reason. Simply put, I felt that if I could find Doug before Suzy found us then he could call her off and sort everything out. But I didn't want Bella to know that Donny's kidnapping was somehow my fault. She already suspected that, and World War Three would be nothing compared to her wrath if I conceded the possibility. I simply needed to find Doug urgently and now Linda was coming to my rescue. I could fix this and Bella need never know how.

I faced her then. "Would you look after Donny while I try and sort this out?"

"What kind of a stupid question is that?" she retorted. "I've been looking after him his whole damn life without him getting so much as a skinned knee and I leave him with you –for only a few weeks– and look what bloody happens. What the hell makes you think I would even consider for a moment leaving him in your care ever again?"

"Mum, come on. I'm not a child anymore–"

"Don't you start, young man. You're coming home with me. You can't think for a second I would leave you with this worthless dog turd for another minute. He isn't responsible enough to care for a bloody house-plant, let alone my son . . ."

And she reeled away into another of her monumental tirades against me. I stared blankly at her as she waved her arms about to emphasise each ridiculous point. Once again I was struck by the fact she was still such an attractive woman, but in a fiery and somewhat frightening way. Incredibly passionate about everything in her life, but doubtlessly the most fiercely zealous about her precious son. Her deepest regret – she's told me this bluntly, more than once– was ever letting me know that I was Donny's father. He was already seven years old by then. She only did it because, at the time, the Social Welfare people told her they could get money out of me to help her raise him and she was between boyfriends and in need of funds. Before that I never even knew he existed. When she gave them my name she never stopped to think that I might have rights too – or that I might want to get to know my son, to be involved in his life. Since that day she has resented every visit I made, every gift I've given him, every minute I spent with *her* son. Every moment of his life I've taken away from her.

Still the tirade continued, ". . . putting you in danger. He couldn't–"

"Bella!" I snapped, cutting her off. "Enough!" She thankfully fell silent but the glare she unleashed on me would have turned a lesser man to stone. "You're right. I failed him, okay? I'm a terrible father, a hopeless role model. All right? But we can recriminate about this another time . . . I need to go. So please, take Donny home." I took a deep breath. "But first, would you both do something for me?"

"What do you need, Dad?" Donny said. His face was flushed. He hates it when we fight. Bella continued to glare at me and said nothing.

"Those company names. MacDoe and the other ones that appear to own the Falcon. Would you Google them for me?"

* * *

Suzy was bored. This wasn't unusual –given her particularly low tolerance levels for inactivity– so sitting in the stolen SUV, staking out Donny and his dad's home, was becoming more than she could bear. Although she'd been there for less than an hour it was already way too long by her standards. Way, way too long.

She tried stretching but found the driver's seat restrictive. Opening the door she got out, leaving the keys in the ignition, and wandered a few steps. She wasn't worried about anyone watching or about the car being reported stolen. There was absolutely, definitively no chance that that was going to happen.

As she surveyed her surroundings she once again decided that Donny lived in probably the worst house in a reasonably nice street. His was one of the only pair of brick and tile units within view and was surrounded by much larger stand-alone weatherboard family homes. Clearly Donny's dad was a loser and needed to try harder.

Leaning up against the SUV's bonnet she stretched out her legs and back. The movement was an immense relief. Surveillance was not her favoured pastime. She hated just sitting around and was always happier when she was moving. Walking, running, dancing, fighting, whatever . . . as long as she was in motion.

She threw a frustrated gaze at the bland brick and tile unit again. There was obviously no one in. If Donny and his dad were coming home with her car they would have arrived by now. So they must have gone elsewhere and she didn't believe for a minute they would be anywhere near Birkenhead. There was no chance of that at all. Big Daddy had sounded far too sure of himself for her liking, and that pissed her off. So that meant, once she finally caught up with them, he would need a bit of a lesson too. Donny had to be punished for escaping while Big Daddy would also need to be shown the error of his ways. Suzy smiled cheerlessly. She was looking forward to that moment.

It was time to move on, she decided suddenly. If the boys weren't here and they weren't in Birkenhead then they might be over in Milford, at Big Daddy's pokey little travel agency. She'd done a quick drive-by earlier, prior to staking out the home, and felt it was definitely worth another look.

Suzy jumped into the driver's seat with a renewed sense of purpose and energy. She was going to find these damn boys and then they were gonna pay.

* * *

"I don't see the point, Adam. How will that help?"

I took a deep breath; Bella was not going to fall over herself to help me do anything. "Honestly, I'm not sure it will. But it can't hurt. Just think about it. The Falcon is owned by someone who's gone to a lot of trouble to hide who they are. And this girl Suzy knows where we live, who I am, what I do. Yet we know almost nothing about her . . . other than that she either owns this car or is working with or for whoever does."

"We could just give the car back, Dad," implored Donny.

"I don't think so. These people held you for three days without making demands. Why? What do they really want? If we can figure out who they are we'll be in a better position to understand what they might want."

"We should just go to the police," he said.

Bella actually frowned at him. She has always had a deep mistrust of the authorities, be that the Police, the Government or the Social Welfare people. I know that some of her past boyfriends have been on the dodgy side of the law and I wasn't surprised when she didn't immediately agree with him. Frankly we probably should have gone to them by this stage but, personally, I had seen enough of the inside of the North Shore Police's interview rooms this week. I shook my head and Bella, completely uncharacteristically, said nothing.

"So what are you going to do?" Donny asked.

"Don't worry about that. I'll be fine. You just see if you can find out anything more about MacDoe, Toroa, Albatross or Yokovich and call me, okay?"

Bella frowned and gave me a funny look, but Donny wasn't giving up easily.

"I should go with you, Dad. You shouldn't go after her on your own."

Bella stepped forward. "Over my dead body."

Another rare moment of agreement. "You stay with your mum, Donny. I'll be all right. I have to go. Call me if you find anything."

They locked the door after me as I slipped out into the early evening.

* * *

Suzy couldn't believe her eyes as her beautiful Falcon hurtled past in the opposite direction just before she reached the Milford shops. The man driving didn't even see her. He was older, probably in his late thirties or early forties, and a bit light on top. Big Daddy. Had to be. And he was on his own. That probably meant that Donny was hiding out at the travel agency, or nearby.

She didn't give it a moment's thought and immediately pulled across the oncoming traffic to pitch the SUV into a driveway. Brakes squealed and a horn blasted but she ignored them both, quickly dropping the SUV into reverse and flying back out into the road to complete the three-point turn with total disregard for other vehicles. Pumping her right foot to the floor she tucked the SUV in behind a silver Audi that was tailing her XR6. It took a considerable amount of self-control to decide to follow until Big Daddy pulled over rather than overtake and force him to pull over. But there was unnecessary risk in forcing her lovely car off the road and she didn't want to scratch it if that could be helped.

Suzy began to hum happily as she followed her quarry.

* * *

Lloyd moved more leisurely. The Asian bloke had disappeared into the alley the moment that Holt exited the travel agency. Lover-boy seemed to be hell-bent on tailing Holt for revenge, exactly as Lloyd and his employer were hoping. Everything seemed to be still going to plan, and that was good.

He stood slowly, nodded farewell to the old lady on the bench and wandered, seemingly aimlessly, away. Once around the corner and out of sight he ditched the shopping bag and slung the back-pack over his shoulders. As he reached the scooter he drew his smart-phone and tapped away on the screen. The GPS was transmitting perfectly. The Audi was heading up Kitchener Road, so Holt was probably going home. He nodded to himself. That would be just fine. He'd already scoped out the little two bedroom unit and it would make a perfectly acceptable backdrop to the unfortunate events that were about to transpire.

Lloyd mounted the scooter and began to follow in an easy and unhurried manner.

TWENTY-THREE

"Nice car, Adam. I take it yours hasn't turned up as yet?"

As promised Linda was waiting on the footpath outside the offices of Picarso Rent-a-Car when I arrived. I had barely pulled up in the Falcon when she jumped in and pointed forward so I took off again immediately.

"No, they've found my car. But that's all part of my long story."

"And it's okay then? Not stripped down for parts?"

"Not so far as I know." I glanced across and duly noted the iPad-like tablet she was holding. "Very flash," I said. "Is this the tracking thingamy?"

"Cool, isn't it. And loaded with a very clever little application for locating lost rental cars when their navigation systems GPS signal is remotely activated."

"I wasn't sure that Picarso had Nav systems in their cars."

"You didn't read any of the brochures I gave you, did you?"

I looked sheepish. "I did look at some of the pictures . . ."

She said nothing, just shook her head.

"So . . ." I ventured. "You know where he is then?"

"Possibly. We have six Toyota Estima people-movers currently rented out from Auckland airport, but only one has a registration similar to the one you gave me. It was hired by a guy called Gavin Wilson on Monday for a week."

My total sum of investigative skills comes from reading mystery novels and watching movies. And in fiction the bad guys always use cash to remain anonymous. So I asked, "Really? Did he pay in cash?"

"Nope, credit card. BNZ issued. And he gave an address in Invercargill."

"Oh," I said, as my hopes began to fade. "So this is probably not Doug."

"Who can say? The address could be fake and the credit card could be stolen. It wouldn't be the first time we've rented cars to people that lie."

My hopes rose back up a little. Of course they would be fake. Doug has had twenty years to work out how to use fake or stolen identities. "So where is he?"

"The car hasn't moved, so it's not too far from here. Take a left up ahead. Head down towards the Wynyard Quarter."

"Really? Why on earth would he be there . . . sightseeing?"

"I don't know, Adam. He's your old mate, not mine. Maybe you could tell me what this is really all about."

I took a deep breath, feeling stupid. We had to stop at a red traffic light and I turned to face her. "I'm sorry, Linda. I want to explain, but I really wouldn't know where to start. I truly appreciate what you're doing here though . . ."

She fixed me with a frustrated glare. "Look, Holt. Let's cut to the chase. No more bullshit, all right? I'm here, right now, risking my job to help you because I like you. Not just because you're kind-of funny, or because you seem to have a good heart, but in some part because of the desperately positive sell-job your friend Brent did on me. He really believed in you and he somehow managed to convince me that you might actually be one of the last available good men out there. But I'm starting to have my doubts, so please . . . clue me in. Just start at the beginning. I'm not as blonde as I look. Maybe I can help?"

The lights went green and I moved the car forward again. I was initially gob-smacked, totally unsure of how to respond. But deep inside I knew that I needed help. I needed a confidant. Someone to talk to and to try and make some sense of whatever the hell was happening in my life at this moment. Linda's mention of Brent and the speech he gave her before he died touched me in a way I might never have expected. I felt a tear form in my eye and blinked it away. Then I made a decision.

As we drove I started talking, right from the very beginning. In a few of minutes of stilted storytelling I had covered off the historic incident on the *Kestrel*, Brent's murder, Doug's appearance at his funeral and subsequent reappearance in Takapuna. Then I roughly outlined Donny's kidnap and escape and whose car we were in and finished with how I thought it was all interrelated and that finding Doug would surely put an end to whatever was going on. There were a lot of gaps in my story and her face was a mask of puzzlement when we turned off Fanshawe Street and into the Wynyard Quarter.

Linda was still trying to make sense of my garbled tale when I pointed ahead. "Look, there. Is that the people-mover?" I said.

She checked her tablet and then the nearest street signs. "I think so. Everything looks about right."

I pulled over about thirty metres away. Even in the fading light the garish Picarso paint-job stuck out like a sore thumb. The registration plate was obscured by a car parked behind it, but I felt pretty near certain that this was the same car I had seen in Takapuna earlier today.

But there was no one inside it.

I scanned the area quickly. This was a new part of downtown, recently revitalized by the council to try and take more advantage of the harbour waterfront. The area was freshly paved and planted, with a line of flashy new restaurants and a kids playground and the usual mix of obscure art pieces and trendy seating. Lighting was minimal though and the early evening gloom made the area looked bleak and deserted.

"Maybe he's eating at one of the restaurants?" said Linda.

"There wouldn't be much else to do around here at night."

"Shall we go and look?"

I turned to her. "Maybe you should stay here?"

She frowned back. "I'd rather not . . ."

I thought about if for a moment. There was virtually no chance of Suzy having tracked the Falcon to Wynyard Quarter. She didn't have the benefit of a fancy GPS navigation system to guide her, so was probably parked angrily somewhere over in Birkenhead. And we had the drop on Doug. And I felt more than confident I could take him down if I needed to. I wouldn't fall for a kick in the crotch again so easily.

I shrugged and spoke seriously. "Okay. But if we do find Doug you'll keep your distance, won't you?"

"Of course," she said slipping the tracking tablet into her handbag and climbing out of the car.

I took a deep breath and followed.

* * *

Suzy was furious. She'd been right on Big Daddy's tail all the way from the North Shore and over into downtown Auckland. She'd seen him stop and pick up a woman and then take off again quickly. But just after that the stupid old bat in the car in front of her had slammed on her brakes to avoid something, probably a stupid pedestrian, and Suzy had instinctively taken evasive action to avoid rear-ending her. She'd spun the wheel and shot out into the oncoming lane, forced to accelerate through a small gap to reach the far footpath and relative safety. But it had cost her dearly.

Once she maneuvered the SUV back into the traffic flow, frustratingly having to avoid other bloody pedestrians and maneuvering with the accompaniment of horn blasts and shouts from other motorists, the XR6 was nowhere in sight.

She remonstrated with herself out loud, cursing her reflex to avoid the collision. If she'd just stayed square-on and simply allowed the SUV to rear-end the other car she'd have been able to keep her XR6 in sight and carry on. Stopping to swap insurance details with the old bat never came close to entering into her considerations. Now she was back to square one.

She kept moving though, determined that she was better, faster, smarter than this bloody man that was driving her car. She could beat him. Out-think him.

What would Big Daddy do?

He'd picked up a woman. Why? Where would they go now?

Possibly on to her place, wherever that might be. In that case she had most likely lost him. Or possibly back to the North Shore, back to his home ground.

Suzy floored it and the SUV leaped ahead, careering around the next left turn. He'd left Donny in Milford, she felt certain of that, so he could be heading back to the Harbour Bridge and over to the Shore. That would make the most sense, wouldn't it? Suzy thought so. She made another quick turn and in moments was onto Wellesley Street and flying down towards Victoria Park and the markets. She got caught at a red light at the bottom of the street, both lanes blocked, but suddenly her eyes lit up and she was grinning again.

On the far side of the park, through the trees, even though it was now almost fully dark, she recognised her beautiful car, the bright yellow colour flashing gold beneath the street lamps glow, as it headed north, up Fanshawe Street, towards the motorway on-ramp to the North Shore.

She let out a little whoop of glee and then stopped cold. The car was slowing, and then turned into the Wynyard Quarter. Big Daddy wasn't going home. Suzy grunted. That was okay too. In fact it was probably better. She felt confident that she could have caught him up on the motorway, but the Wynyard Quarter was only a small area – and most of the roads rounded onto each other. She would find the XR6 in no time at all. She wriggled in her seat and nodded happily to herself while waiting impatiently for the lights to change.

Big Daddy was gonna get his ass kicked for messing her about.

And soon.

* * *

"You know," Linda said. "I can't help wondering . . . If that yellow Falcon belongs to your mate, Doug. Why is he driving around in a rental people-mover?"

I didn't see her point. "Because he's loaned his car to Suzy."

"But you said that Falcon was owned by a string of probably bogus companies. If that's the case, and Doug has all that worked out, why does he need a rental?"

"I don't know. Maybe he thinks it's more anonymous?"

"A Picarso rental . . . more anonymous than an unmarked Falcon? You think?"

Then I saw her point, but I had no answer so just shrugged. "There's a lot about all this that I really don't understand. Let's just find the guy and ask him."

She nodded, smiling. "Okay. Good plan . . ."

Striding purposefully through the light drizzle we had quickly walked the length of the restaurant row already, then turned around and were half-way back to where we started with no sign of Doug. Most of the restaurants were nearly empty so our mission hadn't been all that tough. We reached the end without success and stopped.

"What now, Sherlock?" Linda said.

I frowned and scanned the area around us again. Most of the lights nearby were spilling from the restaurants. Further up the walkway were a couple of dull street lamps and there was a faint glow from one of the oversized ocean launches docked out on the pier. Otherwise everything was dim and quiet.

As we'd walked past the Picarso people-mover I'd checked the registration plate and peered inside. I was certain that it was the car I'd seen Doug fleeing Takapuna in earlier, but there was nothing inside which we could see that would confirm anything. I didn't get it. Why would he come here?

Linda watched me for a moment and then scanned around the area too. She pointed towards the launches out on the pier. "Maybe he got on one of those floating palaces? Maybe he has a rich friend here?"

I shrugged. It didn't seem likely, but then again, what did? He wasn't in a restaurant, but he had to be around here somewhere. "Want to go out and look?"

"Sure," she said, but then pointed to the Mexican restaurant behind us. "But, umm, perhaps I could use the powder room in here first. Too many coffee's . . ."

I nodded and she ducked inside.

I searched the darkness around me yet again. Things weren't going as well as I'd planned. Finding Doug should have been easier. Where the hell could he be?

* * *

Lloyd pulled the scooter over and backed it into a space between two cars. The Audi was untidily parked on the other side of the road, as if its driver abandoned it in a hurry. He shook his head. Lover-boy was an amateur, clearly having no idea what he was doing. And no idea he was being followed. The guy was just running on rage and that was always a mistake.

He took in a quick view of the Wynyard Quarter area and released a small snort of dismay. Not an ideal location. He would have preferred this to go down at his targets home, but that probably wasn't going to happen now. Nevertheless Lloyd wasn't going to let the change of location phase him. Keeping a cool, professional head was what kept him alive . . . and out of the reach of the police.

Clearly Holt wasn't ready to head home quite yet and he could deal with that. Taking in his surroundings further he realised that he wasn't overly familiar with this newly refurbished section of town yet. While it seemed that there were few roads in and out he felt he could turn that to his advantage. The scooter allowed him access through places a car could not pass – and it was almost full dark now with a light rainfall in the air. Reasonable cover for both doing the job and making a clean exit. He shrugged. He could make this location work.

Lloyd moved quietly down the dimly lit road, keeping to the shadows, moving without haste to ensure he did not attract attention. Within moments he passed the yellow Falcon XR6 he had last seen Holt driving and allowed himself a hint of a smile. Lover-boy had done a good enough job of following. Full credit to him. Now all Lloyd had to do was locate them both and his business would be almost complete. He didn't think that finding them would be too hard.

And he felt certain that finishing them both would be even easier.

* * *

About twenty metres from the last restaurant was one of those trendy seating arrangements consisting of brightly coloured shapes –like big blocks of Lego– all stacked up. They looked gaudy and uncomfortable but that seemed to be the thing these days. I didn't get why people liked them, but there's a lot about modern life I really don't get . . .

Anyway, I wandered over and climbed to the top of the Lego stack to get a better view of the area. Doug simply had to be around somewhere. Only exactly where wasn't as obvious as it should have been. I stared back down the line of restaurants and saw nothing new. I looked around in the other direction, towards the big old grain silo's, or water-towers, or whatever they were in front of the tank farm. There were no lights and nowhere obvious that a man would have gone. So I turned my attention to the pier directly in front of me and surveyed the launches, yachts and other water-craft out there. Only one, the largest pleasure boat I have ever seen, had lights on. Perhaps Doug was onboard? To the right of the huge launch was another vessel, also bobbing gently, but completely dark. Something about its shape seemed familiar to me but I couldn't immediately place it.

Suddenly I was falling. My legs were pulled out from beneath me and I dropped awkwardly to bounce off the side of the seats and plummet onto the wet, hard paving stones below. I cried out in pain as my left arm smashed into the ground, twisting horribly and sending searing pain shooting through my wrist and hand and up my arm. I rolled instinctively to take the weight off my injured arm and banged my head against a steel rubbish bin the council had thoughtfully left nearby. The clanging sound reverberated through the still night air as I cursed freely. Then a sharp pain exploded in my thigh as somebody kicked me with everything they had. I rolled away from the follow-up kick and found myself with my back up against the lowest level of the brightly coloured seating.

My left side had taken a battering. My wrist hurt like the devil, possibly broken, and my thigh was locked rigid. I could feel blood oozing down my face from a cut where my head struck the steel bin.

I looked up to see my assailant for the first time.

Cato glared back at me, an evil grimace on his face.

"Now we finish this, ass-wipe," he said as he produced the knife once again.

* * *

Lloyd had a clear view of the assault from the shadow of a building site less than forty metres away. It was going to go down almost exactly as he had hoped. The Asian guy was obviously a bit of a coward, having king-hit Holt from behind without warning. But that was okay. He was getting the job done.

What did disturb him was that the action was all happening out in the open in a very public space. Sure it was dark, and sure there was nobody around at the moment, but that could change very quickly. He would have been more patient and waited to catch his quarry in a less open, less visible position.

He tensed, readying himself to enter the arena and complete his plan. But he was forced to wait and soon found himself shaking his head in wonder. Lover-boy had backed off a little, allowing Holt to regain his feet. That was stupid. Why didn't the idiot just put the knife in him and get on with it?

Now it looked like they were going to dance a little first, maybe even chat about the weather. He checked the time. If the knife-wielding moron got his act together he could tidy things up and be home by dinner time. But it didn't look like the situation was going to play out that way.

Lloyd watched on from the shadows in frustration.

TWENTY-FOUR

"You're making a mistake, Jeremy," I said quickly. "I didn't run Harold down. My car was stolen. That's the absolute truth."

I had managed to get to my feet, but the pain in my thigh had me hobbling badly and my left arm was clutched to my chest, useless to defend myself with. I was backed up against the Lego-like seating feeling very vulnerable.

He snarled. "You're a liar, Holt. I saw you. I saw you driving the car."

"You can't have. I don't know what you saw, or who you saw, but you didn't see me. I wasn't there. I wasn't driving my car. It's all a set-up–"

"You're pathetic. Just man-up and admit it. I damn well saw you with my own eyes. You're a fucking scumbag." He whipped the knife around in the air, drawing my eye, deliberately trying to intimidate me.

And it was working. I was so scared I could barely think. But I'm a salesman by trade, and my default settings are to negotiate. It was all I could think to do. Try to convince him of the truth, that I wasn't the person who had run his lover down.

"I'm sure that's what you think, and there's probably good reason, but I think there's a bigger picture here. I think someone's set this up." He waved the knife again, taking a half-step forward. I gestured wildly with my good hand, desperate to make him stay back. "My car was stolen. I was jogging through Takapuna to retrieve another car when the hit-and-run happened–" He stepped forward and lunged at me, swinging the knife dangerously close. In an effort to step away I tripped over the seating and staggered, only just staying on my feet.

"You have to believe me; I didn't run you guys down. Why would I? What would I gain?"

He flashed the knife again, just to frighten me further. It worked.

"Why? Because you're scared about what my Harold could do to Barclay's business. That's why you did it. To stop him from taking all their accounts away."

Despite my fear I felt my eyes fly wide. My God, was that really what he thought? That I would run Harold Armitage down over business accounts? It was insane, unbelievable madness. Just to consider it was demented.

"Jeremy, that's just not true. I don't work that way. I would never do anything like that to someone else . . . and besides, I have nothing to gain from Barclay and Dodd retaining accounts. I'm not involved there. Brent was my friend, but that's all. I'm not involved in his business–"

"You're so full of shit, Holt. You really expect me to believe that you haven't got a thing going with Barclay's wife, that you're not trying to protect her–"

"I'm trying to help her, sure, but I wouldn't run anyone down to do that."

He danced forward, swishing the knife before me as I shuffled back again. I was starting to run out of walkway. Behind me the pier and its fence were getting close. I kept my eyes on the knife. Cato was ranting now.

"Barclay will have left you shares too, I'd bet on it. You're in this up to your eyeballs you lying bastard. You hurt my Harold bad and now I'm going to hurt you worse." He lunged again, forcing me right back to the fence.

"You're making a mistake, Jeremy. I've been set up. I didn't do it." I desperately searched my mind for something else, anything else to hold him off and a startling possibility suddenly emerged. "Maybe it was Dodd? Think about it. Maybe Marguerite Dodd, or more likely her father, had my car stolen and used it this morning against you and Harold? Have you even considered that's possible?"

He shook his head, an irritated grimace on his face. "You're a worm, a pathetic wriggling worm. I know it was you . . ."

He stepped forward again and I had nowhere left to go. My back was up against a fence, my thigh still so tight and unyielding that I wasn't able to run anywhere. My left wrist throbbed worthlessly. I would have to try and fight him off with some severe limitations.

I thought I was finished, but then, all of a sudden, two things happened.

The first, just as he moved to slash the blade across my chest and draw first blood, was the unexpected, but very welcome, arrival of a car that drew his attention momentarily. A dark coloured SUV came screaming around a corner near the playground and drove straight up onto the walkway, its driver completely oblivious to the rules of the road. As it drove straight at us with headlights flaring both Cato and I stopped and stared, shocked at the sudden illumination of our tussle.

Then the second thing happened.

Momentarily blinded by the SUV's headlights all I saw was the blur of a large object, which I would soon identify as a solid wooden barstool, swinging through the air to strike Cato from behind, across his head and shoulders. He let out a low grunt and pitched forward. I only just reacted in time to sweep the knife in his outstretched hand in a downward slap to stop it from plunging with his momentum into my chest. Instead it took a small slice out of my hip, tearing my trousers, as the man and weapon crumpled to land at my feet.

I stared down at my attacker's inert form for a moment uncomprehendingly before finally looking up to find Linda DeWalt, wide eyed and pale, standing in front of me. She glanced down at Cato, then back at me, then down again.

"Oh, my God," she said. "What have I done?"

I didn't get the chance to respond as the SUV slid to a stop only metres away. The door opened quickly and a diminutive girl bounced out. I recognized her immediately from Donny's description. She was small, olive-skinned and quite stunningly beautiful. Donny had said she looked remarkably like an even sexier Jessica Alba and I had to agree. This just had to be the infamous Suzy.

Our situation had just gone from bad to worse.

* * *

Lloyd watched on in growing concern. His plan didn't look like it was going to work out, at least not tonight, and not with Lover-boy as his fall guy. He shook his head is frustration. Why do these bloody amateurs always feel the need to talk? It just shows a lack of commitment, a lack of decisiveness. Surely, after spending all day following the man he was after he should have just got on with it, like he himself would have done. Talking just confuses things.

Taking a deep breath he re-focused on his task.

He had been surprised when the woman came out of the restaurant and wondered if she was with Holt or just some random do-gooder? Upon reflection he decided that she must be with him. Why else would she risk getting involved with an obvious nutter wielding a knife? A passerby would have simply called the police, not taken such a risk by getting into the middle of it all. Lloyd had been surveying the unfolding events calmly when she walked out of the restaurant to discover Holt's situation. He'd actually been a little impressed when, after clearly weighing up her options –she'd actually pulled out her cell-phone, looked at it, and then put it away again– she searched quickly for a weapon and only hesitated a moment before picking up the heavy wooden barstool. He thought it had been a fine choice. He'd watched on in begrudging respect as she quickly and quietly moved up behind Holt's assailant. He wondered if Holt had been aware of her there. He was talking furiously, saying anything to persuade the crazy man not to stab him . . . as you would.

But it was the arrival of the low-flying SUV that had really taken him by surprise. What was this all about? Another friend? Or a well-meaning passerby who had seen the fight and just wanted to break it up. He watched and waited, silently berating the foolish Asian guy again for choosing such an open location. That had definitely been a mistake. And for talking so much.

Lloyd stayed in the shadows and observed quietly as the driver of the SUV emerged. Then he did a double-take. She moved forward into the light and he became absolutely certain.

What the hell was going on? Holt was his target. What was *she* doing here?

He pulled out his cell-phone and dialed quickly.

* * *

"Hey there, Big Daddy. I'd like to say that I'm pleased to meet you, but you've actually pissed me off quite a bit today."

Suzy stepped forward into the light cast from the SUV's headlights and shook her head in amused wonder. There was a bloke, possibly Asian, late twenties, lying prone on the ground at Donny's father's feet. He looked out-for-the-count. Or possibly dead. A knife was lying less than a metre way.

Interesting.

Then there was a woman, mid-thirties, standing with a bloody great wooden barstool in her hands, looking absolutely terrified. Suzy smiled. She'd seen the woman level the bloke on the ground with the barstool as she'd pulled to a stop moments ago. It had made her laugh.

Absolutely fascinating.

And then, of course, there was Donny's dad. The charming Adam Holt, who thought that he could get away with fooling her into visiting the droll suburb of Birkenhead in search of her XR6. And wasn't he a mess. Despite the blood running down the side of his head she could actually see the family resemblance to young Donny – in the nose, and definitely the eyes.

"Okay," she said. "I am very excited. You guys seem to be having quite a party here. What's going on?"

No one spoke immediately. The woman seemed too terrified to even move. Big Daddy was still trying to get himself

210

together. His face was ashen. Suzy stepped forward into the silence and none-to-gently prodded the guy on the ground with her foot. He didn't react. She prodded him again, this time a short, swift kick. Still there was no reaction. Holt and the woman watched on in silent horror, both shuffling a step back away from her. She bent down and placed a finger on the prone man's throat, waited a few beats and stood up again.

"If you wanted to kill him you're going to have to take another swing," she said to the woman. "He's out, but I don't think he's critical. Do you want me to finish him off for you?"

The woman reacted quickly. "No, please. Don't . . ." She seemed to suddenly realise that she was still holding the barstool and dropped it quickly.

Suzy laughed and shook her head. She was just teasing. "Don't worry, I won't. I don't think you can afford my services."

Big Daddy finally came to life. "You're Suzy," he announced.

"Yes I am, Big Daddy. And I want my car back."

"Take it," he said, fumbling in his pocket for the keys. "I'm sorry for any trouble. Just take it and go." He found them and threw them across to her. They would have fallen short but Suzy deftly bounced forward and plucked them out of the air effortlessly. "It's parked just over there," he said, pointing.

She dropped the keys into a pocket. "Oh, Adam. Surely you're not in a hurry to say goodbye so soon. We've only just got together . . . finally. And I'm curious. Very curious. What is all this about?"

She indicated the man on the ground between them and took a step forward. Once again they both shuffled back, away from her, obviously frightened. Suzy smiled again. She was going to have a bit of fun with Big Daddy and his girlfriend.

* * *

I didn't know what to say. Everything had happened so fast. One moment Cato had been about to stick me like a pig and the

211

next I was face-to-face with the psychotic woman who had kidnapped my son and held him for three days.

I reached out to Linda, wanting to both comfort her and draw strength from her. She had just saved my life and I wanted to thank her, to hold her, but that didn't seem likely. Suzy stood before us. A mysterious and seemingly dangerous enigma. What the hell did she want from me?

She asked the question again. "Come on. This is great stuff. What's going on?"

"I don't know," I finally responded. "You tell me. What were you doing with my son?"

She tilted her head and actually giggled. "Don't worry about that. That was just business. I want to know what this is all about." She prodded Cato with her foot again. "Jealous boyfriend? Temperamental ex-husband? Random mugger? It looked like he was about to knife you up. Why? What is this?"

There was something very offhand about her, like she didn't have a care in the world. I immediately felt that I could tell her almost anything as long as she might find it funny. But if I failed to amuse her she would slit my throat without blinking. Finally I understood why Donny had been so damn afraid of her. She was a very pretty girl, probably only early twenties and very petite but every little movement and mannerism scared the living crap out of me. If Cato had seemed unstable, Suzy made me feel like I was balancing explosives over a naked flame.

I tried not to sound half as nervous as I felt. "He thinks I ran over his friend."

"Really," she bent down to inspect him again. "And did you?"

"No."

She looked back up again and fixed me with a terrifying smile. "Oh, go on. He's well out of it. You can tell me the truth. Did you?"

I shook my head, my mind reeling. "No," I repeated.

"Huh," she said, raising her carefully manicured eyebrows. Then she turned abruptly to Linda. "I saw what you did with the chair. Nice work. I don't give compliments often, but that rocked. Really. Well done."

Linda looked baffled, and then blushed. "Uhh . . . thanks?" She was confused and wary, probably more from my reaction to Suzy than anything else as I hadn't provided her all that much detail of Donny's kidnap earlier. But I also think she too had sensed that Suzy wasn't altogether a nice person. She glanced at me briefly for understanding, I could only shrug, and then wisely she said no more.

"So who ran over his friend?" Suzy said, turning back to me.

"I wish I knew," I said. "I guess it wasn't you then."

She grinned. "Is the friend dead?"

I was pretty sure she didn't really care. "No. Badly hurt, but he'll live."

"Well, there you go. Can't have been me or he'd definitely be dead."

I said nothing, unable to think of an appropriate response.

"Hmm," she said, tilting her head again in thought. "What shall we do now? Any suggestions? I could help you throw him in the harbour?"

I shook my head immediately. "No . . . No, but thank you for the offer."

She laughed. "You're quite the funny man, Daddy-O. Donny doesn't seem to have picked up your sense of humour though. Shame really."

I wasn't sure if she was actually amused or not. I had no idea of what was going on inside her head but I chose to play along. Once again the salesman in me wanted to ingratiate myself, befriend her, try to convince her not to hit me with the barstool and throw me in the harbour. I was convinced that she was capable of it. "I know. Too much time with his mum, I'm afraid. She stifled him."

She nodded at that and smiled again. But without warning the smile slid from her face in a flash. "You really pissed me off earlier. You know, with all that crap about leaving my car in Birkenhead and hanging up on me."

"I'm sorry," I said. "I obviously wasn't thinking . . ."

"I really need to teach you a lesson for that."

"I think I've seen the error of my ways. Maybe we could just–"

The trilling of a cell-phone cut me off. Suzy looked down casually and extracted a phone from her pocket. She checked the display and frowned before answering the call. "I'm a bit busy at the moment."

Then she went quiet, listening. Linda and I stood there nervously, not daring to move a muscle. Our eyes met for a moment and the consideration of running for it passed between us unspoken.

"Don't even think about it," Suzy suddenly snapped. "Don't move!"

As she continued to listen to whoever was calling her eyes flicked back and forth between Linda and I almost daring us to move. Then she glanced at the SUV and spun slowly to survey the darkness around us. As she listened she casually drifted to her right, out of the SUV's headlight beams, and inspected the area around us once again. Suddenly I got the feeling we were being watched.

Realisation swept over me.

Suzy must be working for Doug, and she was on the phone to him right now. Somewhere out there, in the gloom, Doug Masters was watching everything, pulling the strings.

* * *

Lloyd watched quietly from the shadows as the girl took the call on her cell-phone. He had just hung up from the man who was now talking with her and he wasn't happy. Further explanation was required, but Lloyd had reluctantly agreed that that would have to come later. Right this minute the man had said he needed to make contact with her . . . before the situation got even messier.

She was looking about now. She had obviously been told that she was under surveillance and that would piss her off enormously. He had only met her the once, but it had been a long enough meeting to understand that she was a very disturbed individual. Quite different from him, but also quite useful in certain situations. Lloyd considered her unstable and had refused to work with her directly. Regardless of her obvious skills –she was clearly more than capable of handling herself– it was still a good decision as far as he was concerned. He'd heard rumours about other jobs she'd been sent on. Where the level of persuasion had been unnecessarily excessive or where the termination had been gratuitously messy.

He kept very still. He didn't want the situation becoming more volatile, which was usually a near certainty with the girl, and was fairly certain that the man talking to her now would be able to rectify things. He had asked Lloyd to stay in position until she had followed her new instructions. If she didn't, he had been asked to intervene and move her along, then tidy up.

He wasn't happy about that either, once again because his bloody fall guy had chosen such a poor location. Any clean up would have to happen out in the open, right in front of an open restaurant. It wouldn't be easy.

Lloyd took a deep breath and crossed his fingers. Hopefully the girl would make the right decision, do what she was told, and he could still be home within an hour for a late dinner and some serious thinking.

This job had now officially become way too complicated . . . and that simply wasn't acceptable.

* * *

I found myself scanning the darkness around us. Where are you Doug? Where the hell are you hiding, you bastard? I wanted to call out: Come out and show yourself, but I managed to contain myself. Suzy was still in control here.

Linda inched towards me, clearly anxious and seeking comfort. I wanted to put my arm around her but she was on my left and there was little I could offer in the way of reassurance

215

with my injured wrist. I inched towards her too, looking into her eyes. Silently trying to soothe her but feeling hopeless I resolved that whatever happened next I wouldn't let Linda get hurt. She was innocent here. She'd never met Doug; she wasn't part of what had happened to Kieran all those years ago. She was just in the wrong place at the wrong time and it was my fault. God-damn it. It's always my fault.

Suzy shuffled her feet. She clearly wasn't happy. I couldn't hear what Doug was telling her but it didn't seem to be cheering her up any. The conversation went on. Suzy glared at me and muttered something that sounded like, ". . . but he took the XR6 . . ." and then rolled her eyes. She listened for another minute and then finally she said, "Yes . . . Yes, of course I understand." And then with a grunt she ended the connection and groaned, "Whatever . . ."

She slowly replaced the cell-phone in her pocket and glared at me some more. Linda and I stayed silent. I stepped forward slightly, putting Linda behind my left shoulder. It was a small effort but Suzy caught it and laughed.

"If I was you I wouldn't turn my back on that one," she said. "She's pretty handy with a chair. I'd put my money on her dealing to you in a fight."

I tried to sound staunch. "You've got the car's keys. We've got nothing else you want."

She sighed in exasperation and looked over my shoulder at Linda. "Men, huh. What are you gonna do?"

We stood in silence for a minute, just eyeballing each other. Then she sighed again. "Did you like Donny's new haircut," she said abruptly.

"What?"

"I gave him a haircut, while we were on holiday. Did you like it?"

The question was completely out of left-field but I felt sure the correct answer should be a positive one. "Uhh, yeah. Yes. It looks good."

She grinned. "Yep. Brings out his cheekbones."

I just nodded and said nothing.

Suddenly she dipped her hand into a pocket and pulled out another set of keys. She bounced them once in her hand and then tossed them to me. I caught them instinctively in my good hand.

"I'm leaving but I need you to do one thing once I'm gone," she said.

Desperate to please her I said, "Sure, anything."

"Would you clear out the SUV's boot for me . . . please?"

"Clear out the boot?"

"The SUV, there," she said, pointing behind her. "I don't need it anymore, but someone needs to clear out the boot. Okay?"

"Sure," I said. "Will do . . ."

She grinned playfully. "Be sure you do. Right. Well then. See you around." And she abruptly spun away in a balanced pirouette, only pausing briefly to grab a sports bag from the SUV, before skipping away towards where Linda and I had parked the Falcon a century ago.

I felt Linda's hand grab my arm. It hurt. "She's going . . ."

I couldn't believe it either. "Yeah, it looks that way . . ."

"That was the girl who kidnapped your son? She should be locked up."

I simply nodded, completely flummoxed at the sudden change of events. Then it struck me. Doug Masters. Doug must have called her off. Oh, thank Christ.

"What do you think is in the boot?" Linda said cautiously.

I looked at the keys in my hand and then at the SUV. Immediately I thought the worst. A bomb? A dead body? Then, rather randomly, I remembered the scene from The Hangover movie where they opened the boot of the Cadillac and out leapt a naked man who attacked them with a tire iron. Anything could be in there.

"Maybe we should just leave it and walk away," I said.

As if she'd read my mind Linda said, "Did you see The Hangover?"

"I was just thinking that."

"What if there is someone in there?"

"What if he's naked?"

She almost laughed. I was feeling a little light-headed with relief too. "Come on, there's only one way to find out."

The SUV wasn't locked. Suzy had left the driver's door wide open and the headlights on. They illuminated Cato, still lying flat out on the ground. He hadn't moved although I believed it when Suzy said that he was still breathing. Neither of us felt up to examining him though so we walked cautiously around behind the SUV to check the boot. I put my hand on the release handle. I looked at Linda. She stepped away and nodded. I opened the rear door.

There was a man inside.

He was fully clothed. His hands were bound with tape as was his mouth. I'd never seen him before in my life. He looked up as the rear door swung up away from him. His eyes were wide with terror . . . which changed suddenly to hope as he saw faces he had not been expecting. Muffled noise came from beneath the tape over his mouth and he began to struggle, trying to sit up.

I couldn't move. Linda reacted first and reached in to tear at the tape on his face, and then I leaned in to help him rise. As soon as we had the tape off his mouth he started to abuse us.

"Who the fuck are you? What the fucking hell is going on? Where is that little darky bitch? How fucking dare she . . ."

"She's gone," Linda said. "She gave us the keys, told us to clear out the boot, and we found you . . . that's all we know."

"You've got my keys?" He had his hands free now and was pulling himself awkwardly out of the small space he had been crammed into.

"Yes," I said, holding them up.

He snatched them from me and literally fell out of the SUV onto the ground. He cursed and moaned and tried to stand, but his legs were cramped up. Linda tried to help him but he swore at her and pushed her away and kept on scrabbling around, trying to get feeling back into his numb body.

"Calm down. Let us help you," I said.

"Fuck off. Just leave me alone," he spat angrily and forced himself up onto both feet. We both stepped back to let him vent a little. I thought back to Donny's tale of escape from the bach. This must be the owner that turned up and distracted her. Suzy must have forced him in there when she took his car. He would have been crammed into that uncomfortable space for hours. I felt sorry for him. He continued to curse freely and started to take in his surroundings.

"Where the fuck am I?" he said.

"Wynyard Quarter," I said. "Downtown, Auckland."

"Aww, for fucks sake," he said. He staggered around his car looking for damage and then abruptly slammed the rear door closed and shuffled awkwardly into the driver's seat. He started the engine and pulled the door closed.

"Can we help you in some way–", I started to say, but I was wasting my breath. He slammed the SUV into gear and spun away in a ferocious U-turn. Before we could say anything more he was gone.

I watched him fly away up the road for a moment before I felt a tug at my arm.

"Adam," Linda said. "Look . . ."

She was pointing at the area in front of where the SUV had just been parked. The area where a solid wooden barstool lay on its side . . . all on its own because no one was lying inert on the ground beside it.

Suzy was gone. The SUV and its owner were gone.

Cato, and his knife, were gone too.

TWENTY-FIVE

The cell-phone vibrated silently in Lloyd's pocket. He extracted it without letting his gaze drop from the scene before him and put it to his ear. Only two people in the world had this number and he was only expecting to hear from one of them at this moment. "Yes," he said softly.

"Did she leave?"

"Yes." He heard a sigh down the line which he interpreted as relieved.

"No one was hurt?"

"No, she behaved . . . wisely. But there was a man in the boot of the SUV she arrived in. Holt and his girlfriend let him out. He left immediately. Took the SUV."

"Describe him."

He did.

"Shit. Another apology required."

"You know him?"

"Yes . . . don't worry about it."

There was a moments silence before Lloyd said, "I'm on a job here."

"I know, and I'm sorry, but I can't let you complete it."

He was silent again for a beat. He watched as Holt and the woman drifted over towards the Mexican restaurant. "I have expenses," he said.

He heard a soft grunt in his ear, an irritated sound. "I'll cover them. And your fee. Plus a bonus for the confusion."

"I don't know. There's a principal at stake here. I've never left a job incomplete before. My reputation is important to me."

There was a few more beats of silence before Lloyd's caller spoke again. He sounded frustrated. "I'm sorry, but I have to buy out the arrangement. I don't like it and I don't want to, but it needs to happen. Things here are . . . delicate enough. Who are you working for? Maybe I can try and clear things up?"

Holt and the woman were now out of sight, inside the restaurant, possibly calling the police, possibly getting coffee or a meal, possibly just cleaning up. He turned his attention to the man who had somehow managed to get to his feet and stagger away into the shadows behind the restaurant. He didn't look steady at all and was struggling to make his way to his car.

"You know I can't tell you that," Lloyd said.

After a short pause the voice said, "No. Of course not. But tell me, is it someone I know? Better yet . . . is it someone you trust to pay up afterwards?"

He thought about that as he watched the injured man stumble and fall. He just lay there. The guy was in a bad way. Probably had a serious concussion.

"It's not someone you know," he said finally.

"Okay, look. I have to go, but I want you to promise me that you won't complete the job tonight. Go home. Sleep on it. Will you do that for me?"

He sighed. "Sure."

"And in the meantime I want you to think about this as an offer, okay? I will buy out the contract on Holt, double your fee, plus expenses. And it would work out best for all if your other employer was unable to re-advertise the job."

He sighed again. "I'll give it some thought."

"Thank you. I know I can rely on you."

The line went dead. Lloyd watched the semi-concussed man stir, pull himself up to his hands and knees and begin to crawl in the dark along the footpath.

He considered the offer, thinking seriously about this current employer. He had been paid appropriately for the first job, but not yet for the hit-and-run effort. He contemplated how the target had changed so rapidly from one day to the next and he reviewed his earlier concerns that this employer seemed to be losing control of the situation. The thoughts disturbed him.

He watched as the guy managed to stand again, with some effort, and then progress another two metres towards his car. But, as he struggled to pull his keys from a pocket he dropped them and then sank to his knees once more.

Drumming his fingers softly on his thigh he reflected on the situation thoughtfully as a fresh idea began to take shape. He thought about it some more as the injured man continued to scrabble about weakly and soon he started to see some real positives from the idea.

Lloyd had a lot of history with the man he had just finished speaking to and, as far as trust went in his line of work, he knew that the man would honour his word.

But, it had to be acknowledged, he did not feel any of the same confidence in his other current employer. In fact, the more he thought about it, the deeper his feelings on unease grew.

As the injured man finally found his keys in the gutter Lloyd made a decision.

* * *

"Are you sure you really want to do this?" Linda said.

We had cleaned up a little in the Mexican restaurants toilets and I now had a bandage covering the cut on my forehead. It's surprising just how much blood a relatively small cut can spill. My shirt was ruined, but the bleeding was stopped and I was starting to feel determined again.

"I have to. I've come this far," I said.

"You're more obstinate than a mule," she said.

"Do you know many mules?"

She shook her head, refusing to be drawn. "How's the wrist?"

I tried to move it, flexing it slightly. It hurt. "It's okay, I'm pretty sure it's not broken. I'll live."

She gave me raised eyebrows, in obvious disbelief, as a response. Then shook her head and muttered, "Whatever . . ."

We were standing outside again, having thanked the restaurant staff for letting us clean up and promising to come back another night for a meal. Rather surprisingly, they appeared to have seen nothing of the incidents out front and I had told them I was fooling around and slipped over to receive my injuries. My ability to lie was improving daily.

While we were cleaning up I had explained to Linda that the man she flattened wasn't Doug, but another chap who didn't like me for a completely different reason. I had neglected to mention Armitage and Cato before, thinking my tale was already complex enough, but had now filled her in on all that too. She looked besieged, but seemed happier that she obviously hadn't killed him. We were both still quite watchful, just in case Cato reemerged from the shadows, but we had agreed that it didn't seem likely. He's seemed quite badly hurt and we'd already checked around the area, when we first emerged from the restaurant, in case he'd only staggered a few metres and was lying unconscious nearby. But there was no sign of him and I felt sure he was no longer following us. Hopefully he'd taken himself off to a hospital for treatment. Or at least gone home to recover.

"Maybe you should go," I said. "This whole thing has been far crazier than I could ever have imagined."

For a moment I couldn't read the look on her face, then she smiled. "I'm not going anywhere, Holt. Not yet anyway."

I was actually relieved. Having her nearby was lending me a feeling of confidence that I probably didn't deserve.

"Are you sure?"

Her smile broadened. Her eyes were alive. "I know this is wrong, but I think this might be the most interesting date I've ever been on."

I made a funny face. "You've led a sheltered life."

She nodded. "I'd like to stay, if that's okay with you."

I smiled and nodded back. "That's very okay with me."

We stood silently in the dark for a few moments, with light drizzle persistent in the air, before I spoke again.

"I think I know where Doug is."

I took her hand and we moved over towards the Lego-like seating again. I scaled the seating for maximum height and invited her to join me. Then, after rechecking that the Picarso people-mover was still parked where we'd last seen it, I pointed in another direction. "Just before I got knocked off here by that lunatic I saw something, over there. Do you see it?"

"I don't know. What am I supposed to be seeing?"

"An old boat."

She squinted into the darkness. "Across from that massive pleasure-boat?"

"Yes. You see it?"

"I think so."

"That's where he is," I said, feeling oddly confident. "Come on." Still holding her hand I climbed down, leading her along the pier, towards the dark shape. She said nothing until we were about twenty metres from the old boat's stern.

She gasped. "You're kidding me . . . Is that . . .?"

"Yes, I'm pretty sure it is."

As we drew closer the old boat began to take clearer shape within the darkness. It was a long oval shape, with two levels. The stern was also its bow, depending on which direction it was to be sailing. I recognised the oversized funnel and its classic wooden features. The *Kestrel* bobbed gently before us.

"I wonder how long it's been berthed here?" said Linda.

"I don't know. I thought it had been taken to Tauranga and turned into a floating restaurant." I could see it clearly now. "It's definitely the *Kestrel*."

I stopped and stood before it with a feeling of absolute dread. I had studiously avoided any kind of travel by ferry, yacht or any other boat since Kieran died. To behold the actual ferry that was the scene of the worst thing that had ever happened in my life filled me with trepidation.

I felt Linda's hand squeeze mine. My disquiet must have been obvious. Our eyes met and I nodded to acknowledge her unspoken support. Then I turned back to the ferry and walked forward again, Linda's hand still firmly encased in my own, providing the strength I truly needed.

There was no obvious access point. No drawbridge or ramp. No ladder. But getting onboard would only require a short leap to stand on the upper deck. I felt oddly certain that Doug would be onboard, and I thought I knew where on the ferry he would be. But I didn't want to sneak up on him again. That hadn't worked out well the last time. Just thinking about it made my groin tense subconsciously so I released Linda's hand and walked further up the pier. Upon reaching the bow of the ferry I stopped and stared into the inky darkness of the lower deck.

I couldn't see anyone.

I called out, regardless. "Doug. I know you're on there. We need to talk."

There was silence. Linda moved up to join me.

I called out again. "Don't hide from me, Doug. It's Adam. I know you're there."

I thought I saw something move in the shadows, but still the silence remained.

"For fucks sake, Doug. Answer me."

I waited longer, letting the silence stretch out, and eventually a voice drifted back.

"How the hell did you find me this time?"

"I have superpowers, Doug. Like you wouldn't believe."

"Are the police on their way?"

"No, I haven't called them . . . yet."

Another moments silence and then, "You're an asshole, Holt."

"I missed you too, dickhead. We're coming onboard."

* * *

Lloyd had deliberately chosen not to adjust either the seats position or that of the rear-view mirror as he drove across the Auckland Harbour Bridge, back to the North Shore, in the Audi. But he wasn't cramped and only had to lean across a little to use the mirror so that was okay. It was important that he left no clue that anyone other than Lover-boy had been driving the vehicle this evening.

Lloyd extracted his cell-phone once again. He dialed the only other person who had his number, his other employer. The call was answered after seven rings.

"Yes?" he heard.

"It's done. I'm on my way to collect my fee."

"Wait, you're saying that Holt is dead?"

Lloyd frowned. He much preferred when his employers kept their words vague, especially on the phone. The use of the target's name annoyed him and effectively set his resolve to follow through on his revised plan. "Yes," he said.

There was a moment's hesitation, then, "Okay. Thank you."

"I'll be with you in ten minutes."

"You're coming here? Now? Is that wise?"

"No one will see me. Have the money ready."

"I'm not sure you should come here–"

"You wanted urgent. You got urgent. Now I want paid and I want it urgent too. Then you'll never see me again. I will be with you in ten minutes."

Another longer hesitation, then, "I understand."

"You're alone?"

"Yes, there's no problem there."

"Good," he said. "Nine minutes," and he ended the connection.

* * *

Doug Masters made no effort to run this time, nor did he offer us any assistance in getting onboard the *Kestrel* or even attempt to stand up once we finally reached him. He remained where he was, sitting in the darkness on the lower level, his back to the vessels bulkhead, staring out across the harbour as various lights splashed over the constant movement of the water. He didn't even look up as Linda and I shuffled past him to stop on the pier side of the vessel.

As my eyes adjusted to the dim lighting I could see that he was now clean-shaven and looked almost exactly like the teenager I had known twenty years ago.

Without speaking he extracted a cigarette and lit it. He didn't offer us one. I sat down too, not quite facing him but more down the side of the boat, my back to the bow. Linda followed my queue and also sat, just a little further away, within earshot but obviously not intent on being part of the conversation.

I said nothing and waited.

Finally Doug exhaled in a loud and deep sigh. "Never thought I'd see this bloody ferry again," he said. "Let alone sit here . . . with you." His voice was dry and melancholy, almost wistful. He continued to gaze out across the harbour, steadfastly refusing to look at me.

I thought about that for a moment. "You've been away quite a while . . ."

His response was even slower. "I had some stuff to do . . ."

"Like running, hiding. Must have been a laugh a minute."

"You have no idea."

There was silence again. Suddenly I felt tension wash over me. Our approach had been so casual, considering that as far as I knew this man had killed Kieran, murdered Brent, tried to frame me for Harold Armitage's hit-and-run, and arranged the kidnap of my son. Had I walked into a trap?

I tried to push the feeling aside. There were so many questions I needed to ask and after twenty very long years I wasn't going to waste the opportunity.

I decided to begin at the beginning. "Did you kill Kieran?"

He shook his head slowly, not looking at me. "No."

"Then why did you run?"

"I had to."

"Why?" I said, getting frustrated at the brevity of his responses.

"Barclay."

I snapped. "For crying out loud. It's been twenty fucking years. My life was ruined that day. You owe me more than that."

Finally he looked over at me. His expression was grim in the darkness. "Your life was ruined? You whiny little wanker. What about my life? You think I've been swanning around, living it up, living La Vida Loca? You have no fucking idea."

My frustration simmered. "Then why did you run? If you're telling me the truth and you didn't kill Kieran then why run? It doesn't add up."

He shook his head, irritated. "You know why."

I exploded. "I bloody well don't know. I don't know a fucking thing."

He stared at me in silence, frowning, his expression fluctuating between irate and unconvinced. Finally he said, "Everyone I talked to, all the newspaper reports I read, they all said that you and Barclay didn't remember anything, but I knew that was bullshit. Are you honestly trying to tell me you don't remember?"

Desperation flooded through me. "Not a thing," I said. "I remember flashes of us all partying around various different pubs and clubs. Shooters at the London Bar; depth-charges at The Shakespeare; dancing like fools somewhere else . . . but nothing after that. I don't remember how we got onto the ferry. I don't know what happened onboard it, or how Brent and I got home afterwards. I just woke up the next day. Later in the morning. Very, very hung-over. My head splitting. I had a few bruises, but no idea what we'd got up to . . . Brent said the same thing. He didn't remember anything . . . But I think he actually did . . . now. I didn't back then, but now . . . now I think he did remember."

Doug stared at me again, hard. Finally he shook his head. "Well, fuck me . . ."

Being around Doug had a strange effect on me. I found myself retorting like a teenager again.

"No thanks," I said reflexively.

He continued shaking his head. "Christ, but you haven't changed at all. Still far too lippy for your own good . . . And you really don't remember, do you?"

I shook my head. "No. Not a thing."

I think he finally believed me then. He turned away and took a deep drag on his cigarette. Exhaled loudly in an exaggerated sigh. "Fuck me," he muttered.

I waited a beat, actually trying not to speak, but was again unable to help myself. "You're not my type."

Linda kicked me.

"Sorry," I said, apologising to both of them.

"Who's this?" Doug asked, rolling his eyes towards her.

Linda said nothing and looked to me. "Linda DeWalt," I said. "Meet Doug Masters. Doug . . . Linda, Linda . . . Doug."

"You trust her?" Doug said.

"Linda just saved my life."

Doug raised his eyebrows, feigning interest. "You said we need to talk and we probably do. But do you really want her listening in?"

I didn't hesitate. "Of course. Linda's one of the good guys."

He swiveled his head around to face her. "You a cop?"

She shook her head. "No. I'm a sales rep, for Picarso."

"The source of some of my superpowers," I said.

"Are you wearing a wire? Recording this in any way?" Doug demanded.

She shook her head again, "No."

He glared at her intensely for almost a full minute before turning away, shaking his head. He said nothing more. We sat in silence for a while longer before I spoke again.

"You were going to tell me why you ran? What actually happened that night . . ."

He snorted and took another drag on his cigarette. "It doesn't matter anymore. And anyway, you don't want to know, Holt. Believe me; you really don't want to know."

"Brent killed him, didn't he," I said, taking him by surprise.

"Why would you think that?"

"Because he confessed to me . . . in a note."

"Bullshit. Barclay would never confess to anything. And why a note?"

I took a deep breath. "After Brent died his lawyer called me in to see him. There was some stuff in his will that needed to be sorted out. And there was a note, which Brent left for me – but only to be read after he died."

"You're kidding. He left you a note in his will. Seriously?"

"Yes."

"What did it say?"

"It was a bit vague, but it sounded like a confession. He asked for forgiveness. He said that he lied about what happened that night. He urged me to find you . . . He said that you could tell me what really happened."

Doug snorted in disbelief. "He said that in a note? Asked for forgiveness? The fucking weasel. He fucking lied all right. He lied to everyone."

"You know what he meant?"

He ignored me. "And you only got this note after he died?" I nodded. "So he's been lying to you for twenty fucking years and you had no idea?" The scorn in his words tore into me. I suddenly felt small and very tired. All I could manage in response was a vague shrug. "You're an asshole, Holt," he said.

"Maybe I am, but I'm not a fucking coward. If you didn't kill Kieran then why did you run away? You must have done something? Why bloody run?"

"I've never killed anyone in my life," he said.

"Not Kieran, so you say. What about Brent? Did you kill Brent?"

"I wish . . . But, no. I didn't kill Barclay."

"Then why are you back here? Isn't it a bit suspicious that you turn up here again, after twenty years, only days after Brent was murdered?"

He snorted again. "You wouldn't believe me . . ."

"Try me," I said. "You never know what I'll believe."

I spent a moment pondering my own words while he took another long pull on his cigarette and stared at me pointedly. Am I really that naive? Have I spent all of my adult life believing a lie? Doug deliberately exhaled the smoke towards my face to interrupt my maudlin thoughts. Then he spoke again with acid in his voice.

"Brent Barclay ruined my life. He fucked me over and forced me to run and hide, to try and start my life all over again . . . with absolutely nothing. Whoever killed him is someone I would like to meet and shake them by the hand. That bastard Barclay can burn in hell for all I care."

"So why are you here?"

He sighed again then. "The God-honest truth . . . I wanted to be certain he was actually dead. And I wanted to piss on the bastard's grave."

A chill ran through me as I recognised the bitter truth in his words.

* * *

Lloyd stopped at the top of the driveway and carefully scanned the road and houses around him before rechecking that he had everything he needed. Running the plan through his minds eye one more time he stepped through each action and likely reaction, vigilantly considering any and every possible hiccup that could derail its smooth implementation. There were a couple of small concerns but otherwise he felt confident of a successful outcome.

With a final surveillance of the area around him he decided all was in order and drove down the driveway at a sensible speed that would not attract attention. He eased the car to a stop in front of the garage beside his employer's main front door. He had been here before, but only ever on foot, usually leaving his scooter parked a couple of streets away. It was a private setting, the main entrance of the house not visible to any neighbours. It would work well.

He climbed quickly and quietly out of the Audi and approached the door. As anticipated there was no need to knock, he was expected. The door opened as he was still two steps away. His employer stood there, a thick envelope in hand, looking uncertain. He kept walking, the element of surprise his best friend.

Lover-boy's knife glinted briefly in the wash of light coming from inside the house and then it disappeared, buried deeply and with carefully considered accuracy into Lloyd's employer's chest. He knew exactly where to inflict exactly the sort of damage he required for this plan to work. Only one thrust was allowable and it had to create the right internal damage to be fatal, but not immediately. He needed his employer to take at least a minute or two to die.

He twisted the blade slightly, sure that he had it in the right spot, and then stepped back to observe his handiwork. Shock and confusion seared out at him from his employer's face, but no words, no cry of either surprise or pain. That was good, excellent in fact. Lloyd watched dispassionately as the person who had procured the death of one man, the serious injury of another, and had asked him to kill yet again slumped back, away from him, to fall into a heap on the floor.

* * *

"How did you find out he was dead?" I said.

"It was on the bloody news, Holt. It wasn't a secret," said Doug.

"Oh," I said, feeling stupid. "And that's why you were at his funeral."

"I missed most of it. Some idiot chased me outside and into the fucking trees. I nearly broke a bloody toe at one point when I almost tripped over."

"That was you in the wig then?"

"Yeah," he sounded ashamed. "That was me. I fucked that up a bit . . ."

"Cry me a river. You almost broke my bloody neck."

He shrugged it off. "Can you believe how many people were there? Jesus, but that pissed me off. Even the fucking Mayor was there. That son-of-a-bitch must have had incriminating photos of them all. There's no way any of them actually liked the prick . . ." He shook his head. "But anyway, I went back later on . . . fulfilled my dream."

A vision of Doug, standing over Brent's freshly turned grave, urinating, suddenly flashed before my eyes. I felt sick at the thought. Then I remembered our other encounter, earlier today. "But you went to see Claire, this afternoon. Have you been in contact with her all this time?"

He sighed again, but with a different tone this time, a sadder sound. "I just wanted to see her . . . I don't know. I was thinking about trying to apologise, but, well . . . I really don't know why I went there. That was stupid too. I sort-of went there on an impulse. I used to think about her a lot, back then. About how we could have been so good together, if . . . you know; if her brother . . . damn that bastard Barclay . . ."

I stared at him, not knowing what to say. Claire should have been with me, not with this low-life. Surely he didn't think his little fling would ever have stood the test of time?

". . . and then you bounced in and fucked it all up again. You asshole."

I managed to hold my tongue. He should never have been with Claire . . . A frustrated sound escaped me. Doug sighed. We sat in silence for a while, both lost in our memories of the girl we'd both loved.

Linda broke the silence. "What about Donny? What about your son, Adam?"

I started, jolted from my thoughts and faced Doug. He raised an eyebrow rather comically. "Donny?" he said. "Bella's got a kid called Donny. Surely not . . ."

"Yes," I said. "My son, Donny. Bella is his mother."

"Holy fuck, Debbie never told me that. She kept me up to date with our old friends up here and I knew Bella had a kid, but I thought she didn't know who the father was. It was you? You're Donny's dad?"

I nodded. Did I believe him? Did he really not know my connection to Donny? As best I could tell he seemed sincere.

"My son was kidnapped this week," I said.

"What? Kidnapped? But he's gotta be . . . what, about twenty? How would someone kidnap him? And why? You'd have to be fucking crazy. Bella would kill you. She'd rip your nuts off and feed them back to you."

He had a point. Bella can be more than a little scary at times. Especially when the subject was Donny.

"So you didn't know about it?"

"Why the fuck would I know about it?"

I watched his face. He seemed genuinely incredulous. Maybe I am too naive, too trusting, and I may not be the smartest guy alive but my instincts are usually pretty good. I was surprised to find myself believing him again. He didn't seem to know anything about Donny's kidnapping. My confusion only mounted.

After a long pause I said, "You stay in touch with Bella?"

He shook his head. "Not really, but we've caught up a few times when I've come up and visited Debbie. I guess I shouldn't be surprised that she never mentioned you were her son's daddy."

I was shaken by the notion of Bella in contact –and apparently more than once– with Doug Masters, the runaway killer. She'd never said anything to me. Had she actually let my son near this guy? "You've met Donny?" I said.

"No, but I've seen pictures. She's a very proud mother . . ."

I tried to clear away an image of Bella sitting down with him and flipping through photo albums of my boy. Somehow it made me feel more dizzy than angry. Trying to refocus I changed tack to my final area of confusion.

"I guess you don't work in the travel industry . . . but have you ever heard of a guy called Harold Armitage?"

He looked at me blankly for a moment and then shook his head. Either he was an incredible actor –and maybe he needed to be to have survived on the run for so long– or he was telling me the truth. I stared into his eyes and found myself believing him again. Why would he lie to me now?

My mind fogged as I tried to reconcile everything he'd told me so far.

It was highly unlikely, given that he didn't seem to know Donny was my son, that he'd arranged the kidnap and unleashed Suzy upon us. He also claimed, quite believably, not to know Armitage so probably had nothing to do with the hit-and-run that had driven Cato after me with a death-wish. And, although it seemed pretty clear that he would have liked to, I felt almost certain that he didn't stab Brent to death. Yet worst of all – he was adamant that he didn't kill Kieran.

I still understood nothing at all.

TWENTY-SIX

Lloyd moved quickly. Everything needed to happen in a precise order, in a specific way for the police to accept how he wanted this to look. Carefully avoiding treading in any of his employer's blood he stepped over her, as traces of the dark liquid now bubbled from her lips, to quickly find what he needed in the kitchen. He carried the tall chair from the raised breakfast bar back to the main doorway, only stopping briefly at a hall cupboard to select and extract a suitable towel. He wedged the chair against the doorframe and draped the towel over it. The woman he had stabbed lay on the floor, twitching as her head lolled back and forth, her life slipping away. She moaned softly, an unintelligible sound not loud enough to disturb the neighbours.

Next he prepared the gun. It was a Glock, a similar weapon to those that the police are now carrying in their cars. He knew it was already spotlessly clean as he unwrapped it from the small cloth he kept it in but he wiped it down again, just to be absolutely certain. He chambered a round. With a built-in safety mechanism the gun was now ready to fire. Then he approached the dying woman and gently lifted her left hand to press her palm and finger prints onto the gun. This would ensure prints from both hands were on the weapon when it was found. He firmly believed that most people, especially woman, actually carry their guns in both hands, not just the one. He dropped her hand and, continuing to carefully avoid stepping in any blood, placed the gun on the floor near the door, ready for its key role in the upcoming pantomime.

He walked outside to the Audi and opened the rear door. The Asian guy was prone across the back seat, unconscious again thanks to his educated touch. He braced himself, leaned in and dragged the inert form out carefully, ensuring he left nothing behind in the car, no clue that Lover-boy had lain there. Lloyd was not a big man but he was strong. Plenty strong enough to carry the slightly smaller man the few metres to the entrance to the house. When he got there he propped the man onto the tall chair and leaned his shoulder against the door frame. It was a tricky balancing act to keep the unconscious man upright on the chair without being held but Lloyd managed it swiftly and calmly. He stepped back and admired his work. It would do. It would do just fine.

Turning back to the woman he was pleased to find that she wasn't quite dead yet. Her eyes were glazed and the moaning had stopped, but faint bubbles still formed on her lips. He took a moment to rethink through the steps he had preplanned and reassure himself that all was in order. He looked around the lobby area of the house and nodded before picking up the envelope the woman had dropped when he stabbed her and pocketed it. She was wearing a long robe over a V-neck T-shirt and stretchy leggings. She had obviously been relaxed, lounging around, probably watching TV when he called. He crouched and checked in the robe's pocket to find exactly what he expected there. The cell-phone he had given her especially for contacting him, and for him only. He dropped it into his own pocket. He double-checked the set-up. He was ready.

Lloyd picked up the gun and moved to stand behind the woman's head, facing the open door with the unconscious man propped up inside its frame. He lifted her right hand this time and placed the gun deftly within it. Then he thrust the hand and the gun into her robe pocket and dragged it out again, pleased to see that a thread had caught on the weapon. The forensic people would love that. It would prove perfectly that the gun had been in her pocket before being fired. Now came the tricky bit. He needed to aim and then squeeze the trigger while ensuring that he both hit the man in the chest while keeping his hand as clear as possible from the weapon. He knew that as a gun fired it kicked out a very fine spray, and almost imperceptible mist, of burned gunpowder. The forensic people knew this too and would be looking for it. Therefore he needed as much of the gun's powder-burn to cover the woman's hand rather than his own. He knelt over her head holding her right hand on the gun's stock and her finger on the trigger. Slipping his left hand under hers he was able to maintain the weight of the Glock and her hand while maneuvering his index finger over hers onto the trigger. He leaned down further, lining up the shot and then gently pulled his right hand away just before he squeezed the trigger. The weapon fired and kicked back, out of his and the woman's hands. He let it go. It was unrealistic to think that the dying woman would have been able to hold onto the gun as it was fired. It just missed his knee and came to rest on the floor. The bullet found its mark and the man was lifted off the tall chair and spun around and away to crumple onto the ground just outside the door. Lloyd stood. The noise had been loud, a rather flat crack that most people simply wouldn't recognise, but he still had little time now. He imagined that any neighbour who heard it would currently be sitting up, listening, waiting to see if they heard the noise again, wondering what it was. Most would simply go back to their televisions but you could never tell.

It was time to move.

* * *

"I'm a bit busy at the moment actually, Bella. Whatever it is will have to wait," I spoke tersely into my cell-phone. I really shouldn't have answered it, all things considered, but when I saw Bella's name flash up I immediately worried that something else might have happened to Donny.

"This is important, Holt. You need to come home," she demanded.

I sighed in frustration. I had already established that Donny was fine and not in any sort of trouble. Suzy had not reappeared. I took a blunt approach. "I said I'm busy. I'm talking with Doug Masters."

That shut her up, but not for long. "Where are you?"

"It doesn't matter, but I can't talk and I can't come home yet."

"How long will you be?"

"For fucks sake, Bella. What's the big deal?"

"Don't you swear at me, Holt. Don't you dare."

"I have to go–"

"We need to talk, Holt. I'm at your place, waiting. Come home asap."

"Why?"

"I know who owns the car."

"What? The Falcon. Who?"

"Not on the phone. Come home." And she ended the connection.

I stared at the cell-phone in my hand, totally dumbfounded. I wanted to call her back, but I knew that would be pointless. If she wanted to talk face-to-face then nothing would change her mind. Bella was impossible to sway.

Linda looked worried. "Is Donny okay?"

"Yes, he's fine," I said. I turned to Doug. "We have to go. Please, no more fucking around. I need to know what happened that night."

"Let it go, Holt. It really doesn't matter anymore."

I started to get angry again. "Don't feed me that shit. That night turned both our lives upside down and inside out. What the fuck happened?"

He shook his head, frustrating me further. "It's ancient history. Forget about it."

"Let me be the judge of that . . . Please, what happened?"

He turned away, once again staring out blankly over the harbour. He pulled out another cigarette and lit up, drawing things out, pissing me off.

"Doug . . . for pities sake . . ."

His smile was grim. "It was a dark and stormy night . . ."

"Don't be an asshole. That's my thing."

He snorted; an odd semi-laugh and drew on the cigarette again. Then he finally began to talk, softly, slowly drawing a picture of the night that had changed both our lives forever. As his words drifted to me through the cool evening air I could almost see that night unfolding again, almost hear the laughter and smell the despair as it all turned so horribly wrong.

"It all went pretty much as you so vaguely remember . . . up to a point. Yes, we went on a huge pub crawl. The London Bar, Shakespeare, and so many others. Too many others. Yes, we drank far, far, far too much. Especially you and Kieran. I was pretty pissed too, but you guys were practically blind. Brent, well, who could tell with that prick. I'm not sure he ever actually drank much at all but just pretended to. When it came down to it, later that night, he sobered up in an instant, sober like a judge . . . and jury, and executioner."

Something whispered down my spine and I shivered involuntarily.

Doug continued. "The last place we went into we got thrown out of. I don't remember its name; it was just one of those bland, overpriced dance clubs. We were making dicks of ourselves, acting seriously stupid." He paused to reflect and shook his head at the memory. "Do you remember that stupid Kung-Fu song? You know, it was a big hit . . . *everybody was kung-fu fighting, something about being faster than lightning* . . . you know it, I can tell. Everybody knows it. They use it these days for just about every martial arts parody."

The tune was immediately humming in my head. I couldn't help but silently hum the *dah-de-dah-de-dah, de-dum-dum-dah* bit. I had no idea who performed the song but it was definitely one of those classic novelty songs, like *The Monster Mash* or the *Rocky Horror Time Warp*. It was silly . . . *Everybody was Kung-Fu fighting* . . . and yeah, I remembered it. Only I couldn't explain the feeling of disquiet I always felt whenever it came on the TV or radio. I started to get that feeling again.

"You and me and Kieran, we were dancing to it, being silly buggers. Letting fly with wild kung-fu kicks and waving our arms about like we were doing stupid kung-fu chops. We were being dickheads so . . . obviously, we got thrown out. Then someone decided we should call it a night. Probably Barclay, the big wanker. And so we danced and we kicked and we chopped our way down to the ferry terminal. But we went round the back and over the fence and snuck on board, like you used to be able to do in those days. I bet you can't do that now."

I plumbed the depths of my mind, searching for an image that would support what Doug was telling me. I got a brief flash of the ferry terminal area, back then, how it used to be, at night, but that told me nothing. I could have remembered that from any number of trips we made on the ferry before that night. Something about the kung-fu fighting hit home though. Arms swishing, legs flailing . . .

"We kept quiet until the ferry had pulled well away from the jetty, then we came out of hiding, but we stayed downstairs, right about here where the crew can't see you. And we started up the stupid kung-fu fighting again."

The way he said the last bit, with a bitter distaste, registered somewhat within me and my feeling of unease grew stronger.

"And that's when, well, you know, Kieran . . ." he trailed off.

My heart was in my throat. "Tell me," I demanded.

"He died, Adam. It doesn't matter how."

I didn't know how to take that. "How can it not matter?"

He ignored me. "Afterwards, well . . . Brent did his thing. He fixed it. He made his decision and he told me that I would have to run away, take the blame."

"I don't understand."

Doug sighed heavily, drawing heartily on his cigarette. "Brent picked up Kieran, he was already dead, and tossed his body overboard . . ."

My insides froze. I couldn't speak.

". . . and then he turned to me and told me to go and hide, to stay on the boat, that I would have to run away or he would tell the police that I killed him. I had no choice. I had a juvenile record; I'd already spent time inside. Who would they believe – me or Mr Fucking Perfect. I mean, what could I do? I was pissed. He was Brent fucking Barclay, the former head boy, the captain of the footy team, the son-of-a-bitch voted most likely to succeed. His folks had money . . . mine didn't. I was a convicted criminal. He was practically a choirboy . . ."

The bitterness in his voice horrified me almost as much as the words he was unleashing. Brent's note suddenly sprang clear into my mind: *We all made mistakes, but I made the worst. I lied about that night.*

Doug was telling the truth. Surely he had to be. Why wouldn't he be?

"Barclay said that if I ran away he wouldn't dob me in. He said that he'd pretend to have been so drunk he didn't remember anything. I always assumed that you were in on it too. You were pretty much passed out on the deck, but I always thought you heard him; that you saw something . . . that you knew what happened."

I didn't know what to say, but he didn't wait for a response.

"Afterwards, once I'd sobered up I tried to change my mind. I wanted to come back, but it was too late, there was no way back. Brent made sure of that. I called him, tried to reason with him, but he didn't want to know. He told me it was better this way . . . better for him and better for you . . . but not for me. I even asked him for money to help re-establish myself but he refused. Then he hit me with the clincher, the end-game, the show-stopper. He said that if I tried to surface and tell my side of the story he would make me pay, but he didn't threaten me directly."

I stared at him in horror. I didn't want to believe what I was hearing, but it all made sense. Brent was a bully, I knew that. But I never realised the extent of it.

Doug took another long, slow drag on his cigarette. "Barclay told me that if I ever came back then Debbie would have an accident. A bad accident."

My eyes closed involuntarily and I hung my head in shame. I couldn't speak.

"So I stayed away. Made a new life for myself . . . And I'm doing all right. I have a wife and children, two of them. We have a nice home in Invercargill. I had some help and managed to create a whole new identity. I can't travel overseas but I have a job, a driver's license, a mortgage. I pay taxes. It's a good life."

He took another pull on the cigarette and fell silent.

I was lost for words. I tried to speak and faltered. "I'm so sorry, Doug . . . I always thought . . . well, you know . . . because you ran . . ."

He snorted. "Of course you did, Holt. Why wouldn't you? Believing that I was the bad guy would always be so much easier than finding out the truth."

"That's not fair . . ." I started to say, but I had to tail off. He was right on the button. Shame washed over me.

His voice became hard then, dismissive. "Don't you need to get going? You don't want to piss Bella off."

I was still reeling, unable to think straight. I had had it so badly wrong all these years. Doug didn't kill Kieran, Brent did. The note was a confession. I just sat there shaking my head in denial. Desperately wanting it not to be true.

"But why?" I said. "Why did Brent kill him? What did Kieran do?"

He shook his head in frustration. "You still don't get it, do you? Barclay didn't kill Kieran. He just tossed the poor bastard's body over the side like he was a sack of worthless potatoes. But Kieran was already dead."

"You're right. I don't understand. How did he die?"

Suddenly Doug stood up. "We've been over this. It doesn't matter."

I scrambled to my feet too. "It bloody well does matter. I need to know. This has been hanging over my head for half my bloody life. You're the only person alive who can tell me what happened that night. Come on, stop fucking me around!"

We were now face to face and I suddenly saw a faint glimmer of sympathy in his eyes that I hadn't expected. "If I tell you," he said, "you understand that you can never un-know it, don't you? Once you know, well . . . then you know."

I should have stopped there. I shouldn't have pushed him, but I wasn't thinking. I didn't realise then just how bad the truth could hurt.

"Tell me, Doug. For crying out loud, how did Kieran die?"

He glanced across at Linda, weighing up his thoughts and frowning heavily. Something was making this a massive struggle for him. When he looked back into my eyes I suddenly knew and I didn't want him to speak.

But he did. He fixed his gaze firmly on mine and ripped my whole world apart once more. "You killed him, Holt. Kieran Sandford died because of you."

TWENTY-SEVEN

Moving carefully, but with purpose, Lloyd picked up the tall chair and returned it to where he found it at the breakfast bar. The towel had only a couple of small spots of blood spatter on it but had served its purpose well. He would not need to wipe down the chair. Next he extracted the knife from the woman's chest and held it in the air over the towel, careful to ensure that he did not leave a trail of blood drips as he moved outside. Deftly he rolled the knife into the man's hand and lifted both to allow a few drops of blood to fall onto the guy's hand and arm. Then he released both and let them fall. The knife ended up about half a metre from the hand and looked natural enough. He rolled up the towel, he would take it with him; it wouldn't be missed, before then checking that the man he'd just shot was in fact dead. He was. Lloyd allowed himself a small smile of self-congratulation. It was a smart little piece of handiwork. The bullet had hit him squarely in the chest, pretty much right through his heart. An excellent shot.

He removed his GPS tracker from the Audi and then scanned the way he'd left the car. The driver's door was open, as if the man had leapt out in a hurry, urgently. Nice.

He went back into the house to finalise anything that needed adjusting. The gun was lying near the woman's body, the spent bullet cartridge also visible. She was now also dead, having lasted just about the right amount of time to have pulled the gun from her pocket and shot the man who stabbed her just before she expired. He decided not to move anything. He didn't want to disturb any of his well planted evidence.

As he made his way deeper into the house again he stopped to look back, to reconfirm that all was in place and to listen for any signs of concern around the neighbourhood. He heard nothing unusual. Nobody seemed to have noticed. He reviewed the scene and played through it again in his head. The police would think that the Asian man had driven here, walked up to the door and immediately stabbed the woman as she opened the door. They would think that she had then drawn her gun from her pocket as she lay dying and gotten off one lucky shot, killing her assailant before he could do anything more. But her wound had been fatal and no neighbours had heard the shot and coming running. By the time they were found it was too late for them both. A tragedy, obviously.

Questions were sure to be raised about why the man had come here to attack her, and where the woman had obtained the untraceable gun, but that wasn't Lloyd's problem. He made it a point to never ask the question 'Why' when he took a job. It was always best not to know. But since this woman had hired him to steal Holt's car and use it to put the Lover-boy's boyfriend in hospital –or worse, she wasn't too fussed– he had to assume there was some connection that the police would make. And she had told him about the deranged man's attack on Holt with the knife in a café recently – so he knew that the guy had form with a blade. Hadn't he tried to use it again on Holt less than an hour ago? And, somehow, he felt sure that it must all come back to the original murder that he had performed for the woman. That of her husband, which must surely have been an insurance and inheritance job. When he'd been at this house previously he'd seen no evidence of children, so the woman must have stood to inherit everything. Probably a tidy sum if she had had the big guy well insured.

Lloyd took in the scene before him and silently acknowledged the irony. Sharon Barclay was lying dead in a pool of her own blood in exactly the same place that she had arranged for her own husband to die – in exactly the same way.

Funny how things worked out.

He shrugged. Shit happens. She shouldn't have started something she didn't have complete control over. Although he had initially been quite impressed with her. Especially with the staunch way she'd taken the slapping he'd been required to give her after dispatching her husband. She'd barely flinched during the whole thing. Regardless, he resolved to ensure he vetted his prospective employers more stringently in future. He would not allow himself to ever get into such a complicated situation again. He still didn't understand how the crazy girl who suddenly turned up in the SUV fit into the puzzle but he accepted the fact philosophically. Her unexpected appearance had provided him with the opportunity to tidy up his concerns about the Barclay woman . . . and he was going to treble his money on the deal.

And the extra money would be very welcome. He would now be able to afford the trip to Peru, to finally experience the wonders of Machu Picchu. Things had worked out nicely.

Finally he was satisfied. Everything was in place, exactly as he planned. He had the cell-phone, he had the money.

He turned away and slipped quietly through the house to depart via the back door, locking it after himself –of course– and disappearing into the darkness just as he had the last time he visited.

* * *

I recoiled in horror, desperately wanted to shout back at him, deny the accusation, make him retract his words . . . but I couldn't immediately speak. Deep inside my head there was a tiny voice that gradually grew louder and louder . . . *you killed Kieran and you know it, you've always known it, you do remember, don't you, you loser* . . . and I began to shake my head in denial. "No," I sputtered. "No, that's bull-shit . . . I would never have hurt him." But the words faded . . . *you're a killer, a murderer . . . you're nothing but scum, Adam Holt* . . . and a deepening acknowledgement of my own worst fears leached into my bones as I staggered back against the railing, the feeling in my legs departing, the shock almost driving me to my knees. I could feel tears burning at my eyes, trying to escape. I looked to

247

Doug again, pleading silently for him to tell me it was a joke, a bad one, that he'd lied. But he couldn't meet my eyes anymore and turned away to draw deeply on the cigarette again.

"I told you to leave it alone," he murmured, his back to me.

"You're lying . . . I would never have hurt Kieran," I repeated more firmly.

"Think whatever you like. It doesn't change anything."

I felt a hand come to rest on my arm and turned to find Linda's sympathetic eyes boring into my own. I looked away, shrugged her hand off. I felt like I had suddenly become poisonous, unclean. I didn't want her to catch my disease.

"How did it happen?" she asked Doug softly.

He turned. He seemed surprised that she was still there. Regarding her watchfully he pursed his lips before offering a small shrug. "The kung-fu fighting . . . it was a big mistake." He turned his gaze back to me. I gestured silently. Please. Carry on. Tell me. I had to know. I didn't really want to know, but . . .

"Once we were clear of the ferry terminal we came out of hiding and started up with the kung-fu nonsense again . . . singing the stupid song, waving our hands, kicking out . . . we were young and stupid and very drunk . . . somehow it suddenly turned from funny play-fighting to serious play-fighting. I think Kieran made some crack about his sister, Claire, being better off with me . . . and you got a bit angry and slapped him one. That pissed him off and he retaliated. Next thing we know you let fly with one of those big sweeping kicks and took out both his legs. He fell . . . hard. You fell too. You hit the deck flat and pretty much passed out. He landed awkwardly though and his head came down at the wrong angle and smashed into the bulkhead . . ." he pointed vaguely at a solid fixing behind me ". . . somewhere about there. It split his head open, there was blood everywhere. But I don't think that's what killed him . . . Brent and I pretty much agreed that his neck broke as he landed. We both heard a sort-of a crack, a horrible popping sound . . ." Doug was shaking his head as he spoke, obviously reliving it in his mind as he probably had done every day for the last twenty years. "We knew he was dead almost straight away. He just lay so still . . . and the blood stopped flowing . . . and Brent checked that he wasn't breathing. It was unbelievable. One minute he was standing there, fooling around, laughing. And then he was dead."

I sank to my knees. My legs simply couldn't take my weight anymore. I felt sick, desperately so, but nothing came out. I started to feel numb inside.

Doug continued. "So that was when Barclay took charge. I tried to argue that it was an accident but he didn't agree. He said it looked bad, that we could all end up going to jail and that he couldn't have that. You tried to sit up a couple of times but never really made it. That's why I thought you must have seen what happened, that you must have known what you did." He took a deep breath and sighed with a cheerless finality, ". . . and that's it. You know the rest."

I put my head in my hands, curled up on the deck and started to sob.

"It sounded like an accident to me," Linda offered gently. "You didn't do it on purpose. You didn't plan it. You weren't trying to kill anyone . . ."

She'd been attempting to console me for a while. Doug hadn't. He'd moved away around the corner, but he hadn't left. However, no matter how much I wanted to, I couldn't accept her generous point-of-view.

It was my fault Kieran had died.

My fault alone.

The phrase '*if only*' kept reverberating around my inside head. If only we hadn't been so drunk. If only we hadn't been acting so stupidly. If only I hadn't taken Kieran's jibe –whatever it may have been– so negatively. If only . . .

But it made no difference and it didn't make up for what I had done. It was my fault that Kieran was dead and that Doug's life got so badly screwed up. Everything was my fault.

If only I'd known.

If only Brent had let me accept the responsibility.

Doug suddenly appeared in front of me. "I have to go," he said. "And so do you. Pull yourself together, man. It's done. It can't be undone."

I stared at him in disbelief. "But I need to set things straight. I need to go to the police and turn myself in . . . I need to make this right."

"No you don't. That wouldn't help anyone, least of all me."

"But you didn't do anything. You're the victim here. I can go to the police and confess and you can get your life back."

He shook his head.

"Jesus, but you're an idiot, aren't you? Doug Masters is dead. He has been for almost twenty years. My name is different now, and it has been for what feels like forever. I have a family, a life. My wife has never heard of Doug Masters, neither have any of my friends and I don't want them to."

Realisation slowly dawned on me.

"You want me to stay quiet?"

"Yes. Of course I do. Burying that fucker Barclay ends this for me. Doug Masters is a name I never, ever want to hear again. And you know what? Adam Holt is also a name I never, ever want to hear again either. You get that?"

Turmoil erupted inside me. "But I can't just walk away. Not now that I know. I can't let you continue to carry the blame. It was my fault. I need to make this right. I need to square things up . . . I need to talk to Claire–"

He hit me. A big open-handed slap sent me reeling.

"Wake up, you stupid son-of-a-bitch," he shouted. "You need to do absolutely, fucking nothing. If you drag all this old shit up now you will fuck up my life yet again. Everyone I know will stop trusting me. Everything I have, that I've worked so bloody hard for, will turn to shit."

I got angry. The little bastard had hit me again. I lost focus, leapt up and began to advance on him. Doug squared up, lip curled, ready to fight.

Linda suddenly threw herself between us, one hand on each of our chests. "Stop this," she cried out. "For crying out loud. Grow up, both of you!"

I stopped dead, suddenly embarrassed. Doug threw his hands up in the air and then raked them through his hair.

He snarled at me. "You have to keep this to yourself, Holt."

"But I can't, I just–"

"Adam," Linda interjected firmly. "I think you have to."

"What? But that's–"

"Stop and think about it, Adam. If you go to the police and confess, then nobody wins. Nobody. All that will happen is that your life will get even more screwed up; Doug's life will be torn apart again. And just picture the media; they'll absolutely eat this up. They'll have a field-day. They'll hound you, and Doug, and Brent's widow. Everyone involved. Kieran's family will be forced to relive his tragic death. It'll be a circus, but nobody will be any better off."

I stared at her, not really wanting to comprehend, but understanding the wisdom of her words. I hated myself all over again as the realisation of my probable acceptance began to dawn. "But it's not right . . ."

"No," she said. "But it's not entirely wrong either."

We all fell silent for a long time as each of us absorbed the terrible things we now knew and tried to find peace in continuing to keep the information secret. My urge to go to Claire and tell her everything, to beg for her forgiveness, was formidable. But the voice that rose up to deter me the firmest was one that I found exceedingly more disturbing than ever before. *Suck it up, Holt,* Brent's voice in my head counseled me brutally. *Shit happens, you big girls blouse. Get over it.* I squeezed my eyes shut and rubbed my temples, desperate to push his voice from my mind.

Nothing was ever going to be the same for me now. Doug was right. What you know can't be un-known. After spending twenty years desperately wishing I could remember what happened I knew then that I would spend the next twenty years, or even more, wishing that I'd never found out.

Linda spoke again, breaking the hollow silence. "Maybe we should go?"

Doug nodded. Linda took my hand, intent on leading me away. I couldn't think straight anymore and dazedly let her guide me back up to the upper deck. We jumped across to the pier without incident and began to meander away from the *Kestrel*, Doug trailing a few steps behind Linda and me.

"Why did he do it?" I suddenly found myself asking. "Brent, I mean. Why did he go to so much trouble to cover up what happened? I don't understand it. He can't seriously have thought that he would get in trouble?"

I'm not sure who I intended the question for but Linda spoke up quickly. "I would have thought that was obvious . . ."

Doug sneered. "Because he was a spineless, self-centered git."

"That may have been a factor," she said, but in a conciliatory way. "But I don't think that's what really drove him. I mean, I only met him the once, but one thing really stood out for me that I don't think you guys really understood."

"Doug's right. He was a self-centered bully, Linda," I said. "There was only one reason Brent ever did anything . . . To gain advantage over someone else." It hurt me to say it out loud. I'd always known it, but . . . well, there it was.

"Okay, yes. Perhaps he was an opinionated bully and pretty focused on his own well-being. But, after hearing from you guys first-hand about that night, I don't think that self-preservation was the main reason he tried to push blame for Kieran's death onto Doug."

Doug snorted. "Go on then. Enlighten us. Why did he?"

Linda hesitated and then spoke firmly. "Just think about it. Put yourself in Brent's shoes. You have, what, fifteen minutes before the ferry reaches Devonport and your best friend has just accidentally killed the brother of the girl that he is head-over-heels infatuated with."

Neither Doug nor I responded so Linda carried on.

"Brent grew up to become a successful businessman. Obviously he was able to find ways to turn difficult situations to his advantage." She looked directly at Doug. "I'm guessing this, but did you and Brent have existing issues, some reason that he would want you out of the way?"

Doug shook his head. "No. I've thought about that myself. We didn't always agree, but there was never anything like that. I've always believed that I was just in the wrong place at the wrong time. A convenient fall-guy."

She nodded her head with self-belief. "Maybe, but I think that Claire might have been a big factor."

"What?" I said.

Linda faced me. "You were still in love with Claire, weren't you? Even after you'd broken up and she started going out with Doug?"

I couldn't respond but I didn't need to, my silence said it all.

She turned to Doug. "You didn't realise just how much Claire meant to Adam, did you?"

Doug looked confused and shrugged.

Linda turned back to me. "You and Brent were friends since you were little kids, right?"

I nodded. "We met the first day of primary school . . ."

"So there you go. Isn't it obvious?"

I turned to Doug. He looked just as perplexed as I felt. "No," we said in unison.

She groaned. "He was protecting you, Adam. Not himself."

"But that's crazy . . ." I muttered.

"No, it's not. It's obvious to me," she said. "Brent Barclay loved you like a brother. He proved that to me the night before he died, at the Hilton. All he could do was talk you up, try and persuade me not to give up on you so easily. That night on the *Kestrel* – he was shielding you. Not only that, but I think he was probably trying to clear the way for you to get back together with Claire . . . the girl you so desperately loved."

"By pushing me out of the picture?" said Doug.

"Yes," said Linda. "Don't you see, Adam? He was trying to fix it for you."

I thought about it for a minute or two, hating to admit to myself that she might actually be right. Brent was the ultimate control-freak. She'd only met him the once but she had him worked out in minutes. I'd known him for over thirty years and never really understood what he was truly capable of.

I turned to face Doug. "I'm so sorry. I never knew . . ."

He glared at me for a while and then shook his head and walked away without speaking. I didn't try and stop him.

I would never lay eyes on the man I knew as Doug Masters again in my life.

TWENTY-EIGHT

"Just sit down and listen, Holt. Don't make this any bloody harder than it's going to be," Bella told me sharply, obviously in a foul mood.

No sooner had Linda and I arrived at my house, having taken a taxi once we realised we were stranded at Wynyard Quarter after Doug left, than Bella began taking charge of whatever was going on. Donny was already there, seated on the couch, looking confused and tired. Bella was pacing, steadfastly wearing out my lounge carpet, with arms folded, a grim and angry expression carved onto her face. And, to my great surprise, her current boyfriend was in my home too. Donny referred to him as '*Grunter*' and we'd only met once before, very briefly, by accident at a shopping mall. On that occasion we barely managed to offer each other a curt nod of acknowledgment before Bella decided she was in a desperate hurry to be elsewhere and dragged him off in the opposite direction. I knew his first name was actually Grant, but I didn't know his last name. Bella had been with him for almost two years now which had to be something of a record for her.

"What the hell is going on, Bella? Why are you here?" I was not in the mood to chat and had completely forgotten that she had called earlier. If I'm honest I was feeling massively depressed, wallowing deeply in self-pity. I just wanted everyone to leave, to get out of my house, to let me be alone.

She fixed me with a look that would have melted steel. "Your son was abducted, remember? The crazy bitch with the bright yellow car . . ."

It all flooded back in a wave. "Yes, sorry." I turned to Donny. "We met her. That psychotic woman . . . Suzy. She took her car back."

His face lost colour. "Is that what happened to you? Are you okay?" he said.

Only then did I remember that I was still favouring my wrist and had dried blood all over my shirt. "I'm fine. No, all this was something else. It's been, well . . . don't worry about it, okay. She's gone. The car's gone. It's over."

"You've seen her? What happened," Bella demanded.

"It doesn't matter. She found us, somehow. We gave her the car. She was pretty weird, but she didn't try anything. She just took the car and left."

For some reason Bella turned and glared at Grant. He was leaning against the wall near the hall doorway. He shrugged.

I led Linda into the lounge and she moved to sit beside Donny on the couch. I followed and propped myself up on the couches arm above and beside her. Normally I would have done introductions but the atmosphere in my lounge was oddly tense. I was missing something. So was Donny.

"What's going on, Mum?" he said. "Why have you dragged him here?"

Bella pursed her lips and the tension in the room deepened. "That car. The bloody Falcon. Owned by MacDoe Enterprises." She paused and we all waited. She expelled a deep snort of frustration. "I know who owns MacDoe."

Suddenly her call came flooding back to me. "That's right. You said that on the phone before. So you know who Suzy is?"

"I said I know who owns the car, not who the bloody girl is."

"Oh, for crying out loud. Who owns the car then?"

She took a deep breath and exhaled sharply again. "Grant."

All three heads on the couch swiveled to stare at the man leaning against the wall. He gazed back blankly, offering no expression at all. I looked at him properly this time. He wasn't a tall man, but he was lean and hard, like a prizefighter. His hair was cropped short with a few twinges of grey and his eyes were a shockingly bright blue piercing out from a granite-like tanned face.

"Your car?" I said. He nodded fractionally and offered a lazy mumble of acknowledgement. So that's why Donny refers to him as the Grunter.

"She stole it?" I said. He barely moved as he shook his head.

"You gave it to her?"

"It's one I loan her occasionally for business," he said softly.

The room went silent. Donny's jaw was on his chest, I imagine mine was too. Linda just looked confused. Bella was dark with fury. Grant showed nothing.

"Tell them," Bella snapped.

Grant looked at her and a small measure of annoyance finally reached his eyes. "Who's the lady?" he said, flicking his gaze briefly towards Linda.

"It doesn't matter if she's the bloody Queen of Sheba, does it? She obviously knows . . . and she's met your fucking psychopath bitch. Tell them."

I sat frozen in disbelief. Suddenly I could see where this was going, but I couldn't believe it. Grant's car . . . it made no sense.

Grant raised an eyebrow languidly and a mild frown creased his forehead. Finally he shrugged slightly and spoke again, his words mind-boggling.

"The woman you know as Suzy works for me . . . on occasion . . . for special projects. This week there was an issue in regards to some of my . . . business arrangements and I asked her to help out . . . with a confidentiality issue."

The silence in the room was overpowering. I could hear myself breathing hard.

Bella finally spoke again. "Spell it out, Grant. Tell them."

He looked aggrieved, as if he'd already said too much. "Come on Honey-Bell, they don't need details. The boy is safe. That's all that matters here."

She spun on him. I thought I'd seen her angry before, but this was a whole new level. This was Bella on nuclear high-alert. I watched in utter bewilderment. She marched up and stood right in front of him, leaning forward, livid with rage.

"You'll fucking tell them everything. Explain it properly or so help me I will make you so fucking sorry you won't fucking know what's going on."

I had to admire the guy at that moment. He barely flinched. She stayed up in his face until he blinked slowly and nodded with a small sigh. "Okay. All right."

Bella withdrew and glared at him with folded arms as he continued.

"On Sunday morning, when Donny turned up at our place unexpected, I felt that it was most likely that he'd accidentally overheard a very confidential conversation I was having on the phone. That information was both highly classified and time-sensitive and . . ." he turned to Bella with a firm glance, ". . . I will not be offering any detail on that, other than to say that I immediately became concerned that Donny might inadvertently discuss said information with the wrong people. So I made arrangements for him to take a short holiday that would ensure he wasn't able to discuss anything that he might have overheard with anyone. At least until this evening when the information ceased to be of any concern to me. The boy was never in any danger. Suzy was under very clear instructions not to harm him. He would have been dropped back at home, safe and sound, later this evening if things hadn't gone . . . astray earlier on."

I simply couldn't process what I was hearing. Donny had been kidnapped on the orders of this man . . . his mother's boyfriend? It was inconceivable, totally unacceptable. My son had been tied up, held captive. He'd been terrified.

I stood up, suddenly boiling with rage, and advanced across the room. In a flash Bella was between me and Grant, and Donny was there too, pulling on my arm, trying to hold me back. "Don't be stupid, Holt. Back off," said Bella.

"She's right, Dad. Don't do this," said Donny.

"You self-righteous piece of shit. How fucking dare you?" I snarled at the man I only knew as Grant. "What gives you the right to play with someone like that? He's just a fucking kid." I tried to push past Bella but she was supernaturally strong.

Donny pulled me back, holding on firmly. Grant didn't move. He watched me dispassionately. Something about the look in his eyes slowed me down. Outwardly they were blank, uncaring. He looked almost bored. But as I stared at them more closely, wanting to tear his throat out, to hurt him in any way I could, I saw a flash of invitation, a spark of excitement there. It was like he welcomed my attempt to attack him. It felt like he was actually hoping I would get close enough that he could defend himself blamelessly.

After a moment I stopped struggling and just glared at him. "Get the fuck out of my home, you sick bastard. Get the fuck out of my sight."

"Happy to." he murmured and shook himself off the wall, ready to leave.

"Not yet," Bella snapped, turning away from me. "You don't get off that bloody easily."

Grant stopped, raised an eyebrow, and folded his arms. He said nothing.

"Apologise," Bella demanded. He gave her a look that screamed; *you can't be serious*. He said nothing. She glared back. Donny and I exchanged a silent look. We knew that glare, that tone in her voice.

It took an eternity but Grant eventually folded. He closed his eyes for a moment and then exhaled softly before flicking his gaze to Donny. "Sorry," he said.

Donny obviously didn't know what to say or do. But I did.

"That's not good enough. You can't just abduct someone because it suits your purposes and then expect a pathetic apology to suffice. She tied him up. She beat him. The bloody bitch humiliated him. She cut his hair and painted his toenails." The bastard actually smirked slightly when I said that. "It's not funny," I snapped, trying to advance on him again. Bella pushed me back. "He lost his bloody job because of what you did."

Grant shrugged. "At KFC. Big deal. He'll get another."

Bella fumed. "Really . . . Jesus Grant, that's not damn-well good enough."

259

Grant rolled his eyes. "Come on, Bells. It's just KFC. It's not like it was a real job. Don't be so touchy."

Big mistake.

Bella reeled away from me and strode over to use both hands to push him violently in the chest. She hammered away until he was backed up against the wall again. "Touchy . . . you fucking wanker . . . I'll give you fucking touchy. You don't mess with my son, do you hear me. Not my God-damn boy." She ranted away and continued to hammer blows onto his chest and arms. To his credit he didn't fight back. He didn't push her away or try to stop the assault. He just stood there and took it, his expression guarded. Eventually Bella relented and stepped back, breathing heavily from the exertion.

To my great surprise he then looked at the floor and murmured, "I'm sorry."

She said nothing for almost a full minute. Everyone else watched on silently. Finally she spoke softly, her voice determined, still angry. "You'll make this right. Do you under-stand me? Whatever it takes, you'll make this right."

"Sure, Babe. Whatever it takes . . ."

"You'll find him a new job, a better job."

He shrugged. "Of course, no problem."

She glared at him. "But not working for you. I don't want him involved in any of that. You find him a real job, a legal job with a proper, respectable company."

He hesitated. A flicker of annoyance crossed his face. "Sure."

I was still furious and suddenly sensed an opportunity. "He needs a car too. His old Mirage has died. And he needs furniture for his room, and a new laptop."

The look I received from Grant made me want to back away quickly but I held my ground, determined that this man should –in some way– pay for what he'd done to my son.

Bella, for possibly only the second time ever, actually agreed with me. "Yes," she said, pushing him up against the wall again. Holding him there. "He needs a reliable car, so that he can come and visit me more often." She glared at Grant while poking him angrily in the chest, almost daring him to say no. "I think he liked that yellow car, the one that you lent to that crazy bitch. You can give him that. And the other stuff too. Donny can make up a list of what he needs . . ."

For a man who was obviously used to getting things his way, and was clearly able to usually mask his feelings brilliantly, Grant blanched. His mouth turned to a thin line and his brow furrowed markedly. He wasn't bloody happy.

I stuck the knife in. "Thank you, Bella. I think that's the least he can do."

There was silence again. After what felt like an eternity Grant spoke evenly; "Fine. Whatever. Can we get going now? I have things to do . . ." He didn't wait for a response and began to walk casually towards the door.

"Wait," I said quickly. Something was still bothering me. He stopped and faced me without speaking. "Did you have anything to do with Harold Armitage?"

His faced remained expressionless. "I've never heard of him."

"Someone ran him over yesterday . . . using my car."

He raised one eyebrow only. "I've never heard of him," he repeated.

"So you didn't have my car stolen . . . to set me up?"

He offered me a wry smile. "You mean nothing to me, Holt. Why would I do something like that?"

"I don't know. To somehow cover up what you were up to with Donny?"

He shook his head. "I don't know anything about your car, Holt . . . or this man, Armitage. Nor do I want to. Whoever you've pissed off is nothing to do with me." He said no more and turned to leave again.

"Wait," Donny called out, surprising us all. "What about the guy who owned the bach? Is he all right? Suzy didn't . . . kill him . . . did she?"

I was just about to speak when Grant muttered a response. "He's fine."

"Are you sure? Suzy must have taken his car to get back to Auckland. How do you know she didn't hurt him?"

"He's fine," Grant repeated brusquely.

But Donny wouldn't let it go. "What, did she tell you that? And you believe her?"

Grant blinked once, very slowly, and exhaled in annoyance. "He's fine," he said for a third time.

Suddenly Bella was in his face. "You've spoken to him haven't you? You know who he is."

Grant just stared at her blankly.

She turned to Donny. "Where was the bach? What did it look like?"

But before he could respond Grant cut in. "For fuck's sake. It was Sully's bach. I've talked to him, all right. He's fine."

Bella's eyes widened in surprise. "You stupid son-of-a—"

He cut her off too. "We're done here. I'm leaving," he snapped. And he turned again and walked away. This time no one tried to call him back.

Bella stared down at the floor for a few moments, obviously trying to reconcile whatever the name meant to her with what had gone on today. She looked annoyed. Sully was obviously a friend, or at least he used to be. She sucked in a deep breath and expelled it abruptly before turning to brush past me brusquely to get to Donny. She grabbed him and held him, pulling him so close I thought she would crush the breath from his body.

"I'm so sorry, Baby. I am so, so, very sorry . . ."

"It's okay, Mum. I'm okay . . ."

I turned away. Linda caught my eye; I'd basically forgotten she was there. I stepped over and sat down next to her on the couch.

"Your life is very complicated, Adam Holt," she whispered in my ear.

I just shook my head, totally lost for words.

TWENTY-NINE

"For crying out loud, Boyd. How many different ways are you going to ask the same question? I don't know how Jeremy Sung and Sharon Barclay knew each other. I did not introduce them. I have never seen them together. Ever. Not on the street. Not at any travel industry functions. Not in any dark alleys. I don't know."

Boyd just gave me the blank, expressionless eyes once again. "And the last time you saw Jeremy Sung?"

I groaned and leaned forward to bang my forehead on the interview room table. We had been at it for over an hour, yet again. The same damn questions, over and over. The repetition was draining. And this was the third day in a row that I'd been hauled in to the North Shore Police station since the discovery of Sharon and Jeremy Sung's bodies at her home. Surely this had to amount to torture to some degree. Perhaps it's not the same as water-boarding or having electrodes attached to your private parts, but it felt like a never-ending hell to me.

"You already know this. I've answered this question at least a dozen times."

"Humour me," he said.

I snorted in exasperation. "He attacked me while I was standing by my car in Auburn Rd in Takapuna at approximately 2.45 pm last Wednesday. A local man, whose testimony I know full-well you have on record, intervened. He ran away."

This was what Linda and I had agreed on the moment we heard about the deaths. I had to protect Doug. I owed him that much. We quickly agreed that we had never gone to Wynyard Quarter the other night. That I had picked her up from work; we had driven directly to my place, cooked ourselves dinner there and stayed in for the night. We watched a DVD. Nothing else happened.

"In which direction did he run?"

I stopped and stared at him in mounting frustration. "Why do we have to go over this again? Nothing's changed–"

Suddenly the door opened. Millward leaned in and signaled to Boyd that he should step outside. No one spoke. They left the door open and stood on the far side of the hallway.

Looking back I believe that it was a deliberate ploy because seconds later Claire O'Driscoll appeared in the doorway and, upon seeing me in the room, stopped dead. We stared at each other in shocked silence. A uniformed policeman peered over her shoulder and muttered something quietly before reaching out and guiding Claire out of my interview room and away down the hall. I leapt up but found Boyd and Millward back at the doorway, watching me with renewed interest. Boyd gestured me to stop.

"Please sit down, would you, Mr Holt," he said as he re-entered the room.

"What's going on?" I demanded as we both resumed our seats. Millward stepped in and pulled the door closed behind him. He leaned against the wall, saying nothing – as usual.

"You know that person?" said Boyd, his expression still blank.

"Yes," I said. "But you already knew that, didn't you?"

He nodded. "Claire O'Driscoll, nee Sandford."

"Why is she here?"

"She's helping us with our inquiries. When did you last see Claire, Mr Holt?"

I shook my head. "Your inquiries into what? Brent's murder? Sharon's?"

He wouldn't be drawn. "When did you last see her?"

"She's not involved in any of this. Claire was a victim. Her brother died."

"Not involved in what, Mr Holt?"

"The murders. Brent, Sharon, Sung. Claire shouldn't be dragged into all this. She's suffered enough. You're making a mistake."

"What makes you say that?"

I suddenly decided that his open-ended question was too vague. Flashing Claire in front of me must have been a ruse. He was fishing. They were using her to try and flush more information out of me. I'm not a great liar, as I confessed earlier, but I was holding my own. At least I had been up until then. I stopped talking and tried to work out what was happening. I considered calling my lawyer in. Getting the indomitable 'Lurch' Andrews by my side would slow things down a bit. But I hadn't done that so far and I didn't want to suddenly change things. It would look bad. There had to be a reason for Claire being here.

"Mr Holt? Why are we making a mistake?" said Boyd.

I sighed. "I just can't see why you would involve her."

"You think she shouldn't be here. Why is that?"

I couldn't think of a suitable response so I said nothing. Silence filled the room.

"Mr Holt, I think you're holding back on us. Why is it that you think that bringing Claire Sandford in for an interview might be a mistake?"

He was baiting me, deliberately using Claire's maiden name. I didn't like that and frowned at him silently. I didn't want to play anymore.

After a couple of minutes silence Boyd and Millward exchanged a glance. There was an almost imperceptible nod of agreement between them. Boyd spoke again, driving an icy chill through my heart. "Did you know that Claire O'Driscoll was a long-term acquaintance of Sharon Barclay?"

I gaped at him. I turned to Millward and gaped at him too. Both men said nothing and watched my reaction intently. I couldn't speak. I shook my head.

"They met about fifteen years ago. They worked together for a bank. They were both Customers Services clerks in a call centre."

I shook my head again. I had no idea.

"You used to date Claire, didn't you? Way back when," said Boyd.

I nodded. "Yes. A long, long time ago."

"When did you last see her?"

Inside my head little wheels were spinning wildly. "I don't recall . . ."

He exhaled in frustration. "Mr Holt, we have witnesses that will swear that you were involved in a fight at Claire O'Driscoll's place of work –WINZ in Takapuna– with an unidentified man earlier this week. At just about the same time that you claim you had an encounter with Jeremy Sung less than a kilometre away."

I closed my eyes. I had to tell him something. My mind raced. After a few moments I responded.

"Yes. I was there. Some bloke thought I'd jumped the queue. There was an altercation. He left. I left." It was a poor effort, but the best I could come up with on the spot. I was determined still that I would not drag Doug down with me on this. I believed what he told me. I believed in his innocence. I would not ruin his life once again. "I went in there to try and see Claire. It was my second visit. Brent's death had hit me hard and, I know this may seem odd, but I'd only just found out she lived and worked nearby. I just wanted to talk to her. Catch up on old times . . ." I tailed off morosely.

"And did you speak with her either time?"

"Very briefly the second time, and for a few minutes the first. She told me to go away. She didn't want to talk to me . . . to be reminded of the past."

"What did you talk about?"

I didn't respond. I felt I'd said enough and wanted some answers. "Are you saying that Claire and Sharon were still friends? That they kept in touch?"

Boyd contemplated this for a moment. Giving a little before had got me talking once; I was hoping he'd give me a little bit more. Eventually he did. "We're still working through phone records and interviewing other people but, yes, it would appear that they kept in contact. What did you and Claire talk about?"

I ignored his question again. "But what does it matter if they were friends? Don't we know that Sung murdered Brent . . . and then Sharon? I don't see what Claire has to do with any of this."

"All three murders remain open investigations, Mr Holt. And it would be fair to say that there are a number of factors that don't entirely add up."

"Such as?"

This time he ignored me. "What did you and Claire talk about?"

I sighed again. My turn to give a little, so I had to lie again, steadfastly determined not to mention Doug. "Nothing. Absolutely nothing. I asked about her life, her husband and children. I just wanted to talk to her again . . ."

"What did she tell you?"

"She didn't want to talk. She asked me to leave."

"Did you talk about her husband?"

"No."

"So you didn't talk about how he died?"

I raised my eyebrows. I had assumed she was divorced. It's so common these days. "I didn't know he was dead."

"Yes," he said without emotion. "A diving accident, eight years ago."

I said nothing.

"Did you ever talk to Sharon Barclay about her former husbands?"

The shift from Claire to Sharon unsettled me. "Husbands . . . as in more than one? No. We didn't chat much. I didn't know she was divorced."

"She wasn't. She was widowed, twice. Brent Barclay was her third husband."

I gaped at him again. Deep inside something began to tear slowly apart.

He spoke again. "Do you know how her first husband died, ten years ago?"

I shook my head slowly, but an image had already formed in my mind. I knew what he was going to say and I felt like it was me who was suddenly drowning.

"A diving accident, over in Australia." He held my gaze as I felt the colour draining from my face. "The second husband was five years ago, in South Africa. His car was run off the road by a driver who fled the scene. Both men were handsomely insured. No other family. She was the sole beneficiary both times."

My mind raced over the scene that had played out at Greenwood and Associates, Brent's lawyers. Sharon's thankfulness at my decision not to contest the unsigned will. Then I pictured her at the hospital. The agony of loss in her face. The absolute, abject misery that radiated from her sitting in that bed. I simply couldn't reconcile any of it with what I was hearing. Had Sharon killed Brent? Or arranged somehow for Cato to kill him? I felt sick to the pit of my stomach. But then I remembered Claire's sudden appearance in the doorway.

"So you think that Claire, somehow, had something to do with all this?"

Boyd was watching me suspiciously. "Is it possible that she introduced Sharon and Brent somehow?"

I could only shrug. "Brent said he met Sharon in a bar. I never asked for details. They dated for a few months. It was a whirlwind romance and marriage . . ."

"But both Brent and Claire worked within throwing distance in Takapuna. It's not a big place, Claire could easily have watched him and worked out which bar's Mr Barclay liked to frequent. Would you consider that feasible?"

I stumbled over my response. "I don't see . . . but then . . . why . . ."

"Did Mr Barclay ever mention running into Claire in Takapuna?"

"No. We never talked about her anymore . . ."

He paused for a moment, and then asked. "What did you and Claire talk about when you visited her?"

I shook my head and then lowered it into my hands.

* * *

Claire O'Driscoll sat silently in her own little interview room only a few metres down the hall from where she had been deliberately presented to Adam Holt. She was angry, and a little scared, but also filled with determination.

They could prove nothing and she would tell them nothing.

She waited for her lawyer and thought of her children. They would be worried but they would get through this . . . again. Claire was strong. And she knew her kids, and her parents. She knew exactly what to say to help each of them understand. They were fiercely loyal to each other, an incredibly tight family group, moulded together by years of adversity and loss. They would understand that whatever allegations the police threw at her; that the media tossed around; that their schoolmates might whisper; were nothing but lies. Evil, made-up, lies.

They were a strong family. They'd be alright.

A noise in the hallway drew her attention, but no one entered the room. The cops were still harassing that idiot, Holt, down the way. She couldn't believe he was still alive. It just didn't add up. Holt should be dead. He simply wasn't smart enough to have willfully evaded their guy. So something must have gone horribly wrong. Sharon messed up somehow, and big-time. Claire still didn't understand how though. The guy Sharon had been using was damn good. One of the best. It made no sense that Sharon was dead and not Holt.

Claire drew a deep breath and released it slowly, leaning back in her chair to stare up at the ceiling. Everything had gone so smoothly with Barclay. The big, stupid bastard had fallen for Sharon hard, just like Claire knew he would. Like putty in her hands, Sharon had been amazing. And once the set-up was complete the execution had been handled perfectly too. The guy Sharon had used had been brilliant, a rare find. Leaving no loose ends . . . or so it seemed.

Then the issue with the will cropped up, yet Sharon had handled that well too. But the note to Holt had thrown her. Claire hadn't told her about Kieran, about that night on the

Kestrel, about Brent's involvement. Sharon had believed that Brent was chosen randomly. Just some local rich bastard. She was pretty pissed about the history when Claire finally admitted it all after Holt had spilled the beans. That idiot, Holt. If only he'd kept his bloody nose out of it all.

And when they found out about Brent stealing from his own business it almost all went sour. But, once again, Sharon had come up with a great plan to buy some time. She couldn't fix the business problems but she'd so cleverly found a way to both reduce the competitive risk –by putting Armitage in hospital– and distract Holt from looking any further into Brent's death – by making him the prime suspect in Armitage's attack– while they saw out the thirty days her lawyer had insisted upon. Initially it seemed to work fine, but still Holt had kept turning up at Claire's workplace, drawing attention to her, and that had to stop. If he discovered the connection between her and Sharon then the police might too.

Claire sighed at the thought. Here she was, at the damn police station, probably because Holt had been seen talking to her. What was the idiot telling them, right now, in the other interview room? She shook her head in frustration.

The last time they'd spoken Sharon had told her that Holt was going to have a little accident. That he might end up getting stabbed too. This had pleased Claire. Not just because it would stop him drawing attention to her but it would also provide one more step towards revenge for her brother's death all those years ago.

Did she think that Holt killed Kieran? No, not really. Of the three possibilities she had always thought Brent the most likely. He was the greediest of them, the most dangerous, the most likely to murder for gain. But it could have been Doug she had to admit. He had been sweet to her, way back then, but he was always a little unstable. She could imagine Doug killing her brother in a fit of drunken rage. But Holt? Not really. He was the least likely given that he had been such a boring saint. And he was a hopeless liar. Did it bother her that Sharon was going to set her guy onto him? Nope. Not in the slightest.

And yet something had gone wrong. Holt was still alive and telling God-only-knows-what stories to the police down the hall. And her good buddy, Sharon, was dead. Had Armitage's boyfriend really killed her? Claire didn't know. That's what it looked like, but looks can be deceiving – as she well knew.

She stood up and stretched, paced a few steps and returned to her seat. Her lawyer would be here soon and the interviews would commence. But she didn't have to say anything. She knew her rights.

She would tell them nothing.

THIRTY

"The sign says that she was brought back to Auckland in December last year. There's a *'Kestrel Preservation Society'* and they're working on restoring it in order to get it back out onto the Waitemata," Linda said.

"Not as a working ferry?" I said.

"I don't think so. More as a historical treasure . . ."

The idea of this ferry sailing again around the harbour actually made me a little nauseous. But I am probably one of a very small number of people who may be affected that way. Most Aucklanders probably had very pleasant memories of the *Kestrel* and her time working on the Devonport run. I envied them.

Linda and I stood on the pier, once again at the furthest point, and gazed back at the once magnificent old vessel. She bobbed gently on the water, the placid keeper of so many secrets. Linda moved in closer and wedged herself under my armpit, hugging me tightly. I wrapped my arms around her and hugged back.

"Did you get hold of Doug today?" she said.

"We should use his new name," I said. "We should refer to him as Gavin, just in case . . . and no, he's still not returning my calls."

"Maybe you should fly down to Invercargill. Go see him?"

"Maybe, I don't know. I'll keep calling . . . but I don't think he wants the money. I think he was pretty serious about never seeing me ever again."

"You could just post him a cheque, see if he banks it."

I nodded. "You think that would work?"

"Or you could courier him a bundle of cash. Either way is worth a try."

I'd give that a bit more thought. Brent left me money, in his will, and he'd left me a note too. In it he'd said: *Money doesn't resolve things, but it's what I know best and I want to try and atone. It's too little, too late but when you find Doug I know that you'll do the right thing. You always do.* I'm not certain if he meant for me to pass it all on to Doug, sorry, to Gavin, but he did seem to want me to, at the very least, share the money with him. Brent knew me so well. He knew that I was a boy scout, that I would find a way to get the money to him, although I do think he seriously overestimated my ability to actually find him. I got lucky, that's all.

Linda squeezed me. "Seen enough?"

I stared at the *Kestrel* for a few moments more. The sun was beginning to set and light was playing off the water, sending ripples of glitter twinkling over her bows. It was a beautiful sight but I still couldn't find it within to actually enjoy the view. I turned to Linda. Her eyes were a spectacular shade of deep blue and twinkled also. They were warm and bottomless and a gentle flutter arose inside my chest. "Why are you here?" I said quietly. "Why haven't you run a mile?"

She smiled and my heart flipped. "I don't know, Holt. Perhaps I have deeply subconscious problems that make me want to help lame ducks . . ." She reached up and tickled my ear. "Or maybe I have daddy issues and need to resolve some inner turmoil?" She laughed.

I rolled my eyes. "Lucky me," I said.

"Can we go and eat now? I'm starving."

We had a booking at the Mexican restaurant at the entrance to the pier. We'd promised them we would return for dinner one day and, as Brent would attest, I am always pathetically true to my word. I took one final look at the *Kestrel* and, still arm in arm, we began to walk past it, down the pier to the restaurant.

"So how's Donny enjoying the new car?" Linda said.

"I still don't believe that actually happened. I didn't think for a moment that Grunter Grant would actually make good on his promise."

"Seems that Bella really has him by the short and curlies."

I nodded and make a small noise of acknowledgement. The yellow Falcon had been delivered around lunchtime the next day, with ownership papers already completed in Donny's name. We'd been blown away. And when Bella turned up later on with the DVD player –still without the errant remote– we were even more surprised. Since then Donny's received a new queen-sized bed with matching dresser and side-table, a new Playstation (the latest one), and he's been dropping some pretty big hints about a new wide-screen TV. He'll probably get that too. His mum is desperate to win back his trust.

"Did I tell you he got his job back at KFC?" I said.

"No way. Really?"

"As I understand it he went back in there and apologised and told the manager that he'd hooked up with an older lady who was desperate for more and more sex and he simply forgot where he was supposed to be. Apparently he made up a whole lot of graphic bedroom detail and this moron was so impressed by the story that he relented and re-hired him. Can you believe that?"

"And you think it's okay that your son wants to work for this pervert?"

I shrugged. "Donny's happy . . . and he's working, so . . ."

Linda shook her head, pretending to be disgusted. "Have the police stopped hounding you yet?" she said, just to change the subject.

There were still so many questions being asked. Nothing was yet resolved, but it was looking less and less likely that the police would actually charge me with anything. I was still unable to account for my whereabouts when my car was used to run down Harry and Sung, but I had witnesses for the time when Sharon and Sung died. Linda mainly, and Donny.

The police seemed to be having as much trouble as we were connecting all the dots. There were still so many unanswered questions. I couldn't help but feel that there simply had to be something else missing from the equations. And, frankly, I wasn't being much help to them. Especially when they asked about Doug Masters. In fact the last time they raised the incident at Brent's funeral, when I first brought Doug Masters to their attention, I changed my story – now telling them that I wasn't so sure that the runaway man had been Doug. I even suggested that it could have been Jeremy Sung, in disguise. My memory had become hazy. The running man could have been anyone. And they haven't pursued any further questions about the unidentified man that I scuffled with at WINZ so it makes me wonder what Claire has said about that day – if anything at all. It may not be true, but I have heard that she's simply not saying anything and exercising her right to silence.

What I do know for sure now is that Claire lied to me. I should have left it alone but I wanted to go and see her mum, to apologise for everything, to beg her forgiveness about Kieran's death and her husband's suicide. Claire had told me she was dying in a hospice in Whangaparoa but when I phoned around none of them had ever heard of her. So I checked the phone book and was surprised to find Claire's parents listed at an address in Tauranga. I phoned them. Claire's dad answered. He was obviously still very much alive. I hung up without saying anything, I was so shocked. It made me wonder what else Claire was capable of lying about.

So, given all the deceptions, silence and conflicting information, I doubt that the police will ever manage to figure it all out, and even if they did I'm pretty damn certain they'd never explain it all to me . . .

"I haven't heard from them today," I said. "But that doesn't mean much."

"Hmm," was all she said. We'd discussed it at length over the last two weeks. Once Linda also knew about the financial issues at Barclay and Dodd we sat down together and worked up a theory, but it had big holes in it. Holes that we thought only some unknown third person could fill, since we couldn't work out a single scenario where everything made total sense. Regardless, I think we got close.

Here's the way we think it might have happened.

It seemed most likely that Sharon had been a gold-digger who married Brent for his money –and then arranged for his murder– after being introduced to him by Claire (who knew exactly what Sharon was looking for and offered up Brent for sacrifice to get back at him for her brother). It's likely that Sharon then approached Sung, somewhere, somehow, and either paid or coerced him into committing Brent's murder. Therefore Armitage was probably aware. So the plan would have been for Sharon to inherit Brent's business and then sell her shares to Armitage, meaning they were probably using me as a go-between so that no one would suspect their arrangement. But, for whatever reason, Sharon decided to double-cross them (we think she may have decided to keep her shares in Barclay and Dodd and didn't want Armitage causing trouble by going after her accounts) so she stole my car and ran them both over. Only they didn't die and Sung came after me –thinking that I was in cahoots with Sharon– and then went after her having failed to dispatch me. Or she contacted him that night and lured him to her house (she did have a gun, after all?) to try and work out a new deal after finding out that Brent had been stealing money from Barclay and Dodd and her shares were going to be worthless. Only Sung pulled the knife and the rest is history.

Does that make some sense?

I hope so. It's the best we could agree upon.

Whether it's right or not I suppose we'll never know.

Guesswork aside, from his hospital bed, Armitage strenuously denied all knowledge of everything, while his business suffers horribly under the weight of negative exposure of Sung's apparently murderous exploits. The media was rife with speculation and accounts are leaving it in droves, many of them returning to Barclay and Dodd who –too successfully for my liking– have sold themselves as the victim in the whole sorry affair. I felt bad about that. Especially as I became a majority shareholder following Sharon's untimely death.

Things might be different if I hadn't agreed to wait the thirty days before signing away my rights to Brent's original will, but that's how it went. With Sharon unable to lay claim to Brent's assets all his worldly goods were bequeathed to me . . . as per his original, signed, last will and testament.

That means I also inherited a battle, of sorts, with the Dodd's over how to repay the money that Brent stole from his own business. Mind you, the accountants did finally complete their digging and the total owed wasn't as bad as Dodd senior had so vehemently made it out to be. And –and this is the big thing– they also discovered some issues with the way Marguerite Dodd had been accounting for a few things. Not on the same scale as Brent, but misappropriation and fraud on a reasonable scale none-the-less. No wonder she looked so damned miserable in that meeting. It's fair to say that Gerald Dodd is not a happy man, yet he remains determined that all of Barclay and Dodd's financial issues remain strictly confidential. On that we actually agree. So, with two insurance policies and the proceeds from the sale of Brent's palatial home in Takapuna (now the scene of three unexplained murders), I felt confident that we would be able to square away the cost of Brent's wrongdoings without my having to forfeit the value of my shares. The Dodd family would actually have to buy them. It was still under negotiation, and I found it all pretty complex, but I had been assured by my rangy and dogged lawyer, Lurch, that I would come out of it all in the positive. In fact, somewhere in the very positive. Whatever the final figure was I had already determined that no less than half would go directly to the man I now know as Gavin Wilson as reparation for past transgressions against him.

To my mind he deserved it far more than I did.

Somehow I was going to have to find a way to live with the gnawing guilt that I found myself carrying each and every day.

Kieran's death that night had been my fault.

On a good day I try to convince myself that it was an accident, nothing more than that. But I haven't had too many good days recently. Most days I've spent drowning in self-pitying remorse, haunted by images of drunken stupidity. But then I think of Brent and I wonder . . . How could he possibly have thought that obscuring the truth and destroying the life of another man was the right thing to do? He was my best friend, and I was his. But would I have done the same thing if the situation had been reversed? No. I'm pretty sure I would never have even dreamt of it.

And still, the 'If only . . .' scenario's play endlessly inside my head. Doug was right. There is no going back.

"Do you think they'll remember us?" Linda said, surprising me.

"Who?"

"The Mexican restaurant people. Do you think they'll recognise us?"

"Maybe if I limp and pour some blood over my head."

She grimaced. "Maybe we should go somewhere else?"

I shook my head. "No, we can't do that. I made a promise."

She stopped walking and looked at me. "You really are a bloody boy scout, Adam Holt. You know that, don't you?"

"I come with many faults. What can I say?"

She smiled again and my heart gave another little flip. "Say nothing. I happen to like boy scouts."

Maybe there's no way that I can go back and change what happened but, for what it's worth, I am determined to find ways that I can atone, for both my actions and for Brent's.

It will never be enough, but it's the best I can do.

* * *